The Heart That Died

1

"She's here!"

Those to words erupted from Tamara like the scream of a boiling kettle.

The tall girl slammed the door to the back room of Charlie Durant Investigations behind her and leaned against the oak effect paneling like it was the only thing keeping her upright. Excitement zinged off her like lines of comic book radiation.

"She. Is. Here," she said again, her words landing with the rhythm of a cop's truncheon.

"Okay." Still about three quarters of the way asleep, I made an effort to rise from the sheets of the disheveled sofa bed. "One, dial the drama down a notch and two, *who's* here?"

"She." Tamara was practically vibrating. "*Her*. The mystery blonde who hopped out of your rescue attempt. She's sat out front right now."

"What?!" Any remnants of sleep flew away from me as a sudden jolt of adrenalin hit me like an ice-cold shower and a quadruple espresso.

Tamara rolled her eyes.

"Look, I'm not sure how many other ways I can put this, but remember the dame you've been mooning over like a schoolgirl for the last few days? The oh-so mysterious woman who skipped out on your white knight routine? Well, she's curled up in our office like a housecat right now, sipping bad coffee from a chipped mug while Howard spins her some cockeyed yarn."

"You left her alone with Howard?"

"I... dammit! Just make yourself presentable... quickly!" She took a deep breath, plastered on her best smile, and swept out the room.

I kicked away the thin blanket covering me, dragged on my slacks, and padded to the door Tamara had left open just enough for a curious eye to peek through, fastening the last two buttons of my shirt as I got there.

It was her, alright. She was dressed in a pristine white blouse and gray slacks slightly flared at the ankle. The same light swing coat she'd worn on the night we almost met was slung over the arm of the chair she perched on like an afterthought and a slim cigarette slowly burned between her slender fingers, completing the picture of composed elegance.

But there was something about the way she sat, a half-buried energy, as if she'd run a long way to get here and was about ready to run some more. Despite the thick layers of foundation and eye-shadow, it was pretty clear she'd been crying.

Perhaps sensing the burn of my gaze, she turned toward the door I lurked behind and, for a second, the world stilled as eyes so very like those that haunted my every waking dream once more flashed my way. Inside me, a fuse I could ill afford to let burn flared into life. I wanted to rush in, wrap her in my arms, and swear on whatever I used for a soul these days that it was going to be okay—that I was going to *make* it okay—but I stayed my hand and listened. Because Tamara was asking my mystery woman for a recap.

#

You see, every story has a 'once-upon-a-time'. A beginning you can trace back through a million events on a million different days. I guess, for me, that first domino fell on a rain-soaked Thursday night, at a bar called Callaghan's Champagne & Cocktail Lounge.

Callaghan's had been a classy joint once-upon-a-time, back in the days before Prohibition. It was the kind of place where men talked serious business over serious Scotch while the women they wore like silk scarves sipped Champagne cocktails and compared their hard-earned finery with narrow eyes and worked out how they could get more of both. Those were heady times—nights that were filled with manufactured glamor and gangland mystique in equal measure. But time passed by and so did the silk and the cigars, put to death by the twin curses of Depression and Prohibition.

But Callaghan's survived.

It was meaner and leaner than those days, sure, but through every trial and every tribulation it stayed open for business.

The piano that played jazz standards disappeared, and second-rate rye replaced the Scotch and the Champagne, but Callaghan's itself endured—thanks to the patron of the establishment and the man I had business with on that first, fateful night.

Patrick Callaghan was a fireplug of a man with thinning, fiery red hair and a wire brush beard. He bore down on me that night like a flaming comet, tearing off his stained butcher's apron to reveal a white T-shirt busy playing peek-a-boo with his generous gut.

"With me." He barked, tossing the apron to Kenny, the head bartender, without breaking stride.

I knocked back my drink, and followed behind, landing the opposite side of a scarred table to the right of the bar.

"You have everything I asked you to get?" he asked with a refreshing lack of small talk.

"Yup, and a little more besides. It wasn't *too* tricky to get, but bribing Tal's guards cost me nearly double my initial estimate."

Callaghan raised one bushy eyebrow. "We already fixed the price."

"And I'm not angling for anything more than we agreed." I

raised my hands, my fingers splayed. “I just thought you should know is all.”

“And now I know.” Callaghan’s blue eyes fixed me with cold reflection like I was a casket he was planning to close. After a less than comfortable pause, he flashed me a broad grin. “Okay, Charlie, why not show your uncle Patrick what you’ve brought him? If it’s the goods then I might see my way to covering your ‘expenses'.”

I weighed the situation, and slid a fat Manila envelope rescued from the inside pocket of my jacket across the table.

“Good call.” Callaghan snatched up the envelope and worked the string securing it. “After all, we wouldn’t want people thinking I’m not a reasonable man, now, would we?”

I kept my eyes on my drink and said a deliberate nothing.

Because Patrick Callaghan wasn't just the man with his name above the door. He was also the man behind every shady deal east of Ashmole—the silent partner of every pickpocket, panhandler, and con artist—whether they knew it or not. Any enterprising individual who forgot about this unannounced agreement and failed to pay him his cut got remembered for all of the wrong reasons. I knew of at least five such object lessons in the past year alone, one of which involved a pneumatic press and a pair of bolt-cutters. No, ‘reasonable’ wasn't a word that fit Patrick Callaghan all that well.

“This is good work, Charlie,” He held one photo up to the light like he was examining a diamond through a jeweler’s loupe. “It looks like you’ve got Mr. Igor Tal right where I want him. Yeah, real nice work, Charlie.” He tore his eyes away from the photo and flashed me a broad grin. “For a skirt.”

I stretched my legs out under the table and let my gaze drift up to the ceiling fan busy pushing cigarette smoke around in lazy circles. “Sure, Mr. Callaghan,” I said. “Funny. Real funny. Because everyone knows a woman could never cut it in this line of work, yeah? She wouldn’t have the guts would she? She wouldn’t have the... balls.”

“Aw, come on, Charlie." Callaghan’s grin stayed where it

was, but his voice softened a little. "You know I don't mean nuthin' by it."

And the hell of it was, I did.

Patrick Callaghan had been the first of the city's major players to see past the problem of my sex and through to the 'skills' I brought to the party, something even Mother Yeager hesitated over, and the jobs he handed me—finding certain items and getting dirt on certain competitors—were, outside of the irregular dribble of worried husbands and wronged wives who knocked on my door, the closest thing I had to a regular, bill-paying gig. It didn't make his 'jokes' land any smoother, though.

"Sure thing, Mr. C." I let my gaze fall to my almost empty glass. "I get it—I *always* get it." I tossed back the last few drops of brandy and tapped the glass with the nail of my index finger. "'Course another of these might help dull that pain. So, what do you say? Buy a girl a drink?"

Callaghan's eyes sparkled. His rumble of laughter crashed through the room like thunder. "What do I say?" he dragged a hand across his mouth and his grin faded like a magic trick. "By all the saints and their long-suffering mothers, Charlie Durant! I say you're a no-good, freeloading crook, that's what I say. I guess I like you all the same, though. Not in the same way our friend Kenny over there likes you, God help him, but maybe a shade or two more than I should." He leaned back, the chair creaking under his bulk, and motioned to the bar for more drinks. "All things considered."

I might have said a little more, but before I could, the bar's door flew open, and my past blew in.

#

The first figure was a real prize, blessed with pinched features and a soft-boiled stare. Slim as a switchblade and twice as sharp, he wore a painfully new suit that whispered menace and bad decisions in equal measure under a deceptively expensive trenchcoat. His wet, blondish-brown hair made me think of empty beaches on a rainy day. Everything about him made my toes curl and my fingers itch.

And then there was the girl.

At a guess she was in her mid-twenties—short and slim with the kind of quiet poise you only see in people who've practiced in front of mirrors. Her dress, white cotton decorated with a pattern of red roses, peeked out from beneath a woolen swing coat. Her soft blonde curls were mostly hidden beneath a cloche hat. Red kitten heels and a very nearly matching clutch held tight against her chest like a shield put the period on her look.

Together, the two were mismatched bookends. Him all sharp corners and silent threats, her a soft echo of innocence—but that wasn't what made me sit up and take notice.

It was *her.*

Because the girl with the blonde curls was a perfectly flawed replica of a ghost I'd tried to banish a long time ago. A ghost that pulled on my mind, dragging it back to the day I wanted to forget more than any other, and raw emotions that I *needed* to.

The thin man peeled off his trench coat and hung it up like he wasn't expecting to stay too long. The dame lingered in the doorway, her big brown eyes working overtime as she cataloged every potential danger the bar held. She was trying to show the world a big brave girl, but every nerve she had was drawn as tight as piano wire. Her mouth might have been closed, but inside she was screaming for help. And I *heard* her.

His coat safely deposited, the goon straightened his suit jacket with a sharp tug and made a beeline for a table. Something in the way he moved, all tight and hunched, made me think of something sharply slinking, with yellow eyes and needle-sharp teeth—a polecat, maybe, or a weasel. The Weasel barked a drink order at the back of Kenny's head, whiskey on the rocks for him, Gin Fizz for the dame, and jammed a toothpick from the glass on the bar between his teeth, letting his soft-boiled gaze wander the bar for someone dumb enough to meet it. His weak impression of Gary Cooper found only the well-studied apathy of men who knew to know better.

I switched my attention to the woman. She was trying her hardest to disappear under the weight of the too-admiring glances Callaghan's more sociable types flashed her. The shy, almost apologetic smile with which she greeted those leers simply screamed '*leave me alone!*'. The trouble was, I wasn't entirely sure I could.

"Know 'em?" I asked Callaghan, my gaze flicking to the unlikely pair.

"Can't say I do. Why?"

"The ring." I kept my eyes glued to the depths of my brandy. "Right hand. Pinky finger... it says the guy belongs." The item of jewelry I'd spotted was a silver-plated brass signet ring pretending to be something finer. Its bevel was inlaid with some dark stone—either onyx or jet and engraved with a silver hand, palm up and fingers splayed.

"The Brotherhood of The Hand, huh?" Callaghan sipped his drink and studied the glass like it held the answers to all of life's mysteries. "Serious business, then—not that it's any business of ours."

I shot him a wordless nod and risked another glance towards the girl.She was talking fast now, her hands moving in small, pleading gestures, her eyes, wet with the promise of tears. Her gaze shot between the face of the man opposite her and the rest of the room, like she was looking for a friend—any friend. The Weasel just worked away at the toothpick behind a nasty little smirk that made my guts flip. Both drinks remained untouched.

"Leave it be, Charlie." Callaghan leaned in, lifting my empty glass from the table.

"Take the advice of an old man. You get involved in this and it gets messy—and messy ain't ever been good for business." He rose and then turned toward the bar. "Messy ain't good for *anything*."

It was good, hard earned advice from a man who knew his way around 'messy', but a little too much of my past was bleeding through the walls.

The same script, a different actress.

Almost like I'd summoned her ghost, my mind returned to that *other* girl and that *other* day, but I bit down on the memory before it could get problematic and focused on the present.

I couldn't make out the girl's words against the subdued thrum of the bar—not even with *my* senses, but the streaks of mascara cutting down her cheeks and the twists at her handkerchief meant I didn't need to.She was asking, no, *begging*, the man for something.

And just like that, the years rolled back—rewound by the single word spilling again and again from the lips of the too-familiar blonde in the white dress. The same word that haunted every dream I ever had. The word was *Please*, but the word wasn't working.

The Weasel's cruel smirk threatened to set up shop as a permanent feature, stabbing me in the gut and twisting the knife. My treacherous fingers started tapping out a staccato rhythm on the tabletop, laying out the beat for a hundred bad decisions. In the stillness of my chest a drumroll of sublimated fury waited for the inevitable crash.

Almost as if he'd read my mind, The Weasel slammed his fist onto the table hard enough to make the ice inside the glasses jump. The girl stopped mid-sentence. Reaching into his coat, he drew out a thick, cream-colored sheet of paper and a sleek fountain pen, laid both in front of the dame, with faux-ceremony and barked the obvious order—one word, as sharp as gunfire and twice as deadly.

The effect was instantaneous. The too-familiar dame stood as tall as her diminutive height would allow, her tears drying as if someone had turned off the faucet. She wasn't a victim anymore, but a primal, legendary creature of righteous fury. The untouched Gin Fizz flew into The Weasel's face, the highball tumbler hitting the floor by his feet with a sound that rang like an alarm bell. Heads turned. Conversations died as the whole bar held its breath. In my mind, a silent cheer yelled, *finally!*

"No!" the woman shouted. "I won't sign. You understand? I won't! Not now! Not ever!" Without waiting for an answer, she turned and strode toward the exit, spilling her chair to the floor as she went. At the door, she stopped and turned, looking back through the haze with tear-stained eyes.

Looking at *me*.

Then she turned and disappeared out of the bar and out of my life forever.

Or, at least I guess that's how it *should* have gone.

#

That all happened four days ago, and now my too-troubled blonde was perched in my office while Tamara asked her all the obvious questions.

"And it's this mystery woman you say came to your rescue that you want us to track down?"

The young woman tapped ash off her slender cigarette with a practiced flick and the flaky residue floated onto the abused saucer hijacked from the windowsill to pull double duty as an ashtray. "Well...no. Not exactly. See, I'd seen this woman before, earlier that same night, in a bar called Callaghan's, so I took a guess she was either a regular there or knew people who were." She paused, buying herself the time and mental space to line up her words. "Now, I'm no kind of hero, Ms. Quinn" she continued. "And I can't say I made the decision lightly, but I needed answers, and this woman seemed like my best chance at getting them. So I choked down a little liquid courage, threw on my coat, and made my way back. It was Kenny, the bartender, who gave me a name—Charlie Durant, he said—runs a detective agency on Revello that specializes in the off-beat and the downright weird —all of which sounded kinda perfect, given the mess I'm in."

She stared at Howard, a sudden hardness in her beautiful eyes. "Trouble is, either I'm real bad at descriptions or somebody here needs to make with some real fast talking. Because whatever the sign on the door might say, *you...*" Her accusing finger jabbed toward the slack-jawed Howard "...sure as hell ain't Charlie Durant."

2

It looked like the jig was up. I ran a hand through my bed-disheveled hair, trying to flatten the rough edges into something halfway respectable, rolled my shoulders, and, summoning what little dignity I had left, strode into the room.

"I believe you might be looking for me," I said, trying for laconic poise, even though my palms were damp.

The too-familiar stranger who'd just called Howard out half-rose, trailing an aura of dry smoke, white petals, and quiet vanilla behind her and then fell back into the chair, hiding the clumsy slip by reaching for another cigarette. Her fingers trembled as she tried to coax her lighter into life. On her third attempt, the flame caught.

"Well, what do you know?" She sat back, her head raised in a display of composure that didn't quite convince. "Two Charlie Durants for the price of one. Ain't I the lucky girl?"

I leaned a hip against the desk. "Maybe. But why come looking for any Charlie Durants at all?"

"Because I've got nowhere else to turn, Ms. Durant, that's why." She blinked once, her eyes glossy with unshed tears. "I'm in trouble. Real trouble. And The Hand are just the tip of it."

I let my eyes drift to Tamara, who replied to the silent question with an almost non-existent nod.

"Start at the beginning," I said. "Don't leave anything out."

#

Her name was Rose Chamberlain, a waitress with stardust in her eyes and a story you've probably heard a hundred times before—girl chases dream, dream runs too fast. But Rose's version held a twist.

"It all started with the nightmares," she said, her eyes flitting between Tamara, Howard, and me. "Or, I don't know, maybe a touch earlier. I know I hadn't been sleeping well for a while—blamed it on the double shifts I was pulling to pay the rent hike, but now..." Her voice caught on some hidden emotion. "They say everyone has dreams, Ms. Durant, even if you don't remember them, but I'll always remember my dreams of the well-dressed man... always."

I leaned in, my eyes not quite meeting hers. "Go on."

"It starts in this big room—a study, I guess. All mahogany furniture, carpets deep enough to lose a shoe in, and expensive air... and, sat behind a desk the size of a dinner table, *him*."

"Can you describe this man?" I asked.

"Sure—dark hair. Expensive suit. Saltwater tan—the kind of guy who knows he owns the room. The kind of guy who owns every room." She exhaled smoke. "Anyway, on the desk there's this clay bowl and he pours something red and thick, and definitely *not* wine into it from this tall, cut glass decanter."

I swallowed hard at the obvious candidate for the 'something red'.

"And he starts chanting—not in English or any other language I know—and the room starts to hum like an old fridge. My skin starts to crawl. My molars vibrate. I taste a tang in my mouth like I've been licking pennies. And *that's* when he looks at me. Not in my direction, you understand. I mean *At* me... like his eyes are drilling into my soul, peeling me open layer by layer and leaving me with no lies left and no secrets to tell... and then he laughs."

The silence that followed that last word was hard enough

to chew on. Tamara's pencil hovered above the paper. My gaze slid away from Rose's a second before our eyes could meet.

"The sound of that mirthless laugh spills into the room like it's leaking from a busted radio," she continued. "And, all of a sudden, I'm a moth and his shit-eating grin's the moon. The whole room tilts as gravity gives up on me, and I'm tumbling, end over end, into a mouth that eats light and spits out death." Rose's hand shot to her mouth like she was trying to stuff the words back in. "When I come to, I'm soaked in sweat, twisted up in my bed sheets like I lost a streetfight in the middle of a hurricane—Mrs. Lukic across the hall says I've got one hell of a scream on me."

"You mentioned chanting?" Tamara's cool, clinical voice cut straight through Rose's growing distress. "I don't suppose you caught any of the words?"

Rose scrunched up her nose. "I think one sounded a little like 'tea-kettle,' and another maybe 'racecourse' but there was nothing that made a lick of sense. Why? Is it important?"

"Could be." I pushed away from the desk and drifted over to the office door, peering through the frosted glass of the small window into the corridor beyond. "Anything else?"

She arched a brow. "Well, I could finish my story."

I turned back to the door, letting the frosted glass swallow the grin curling the corners of my mouth. Tamara let out a soft snort that she tried to cover with a cough.

"For three whole weeks that same dream returned," Rose continued, her voice stretched thin and serious once again. "The same room. The same chanting. The same feeling of falling through the world. Any sleep I got left me feeling more and more exhausted until I started seeing shadows in every doorway and demons on every corner."

"And?" Howard asked, the big guy more focused than I'd ever seen him. "What happened next?"

Rose took a breath she let out slow. "And then things got *really* weird."

#

Shadows in every doorway and demons on every corner.

The words dragged my mind back to Callaghan's and the decision I'd made to trail behind The Weasel as he pursued the girl I now knew as Rose Chamberlain. The lanky goon scurried between the raindrops like the sleek predator I'd named him for, slinking from streetlight to streetlight. The overhead illuminations reflected from the rain-slick paving, lending an unearthly glow to the ion-charged air, but I kept my distance and my patience.

Ahead of the Hand goon, the girl who'd defied him marched past the shuttered windows and dead-eyed doorways of Crows Nest Street, her heels clicking out a staccato rhythm. At the window of Hannigan's General Store, she stopped to remove her shoes and massage the heel of one foot.

And that's when she saw him.

Messy.

She bolted. The frantic, syncopated slap of bare skin on wet concrete echoed down the street, and the Weasel picked up his own pace. This wasn't business anymore. This was pride and ego. This was personal.

Messy ain't good for anything.

The petite girl turned into the cramped maze of backstreets and deadly shadows known as The Warren, a place where a wrong turn could prove lethal. Through this dank labyrinth we ran, three storm-tossed souls fleeing through the driving rain.

As we reached the exposed guts of a row of failing, third-rate diners, where the stink of rotting food and rancid grease hit like a wall, Rose glanced up. Her nose wrinkled. Her foot caught a crack—a stumble that cost her dear.

Because now The Weasel had her.

#

"Ms. Durant?"

I blinked. Rose was staring at me with something like concern.

"Sorry," I said, reaching for a cigarette I didn't have. "You were saying?"

"A contract," Rose continued, watching me carefully. "The next morning, there was a contract sitting on my kitchen counter. Thick paper covered in red symbols, with a dotted line signed with the same symbols and another awaiting my name." Once again her attention drifted from Tamara over to Howard and then to me. “Now, I’m no lawyer, Ms. Durant, but I’ve read enough stories featuring a signature and a scream to know that there was no way, not in this world or the next, I was signing anything—I tore the damn thing into strips, balled them up, and tossed it in the trash, figuring that’d be the end of it.”

I finally peeled my gaze from the small window and met her haunted, tobacco-brown eyes again. “I’m guessing it wasn’t.”

“Not even close. The next morning, the damn thing was sitting in the exact same spot begging for a signature, so I tore it up again—and the next day, and the next—I ripped it, burned it, flushed it... but every time the damned thing was waiting by the coffee pot the next morning.”

“Could anyone have gotten into the apartment?” Tamara asked, beating me to the punch by half a second.

Rose shook her head.

“Nope. The door’s got two locks, a chain, and a deadbolt, and by the third day, the place was locked up tighter than the chastity belt on a prison guard’s daughter.”

“Windows?”

Another head shake. “Fourth floor. No fire escape. No balcony. No ledge. Not even a handy gargoyle to dangle from.”

I handed Tamara a look she handed straight back. A silent exchange that only needed raised eyebrows and gut feelings. There was something we hadn’t got to. I could hazard a guess what that something was, but it never hurt to make sure.

“But that’s not the end of the story, right?”

"You're damn right it's not." Rose sighed. "I'd thought about calling the cops, but I figured I'd be wasting a dime, because anyone who spins the boys in blue a yarn like mine only wins themselves a rubber room and a complimentary strait-jacket."

"But?"

"But that damned contract had been haunting me for five whole days and I needed to tell *someone*. I was getting cooped up..." She tapped the side of her head. "In here. Tom Moody's, the diner I worked at, had let me go a few days back—apparently screaming in the face of customers who nudge you awake is kinda frowned on—I still had a few friends there, though. So, I asked Babs, a nice girl, would be kinda pretty if it wasn't for the nose, out for coffee." She caught my expression and got back to the point of the story. "I spun her a story about a jealous ex giving me grief and she ate it up with a spoon. The following night, I invited her round to mine and up she turned, armed with a cheap bottle and a mind to tear down the entire male species. I put on my act of finding the contract, tore it up, and tossed it right in front of her—she just nodded in a knowing, sad kinda way and poured us both another drink. Babs never could handle her gin, so I wasn't surprised when she passed out on the couch."

"And the next day?"

"Not a goddamn thing." Rose's voice was as brittle as glass. "Not on the counter and not in the trash. It was like the contract never existed." She paused, exhaling another soft huff of air. "I got Babs outta there, salvaged what was left of the gin and got myself into some quality sedation. All that time I'd been clinging on, telling myself I wasn't crazy, but I guess I wasn't sure any more." Her liquid eyes found mine again. "And that's when *he* showed up."

"He?" Again, I suspected I knew but I wanted to hear it from her lips.

"Our friend from Callaghan's," she confirmed. "Same slick suit. Same grease-ball hair. But playing a hell of a lot nicer than you ever saw. He told me he represented a man of 'considerable means'." Rose rolled her eyes. "He never gave me a name."

She paused, gazing longingly at the coffee maker we keep by the back room door, and Tamara fetched her a fresh cup of our thin coffee while I took a perch on the desk, letting the pieces settle in my head.

The alley. The dreams. The contract.

"Anyway, he said this 'means' guy wanted to 'secure my services.'" Rose continued. "Exactly *what* services, our friend kinda danced around—the work was light, legal, and entirely moral, though—his words, not mine—and in time, this 'benefactor' would make me a wealthy woman." She set the cup down, her eyes a little too bright. "Now, I don't have a fancy degree or my name on an office door, Ms. Durant, but I know when I'm being sold smoke. I told him exactly where he could stuff his 'offer' using language that would make my old mom chase me with a Bible and a bar of soap. He just buttoned up his coat, tipped his hat, and handed me this." She reached into her coat like a magician pulling a rabbit from a hat and produced an envelope. "Inside was the Houdini contract, a handwritten letter, and a C-note crisp enough to shave a leg with."

Howard let a low whistle slip between his teeth.

The paper inside the envelope was thick, smooth and as cold as guilt; the penmanship upon it curved and controlled. I let it sit in my palm for a moment, testing its weight, and read:

My dearest Miss Chamberlain,

Please accept this token of my esteem, delivered to you in good faith by my trusted associate.

The services I require of you are, as explained, entirely proper, both in the legal and in the moral sense, and will demand little of you beyond your presence and your discretion. Should you choose to accept this offer, you will find me a most generous and considerate employer. A man who possesses both the means and intent to richly reward your loyalty and put an end to all your present difficulties.

Kindly telephone my associate at St. Germain 0153 within the next twenty-four hours to confirm your acceptance and the ne-

cessary arrangements to retrieve your signed contract will be made.
Sincerely,

A Friend

I passed the letter to Tamara, who scanned it and handed it back like it made her dirty. "Still smells like smoke to me," she said. "More so."

"Yeah, that's why I decided to keep the hundred bucks and ignore the rest." Rose's eyes dropped as she sank into the memory."... Right until my sister fell asleep."

"She... what now?" Tamara's reaction was bullet fast and aimed straight for the heart.

"My sister, Grace." She underlined the name with a subtle hitch. "Three days after I got the letter, she'd just... stopped. It was like she'd fallen into some kind of coma. The docs at St. Jude's ran every test they had but came up with nothing but shrugs—I found out the morning *before* she was admitted... by mail."

"Another handwritten note?" I could already feel where this was going.

Rose nodded, her lips tightening around the memory. "The writer said he found Grace's condition *'regrettable'* but he would be more than happy to cure her... if I signed the contract. He also offered me a demonstration. A 'test' he called it."

"Test?"

"Yeah. I was to be at Grace's bedside, at four P.M. sharp the day after the note arrived," Rose said like the words might break apart if she spoke too loudly. "And then, at that point, I'd be... '*shown*'."

The word hung in the room like a storm cloud that had our names. I shifted my unlit cigarette to the corner of my mouth and, with a look, urged Rose to continue.

"I went to the hospital and pretty much begged the doctors to let me sit with Gracie." Rose took a breath, raw emotion shining in her eyes. "I held her hand, counting each shallow breath and every tick of the clock. As the minute hand crept up to the hour Grace's eyes flew open. Her head thrashed like she was trying to tear herself away from arms only she could see. 'Rose!' she screams, 'Rose, I'm so lost! So very lost! Rose, help me! Please!'"

I heard the fear and desperation echo in Rose's voice.

"Then she looks up at me, and for a moment there's recognition—she reaches out..." Rose extended her hand into the space between us, her fingers trembling. "...but falls back to the bed again like a ragdoll. I think she was unconscious before her head hit the pillow."

"And that's what took you to Callaghan's," Tamara cut in. "You wanted to sign."

"To refuse," Rose corrected, a sudden steel in her voice. "Or, I don't know, maybe. The 'invitation' included in the note gave me twenty-four hours to decide one way or the other and that wasn't enough. It wasn't until he pulled out that contract and ordered me to sign that I threw my drink in his face as a firm 'no' and ran."

Howard's eyes gleamed. "But what if he caught you?"

"Oh, he did." Rose's smile faded. "He caught up to me in an alleyway in The Warren... and that's when Charlie here appeared."

#

'Appeared'. The way Rose said it made it sound like some kind of magic trick, but it wasn't... well, not exactly. I simply pulled back from the struggle, letting the steam of a nearby vent and the big city shadows cloak me—but I could still see The Weasel's pawing hands and the way she so desperately tried to shrink away from them. I could still see the string of spit that hung from the goon's lip like some obscene spider web, could see the way his hips twitched in the way weak men think represents sexual power and the narrow blade that appeared in his free hand. But, instead of charging forward, I buried the raging desire threatening to overcome my carefully built resolve and allowed myself to fade away from human perception, becoming just one more ghost in the rain-clad night.

"I believe the lady said no."

It was my mysterious blonde woman who saw me first. Her eyes widened, gleaming in the kind of look that doesn't know whether to cheer or scream. The Weasel turned and followed her gaze, the corners of his mouth twitching in sardonic humor as he saw me.

"A dame?" he drawled, drawing out the word like a bad joke. "Another goddamned dame?" His gaze, slow and dangerous, rode from my boots up to my face, taking in every attraction along the way. "Well ain't that peachy," he continued. "I'm kinda busy right now, sweetheart, but, you know... if you don't mind taking a number..."

And *that's* when I kicked him.

As you've probably figured by now, I'm no delicate, demure debutante, or the kind of damsel who gets distressed too easy, but there's a part of me, the part I've learned to keep a tight hold on, that thirsts for raw and beautifully reckless violence—something that would have to wait... for now. No, I had to be surgical, precise—I had to wait.

The Weasel landed against the wall, shook his head to clear it and, as his knife leaped into his hand, circled to his right and anticipation, as sharp and cold as a winter's night, slithered through me. When it eventually came, his attack arrived with all the fury I could have ever hoped for. He lunged at me swinging his stiletto in a wide sweep, but I swayed back and felt wind kiss my throat as the knife whistled past. Then I stepped in, caught his wrist mid-swing and twisted like I meant it.

With a dry, meaty snap, something gave way, causing the Weasel to scream and drop the knife, but, before the blade had time to hit ground, I kicked out, sending it skittering into the fallen trash.

Disarm assailant. Check.

He staggered back, cradling his arm like a busted violin,

his sneer gone, but I wasn't done yet. Not nearly. Using the broken arm as a fulcrum, I twirled and slammed an elbow into his gut, and, as The Weasel doubled over in pain and shock, introduced his falling face to my rising knee. The two met with a satisfying crunch, and a warm splash I tried my hardest not to think about.

Pushing down on the silent scream, I clenched my jaw, and finished the fight with a cross which damn near turned the greasy pervert all the way around, then, before he could regain his balance, brought my boot down on the back of his knee, dropping him to the ground like a bag of wet laundry. A kick to the side of his head was enough to make sure he stayed there.

The fight done, I damn-near collapsed against the wall, my fingers fumbling for the solid reassurance of the bricks and the mortar. The Weasel's nose was broken, blood was streaming down his chin, and The Thirst, that dark and needful craving I carry inside me, uncurled and bayed to be sated.

Your name is Charlotte Amálie Durant, I recited the well-practiced words to halt the rush of sensation. *And you are a good person.*

Because this was a different kind of fight. A fight I was actually in danger of losing.

It took time, but eventually, when I felt I'd recovered enough, I turned to check on the woman.

Who wasn't there.

#

"I ran."

It was as if Rose had tracked my thoughts.

"Charlie and the goon were going at it pretty hard, so I did what any sane person would and made for the hills. I guess it took me the best part of an hour to get home, and *this...*" She dived into her pocket again and produced a creamy sheet of paper. "...was waiting for me on the kitchen counter when I got there."

She sat back, her hands flying to her face. “It’s a hell of a story, I know, one I’m not sure even *I* believe, but it happened. So tell me, Ms. Durant, do you think I’m crazy?”

I struck a match and finally lit the cigarette I’d been chewing on. Smoke curled away from my lips like a secret in shades of bluish gray.

“No,” I said. “Not crazy. We’ve danced with some pretty strange situations here at Charlie Durant Investigations, and for us a lot of what you describe is just another Tuesday.”

She blinked. “Then... what do you think?” Her voice was as brittle as pond ice.

I glanced at the faces of Howard and Tamara and found the answer to her question. "I think you need help, Ms. Chamberlain," I said. "Help I know we can provide. I can't say I've much of an idea what any of this means yet, but there is one thing I can promise you— we *will* find out and, until we do, we *will* keep you safe." I crossed to the window and looked down at the rain-strewn big city night. “In short, Ms. Chamberlain, I guess what I’m saying is I think you've just hired yourself a detective agency.”

3

After Tamara left with Rose to check on the sister in St. Jude's, I did what I always do when a case gets under my skin.

I poured myself a drink.

Howard lingered by the door, his hat clenched in his hand. I could see the questions stacking up behind the big man's eyes like so many unpaid bills.

"Go ahead," I said. "Ask."

"I guess I mainly want to know if I did okay?" The child-like uncertainty, coming from a man with a look and a build ripped straight from a dime-store detective novel, was almost disconcerting.

"You did fine, Howard. Tamara would be proud."

"Right." The big man blushed ever so slightly. "And this reappearing contract business, I guess that's another of those things that's going to be part and parcel of the job, yeah?"

I allowed myself a weary smile and gestured to the client's chair. "Sit down, Howard. Let me tell you how we got here."

Howard Gold had been Tamara's way of drumming up trade with those who needed to stay in the dark about my darkness. A man to deal with the walk-ins, lost pets, swindling employees, and straying husbands. Not that it was my more monstrous side that alarmed those blissfully ignorant people. No, the issue that stuck in those workaday folks' craws faster than my fangs ever could was my *gender*.

"You see, a woman's place in the world hasn't shifted all that much in the couple of centuries I've been alive," I said to the big man. I mean, sure, we'd clawed our way to the vote and could collect a paycheck, but despite those oh-so modern headlines, the America of 1934 still played a man's games by a man's rules."

It was true. In these United States, a woman could be almost anything she wanted, so long as what she wanted was quiet and proper, but the picture the general public held of a P.I —a picture reinforced by actors such as William Powell in The Thin Man and just about every pulp rag on the newsstand—was of a grizzled, gum-chewing hunk—a lone wolf in a rumpled suit, good with a gun, handy with his fists, and always, *always* a man. No, no matter how much my preternatural strength and stealth suited me to the role, a female private detective was always going to be a bridge too far—the kind of bridge some people would burn while you were only halfway across.

A man was what our 'normal' clients expected, so a man was what we gave them. The nervous walk-ins with their petty thefts and wandering spouses never once questioned the qualifications of the square-jawed man behind the desk. After all, Howard *looked* the part, and for them that was enough. They weren't to know that two months ago his biggest claim to fame was a quarter-page toothpaste ad in *Home Companion*. I doubt any of them even *saw* the secretary busy taking notes behind him unless they were the type to notice a woman's legs before her brains.

"So that's the setup," I said. "You're the mask. I'm the face underneath."

Howard nodded slowly. "And this Rose Chamberlain blew the whole thing wide open."

"Yeah."

"And do you think she knows about... you know—" He gestured vaguely at me. "The vampire thing?"

"No, not yet," I said. "And, if I'm good enough, she never will."

Howard nodded, glanced at the hat in his hands again and then at the door. "Well, Tamara will be home by now, but if you're okay on your own..."

"Goodnight, Howard," I said. "Don't forget the light on your way out."

#

I guess by now my 'secret' is out, so let's lay it bare. To the upstanding, cheerfully oblivious, 'normal' folk of St. Germain, I'm a secretary, an office manager or, to the select few, a Private Investigator, but to those who have their eyes peeled a little wider—the Patrick Callaghans, Mother Yeagers, and Igor Tals of this world—I'm a card-carrying, shadow-haunting, blood-sipping anomaly. An undead creature of the night with over two hundred years trailing in her wake. I am, in short, a vampire—only a little more Marya Zaleska and a little less Nosferatu.

Because I might be a blood-drinking monster in the middle of her own personal prohibition, with a couple of centuries of bad dreams trailing in her wake, but I'm still a woman with bills to pay—a reasonably modern gal, who's just looking to get by. But angry mobs don't tend to ask how you're doing before they reach for the pitchforks, and they're not big on personal circumstances, either. It was true of Europe back in the day, and it's true of 1930's America. The Volstead Act might have died a welcome death but some drinking habits still get you noticed.

It's something I've learned to adapt to over my long undead life, something that led me to add a little discretion to my moonlit indiscretions and find a friend or two to help me out along the way—people who saw past the horror movie clichés to the woman underneath—people who knew how to keep a secret.

And, as if on cue, a familiar figure detached itself from the shadows and crossed the street toward the office. I tossed back the remnants of my drink and waited for Tamara Quinn to climb the stairs.

#

"I had to wait," Tamara said. "While our new client was here, I couldn't say a word, but the thing is, *it* talked to me."

"It?" I asked.

"The Machine." She rolled her eyes as only Tamara could, dumped her coat on the chair we keep for clients, and marched into the back room. "It was yesterday, while you were taking a well-earned coffin break."

"You mean while I was asleep on the sofa-bed."

"Well, yeah." She reappeared with a sketch pad. "But still... It was daylight, and you were out the game, so I made the initial enquiries and was going to bring it to your attention when you woke up—if only Rose hadn't got there first... anyway, look."

She placed the pad before me, the pages opened to a grisly scene captured in pencil. In the foreground lay the body of a blonde, petite woman. A body torn in places no body ever should be. Her legs were unnaturally splayed, one arm reached eternally above her head for help that would never come. The other lay beside her as limp as a bird's broken wing. From a forest of cuts her life's blood trickled and flowed into the gutter to join with the rain and disappear into the hungry mouth of a nearby storm drain.

"It's her, isn't it?"

I peered into the macabre image again. The face was twisted away, but the hair color coupled with the small build...

"No," I said. "It can't be. You say The Machine gave you this yesterday, but we all saw Rose alive and well tonight."

"Unless it's a warning." Tamara sat down and helped herself to a double finger of brandy. "I mean that's not unknown."

She had a point. 'The Machine' as we called it was a semiconscious device of unknown origin that Tamara had picked up on a foray through the city's very blackest markets. A device whose one and only party piece was the forcing of visceral, muddled images and sensations into the mind of those who touched it—messages, auguries, and yes, sometimes even warnings.

Most of it was housed in polished mahogany, maybe two feet by three. From one of its longer sides, a copper pipe curled in a way that was a little too organic before vanishing into its casing like a snake. A narrow window in the lid of the box exposed the guts of the thing—brass cogs that turned with the rhythm of a beating heart and a hexagonal drum that spun in five separate directions at five different speeds, their faces etched with eldritch symbols that hurt the eye. From somewhere deep, deep inside a nameless *something* glowed a pale and sickly green.

"But what did you see, exactly?" I asked, returning to the vision The Machine had gifted Tamara. "What did you *feel?"*

"Nothing good." She shrugged. "This girl, whoever she was, running for her life and bleeding hard. Her lungs were on fire. I felt gloved hands grab her and a hard stab of ice-cold steel, right here." Her fingers hovered over her chest, tapping once. "And that's where it ended. There was one last burst of pain, and then... nothing."

I looked down at the sketch again, holding the paper close to my eyes, searching for any hidden detail.

"I guess, if you're sure, it doesn't really matter," Tamara said. "Rose changed her mind about the hospital. She figured it was too late for visiting hours, so she went straight home, but I took the address and asked a couple of Dvargn who still owe us for that Runeshield affair to keep an eye on her door for us while we work out where to start." She sat back and nursed her drink, treating me to an uncomfortable silence.

"Then what's wrong?" I asked her.

"Wrong? Why would anything be wrong?"

"Because I know you Tamara, that's why."

#

It was a shade over three and a half years ago that Tamara Quinn, the only daughter of one Thomas Quinn, a career cop with a sharp temper and a granite reputation, decided she was going to dig into the deaths of three bottom-feeding torpedoes working for the Yeager mob—men, or almost men, that the cops barely bothered to tag and bag. Sick of being told no, she set out to prove a woman could be a credit to the SGPD, and not just as window dressing in a badge. She faced the city's shadows with both sleeves rolled up, asking hard questions of even harder customers and demanding quick answers.

Her investigations led her to some uncomfortable truths about exactly what passed for 'normal' in St. Germain. In the margins surrounding everyday life she found names most folk weren't supposed to read. *Wichtel. Heinzelmännchen. Domovoi. Puck.* The names of the old-world goblins and sprites that made up the grist to the mill that powered St. Germain's smuggling, gambling, and drug rackets, and *Dvargn*, who are sometimes called Dwarves, although never to their face, at least not twice, and are renowned guards and ingenious devisers of wards and protections. Names that led her my way.

Not that they ever should have, but, in order to save himself any further pain, a Hob with a brand-new limp handed her the name and nature of the woman who gave it to him, and, just like that, all roads led to me.

I'd say that finding a grim-faced Tamara waiting in the dark of your apartment with a loaded crossbow aimed squarely at your heart would be enough to unsettle anyone. I know it gave me a moment of pause.

"Sit down." She indicated the chair arranged opposite her with the barest flick of her head. "The bolt loaded in this bow is crafted from solid hawthorn, tipped with a mix of silver and thrice-blessed iron." Her voice was quiet and deathly calm. "A combination that is custom built for killing... *Vampires!*"

I swallowed a smile and tried for a slow, solemn nod.

"Silver-tipped hawthorn, huh? Yeah, that should do the trick, alright." I opened my coat, moving nice and easy, my eyes asking her a question, and fished a pack of smokes from my inside pocket. "Of course, you'd be amazed at the wide range of things you can kill with a metal-tipped bolt of hardened wood, fired directly through the heart at point-blank range. But you are here to kill me, and I get that—what I don't fully understand is why?"

"I have my reasons," the tall girl with the dark curls and the crossbow said.

"Of course you do." I tapped a cigarette against my palm and jammed it between my teeth. "Probably a whole bunch of them. But before we move on to the 'killing me' portion of the evening's entertainment, why don't we narrow it down a touch? After all, there's a certain peace that comes with knowing you've killed the right monster for the right reason." I struck a match and let the flame burn for a moment. "You strike me as the type of gal who gets things done—probably the woman who's causing such a buzz around certain parts of town—but all I'm asking is that we take a minute to reflect, and make sure you're sure. After that, you can fire as many of your special bolts in me as you like. I promise."

It was a gambit that shouldn't have worked. But Tamara—headstrong, stubborn Tamara, was—*is*—nothing if not spectacularly thorough. In the end it took thirty-seven minutes to convince her not to kill me that night—eighteen for her to realize the murder victims had a little too much blood left in their veins, and the rest to work out what to do next.

It was a visit to the Hob who supplied Tamara with my name that put us on a scent which eventually led to a lieutenant in the Yeager outfit, the very same mob that all of the deceased had worked for. I guess ambition is a funny thing. Tamara wanted to slap the cuffs on the murdering bastard right then and there and I wanted to do a whole lot more besides, but Mother Yeager wasn't having any of it. The career-minded assassin never did see the inside of a cell, and I never found out when Tamara got her hands on her father's cuffs, either. I guess sometimes, ignorance really is bliss.

Our association might've ended right there and then, if not for an 'invitation' from Mother Yeager— the ultimate head of the Hydra-headed Eastern European outfit—to locate a suitcase the privacy of whose contents she was real clear about. Don't ask questions and *don't* get curious. One overly complex kidnapping and two murders later, Tamara finally floated the idea of making our alliance official. It wasn't the likeliest of partnerships, but somehow it worked. Tamara learned to trust the woman behind the vampire, and I learned to trust the instincts of Tamara.

#

"What's wrong is this whole deal," Tamara said, answering my question. "The contract. The dreams. The Hand. It all feels... bigger, somehow, than our usual cases. It feels like..."

"Caster business?"

"Yeah," she said. "Caster business."

I took a slow sip of brandy, the alcohol working on me like a liquid hug, and weighed her words. The Casters were the loose cabal of magic users who cloistered themselves in the more manicured end of St. Germain that lay to the north of the River Lyff—a neighbourhood where the air smelled less like trouble and more like the money that paid for it.

But the real difference was in the nature of the power they wielded. You see, those who eked out a living south of the Lyff's waters had magic—bone-deep, *natural* magic—in their blood, but the Casters' power came through rituals, symbols, and artifacts. Spells inked in dead languages. Trinkets that hummed and sparkled. Their power wasn't theirs. It was borrowed. Stolen. Twisted and corrupted. And as hard as they worked to get it, they worked twice as hard to keep it.

"Okay," I said slowly. "Let's say you're right. The Casters are toxic company on a good day. We'll have no contacts to call on, not a single favor to cash in, and you know they'll circle the wagons real fast." I leaned forward, my brandy catching the low light like melted amber. "No, any venture into Caster territory leaves us blind, helpless, and hated. A bad hand to play."

"So?"

"So, we take this one slow and steady and we stick close to

home. Before we even think of setting foot on enemy turf, we do our homework and find out exactly who Rose's dream-guy is and exactly what he wants."

Tamara chewed it over, eyes narrow, her mind working.

"Makes sense, I suppose," she said.

"Good," I said. "Which leaves us with the thorny question of where to start that homework."

"Well, there's The Hand," Tamara mused. "Your friend in the alley might not have been sharing, but someone in that nest of vipers knows something."

"Sure," I said, my tone dry as dust. "And as with The Casters, we stand a better chance of being killed to death than getting any answers."

"The sleeping Sister then?"

I finished my drink, studied the empty tumbler like it might change its mind, and reached for the bottle. "Not to be negative, Tam, but do you really think we'll get all that much from a woman in a magically-induced coma? No, I think if we're going to get anywhere, then this time we need to start with the devils we know."

"Meaning?"

"Meaning we call on Mackenzie."

4

"Okay. So, to be clear, you're telling me magic, and we're talking about the real-deal, spells-and-sorcery stuff, is real."Rose Chamberlain sat with one hand wrapped around a mug of watery coffee and the other tucked beneath her chin, her flawless face twisted in disbelief. "And not only that," she continued, staring into the depths of her beverage, "but some mysterious, nameless *someone* is aiming said magic directly at me?"

It was the night after Rose had told us her story and a whole two hours after our consultation with Mackenzie Hoyte. Tamara, Rose, and I were gathered around a chipped Formica table in one of the city's numerous late-night coffee houses.

"That's about the shape of it," I said, watching the steam coil from my cup like the spirit of caffeine.

"Right, and all of it—The Hand, the nightmares, Grace's condition, that contract. The... what did you call it again?"

"*A Binding*," Tamara supplied, her gaze sharp.

"Right. This... *Binding* was cooked up to get me to sign away my soul. And to do so *willingly?*"

"Enthusiastically, you might say."

Rose narrowed her eyes. "And you found this out how?"

#

"You're late," Mackenzie Hoyte had grumbled as I pushed open the door to the office-cum-store he kept on the corner of Wellington and 8th, earlier that same evening. He was a small, disheveled man with a thin face, thinner hair, and the air of a distracted scarecrow. His un-ironed suit, a charcoal-gray number from the bargain end of a department store clearance rack, was impressively stained. He hadn't shaved that morning, and probably not the morning before either. But his pale, bloodshot eyes still held the intellectual fire of a man who'd once lectured at places equipped with marble steps and Latin mottos, the one telltale sign that the mind lurking behind those eyes had once counted among the world's sharpest—in certain, very specialized fields.

In keeping with his outward appearance, his place of business was worn and chaotic.

Almost every available surface was weighed down with piles of yellowed manuscripts. The small table he stood beside practically groaned under the weight of layers of parchment and cracked leather folders. Even the twin chairs that flanked it were buried beneath an avalanche of academia. A musty, sweet scent birthed by the reams of ancient time-stained paper tainted the air like vanilla that had been left out in the sun too long.

Tamara sniffed at this heady atmosphere and frowned as she followed me in, her booted feet falling with heavy percussion on the bare boards.

"I thought we had an arrangement," Mackenzie huffed, glancing at Tamara with barely disguised disgust. "First dark you said. You, the document, and two bottles of the least offensive merlot you could find, and you were to leave *that...*," he jabbed a callused, ink-stained finger at Tamara like he was casting a hex, "...at home!"

To give Tamara her due, she didn't even blink.

"Aw, come on, Mackenzie, you know you don't mean that." I set the wine on the corner of the table, brushed off the only chair not buried beneath a dozen centuries of paper, and dropped into it. "You got off on the wrong foot, sure, but Tamara apologized, remember? And she's promised me it won't happen again."

"Well... I suppose, as you're here." Mackenzie sniffed. "But if she so much as *touches* one single scrap of paper, or even *thinks* of 'tidying' then you're *out!* And I mean *both* of you!"

"Trust me, Mackenzie," I said, glancing at Tamara, who stood in the shop's doorway like a thundercloud in heeled boots, glancing around her like she was mentally alphabetizing Mackenzie's books just to spite him. "Tamara's going to behave herself this time. Aren't you, Tam?"

I didn't wait for an answer. "Good. Now, if we're all a little less unhappy, perhaps we can get down to business."

I reached into my coat, pulled out the sheet of paper that had haunted Rose Chamberlain for so long, and laid it on a mostly uncluttered patch of table.

"We think this is Caster-wrought. Some kind of contract, maybe?"

Mackenzie picked the document up with the kind of reverence usually reserved for relics and loaded guns and brought it to his nose like a perfumer sampling a classic scent, his brow furrowing deeper and deeper with every breath. Only after this ritual was complete did he rescue his glasses from his unkempt hair, perch them on his nose, and turn his attention to the symbols. As he read, his lips moved, his index finger trailing along every line.

When he finished, he flicked an unquiet glance my way. Then, with the slow deliberation of a man folding a death warrant, he smoothed the document's creases into place, laid it on the table, and sat back, venting a low whistle that hung in the air like a storm warning.

"This is serious business you're getting mixed up in, Charlie," he said. "And I mean *real* serious. Are you acting on a client's behalf, or for yourself?"

"A client," I replied. "And we passed serious a long while back."

Mackenzie arched an eyebrow. "Pressure to sign?"

"You might say. My client's sister is in St. Jude's, in a coma the writer of those symbols claims responsibility for. Every now and then, she wakes up to scream."

With a creak, Mackenzie rose and shuffled toward a stack of ancient tomes a sneeze away from disaster. One hand rose to stroke the spines of the heavy, leather-bound volumes like they were pets. "The document you've brought me," he said, "is called a *Binding*." He stressed the word like a pronouncement of doom. "And yes, it is a contract—of sorts. A rare and ancient magic that calls upon the power of entities I'd rather not name out loud to form an unbreakable bargain."

#

"Geez." Rose let her attention wander to the diner's plate glass window and the late-night stragglers slinking along the street underneath the blinking neon light that declared the place 'open'. "And to think I asked you if *I* was crazy!"

I trailed a spoon through the thin crema pinwheeling lazily on the surface of my coffee and tried to find something close to the right words. Behind the counter, a woman with too much hairspray and too little interest in her customers flipped through a bridal magazine and looked up long enough to be unimpressed.

"I know," I said, my voice a little scratchy around the edges.

"But what you've got to understand is... St. Germain... it isn't your average postage-stamp city. It's had its fair share of immigration, just like any other place that promises freedom by the foot, but the folks who bedded down here were always a different breed—outsiders, even in their own countries. When superstition and oppression chased them from the Old World, it was St. Germain that welcomed them in, and, as it became their home, it became the home of something else, too. The home of..." I shot Tamara a desperate look.

"...of magic," she finished, trying not to make the word sound like a weak punchline. "It became the home of magic."

Rose didn't say anything right away. She just sat with her hands wrapped around her cup, warming them on the cooling coffee and the last sane thought she had left. After a while she nodded, the gesture aimed more toward her own internal dialogue than either of us.

"The home of magic," she said. "The *actual* home of magic. Well, ain't that something."

Her voice held that flat-edged drawl people sometimes use when they've run out of irony.

"I was warned, you know... even before I caught the Greyhound with my little suitcase full of dreams. My mom. My dad. Hell, even Mary Travers who once braided my hair and swore she'd never lie to me. All of them explained the dangers of the big bad city. The muggers. The rapists. The sleazy talent scouts who'd chew me up and spit me out—but magic?" She snorted a short, humorless laugh. "No, not one of 'em mentioned magic. Weird, huh?"

A ripe silence, as heavy as a rain cloud, hung in the air. A silence it took Tamara to break.

"It's a lot, I know." She set her cup to one side and cleared a space between herself and Rose like she was laying out the cards for a hand she didn't want to play. "And when I say I know, I mean I *know*. I've been there, you see. I've sat where you are now —felt the exact same disbelief and uncertainty clawing away at my insides. It was as if the whole world had suddenly changed shape on me. Everything was suddenly different, and nobody had thought to let me know." She didn't look my way. Not once. "But think about it," she continued. "The dreams, the contract, the... *Binding*. Think about all those strange coincidences and midnight experiences you told yourself couldn't be real while the sun shone bright and the birds still sang. Doesn't magic explain all of it? Doesn't it *fit*?"

Rose didn't say a word. She just kept staring through the plate glass window at the city sprawled in a hundred shades of rain-soaked trouble, its neon lights flickering like a failing heartbeat.

"I... I guess." Rose's voice cracked and something behind her eyes cracked along with it. "But that would mean..." She trailed off, and when her voice returned, it was filled with something raw and lonely. "Oh, Charlie, it's all real, isn't it? The contract. The dreams. That smooth bastard and his hungry, hellish stare, all of it. I'm not imagining it. I'm not insane."

You can blame it on a too-long life dressed in midnight shadows, but I'd almost forgotten how hard it is to have the veil of everyday life pulled back to reveal the marvels and horrors that lay beyond.

Rose's ordeal had cast her adrift in a sea of self-doubt without a single soul to confide in, but Tamara's words—her simple understanding—were like a beacon guiding her to dry land.

"It's okay." Tamara reached across the table and squeezed Rose's hand to stress the point. "Charlie and I, we're going to *make* it okay. And I mean all of it... I promise."

#

"You see, there are two types of Binding, Ms. Durant," Mackenzie said. "And both call upon these *'patrons'* to enforce their promises. The first, a *Minor Binding,* is a devil's deal with a ceiling in both price and reward. An ugly thing, but manageable.

"And this?" I asked.

"This..." His voice dropped low. "This is a *Major Binding.* The heavy stuff. An infernal bargain that grants the first signee *real* power and in return, demands a far larger fee from the second—the sacrifice of what some might call their everlasting soul, although that's an imprecise term, to forces you can't even begin to imagine."

"But why?" Tamara asked, her voice quiet. "What on earth could possibly be worth signing your soul away for?"

Mackenzie glanced at her, any trace of his earlier grievances gone.

"Power." He spat the word like it was poison. "It's nearly *always* about power, Ms Quinn. Remember, not everyone was born, or... " He flashed me an almost apologetic smile. "... *reborn*, into magic." The 'Casters', as some have taken to calling them, have to beg, borrow, and steal for theirs. It's why they write their spells, forge their charms, and whisper to things that should never-ever be heard under the full of the moon—to gain access to gifts never made for them, but the further they reach for that power, the more that power reaches *back*."

I picked up the Binding and stared at the sigils, my mind working.

"So, what? My client signs this and suddenly becomes the surrogate sacrifice of some Caster creep looking to get his hands on some magic?"

Mackenzie smiled, tight and humorless. "Yes, I believe so."

"Then, I guess we've got our 'why'." I returned the folded paper to the table. "And a method that points the finger at a couple of hundred suspects, too."

"There's something else we've got, too," Tamara said from the doorway, her arms crossed. "We know our mysterious dream guy's more than just ambitious. He's got to be the kind of bastard who'd burn down a house just to warm his hands. I mean, why go straight to mental torture and emotional extortion? Why not run some kind of play before resorting to the heavy stuff? If it were me, I'd bury The Binding under a receipt or a waiver and hand my surrogate the pen."

"No dice, I'm afraid," Mackenzie said, working something loose from his teeth with the edge of his tongue. "Any surrogate has to *want* to sign. And I mean with all their heart and all their soul. The intent has to be *pure*. No tricks. No loopholes. No 'gotchas.'"

I thought about Rose's story. The terror of the dreams. The offer of riches. The sister left tortured and insensible in the hospital. The Binding which kept re-appearing like a vendetta. This wasn't some simple back-alley mugging we were dealing with.

This was a *campaign*—a slow, methodical squeeze.

"Your client needs to stay strong, Charlie," Mackenzie said like he'd read my mind. "As I said, a Binding is serious business. It takes far more than whispered words and a lucky rabbit's foot to craft something of this magnitude. I'd guess whoever created it has got real juice and that kind of power doesn't come cheap." He stood, his shadow falling long against the parchment and dust. "You're looking at a war of attrition, Charlie, a long, slow campaign of magic and terror, and the pressure is only going to build from here on in. So if you're set on standing by your client, you need to be prepared to feel some of that pressure too. Right down to the marrow."

He stepped closer, his eyes catching the hooded light in a way I didn't like. "I suggest you buckle up, ladies, because whoever this guy is and whatever he has in store for your client, there's one thing I *can* promise you... it's not going to be pretty."

#

"A war of attrition," Rose said quietly. "That's really what he called it."

"Yeah." I met her eyes. "But here's the thing, Rose, wars can be won, and this is a war I mean to fight, and fight hard."

"But why me?"

Rose clung to Tamara's hand like it was the last rung on the ladder to the lifeboat, dabbing at her eyes with the cuff of the powder-blue sweater she wore under her swing coat. "I mean, I'm nothing special—just one more girl who's never done anything worth a damn her whole life through and probably never will, so why pick *me*? And who is this guy? Do I know him? Did I hurt him somehow? Serve him coffee? Smile at him a little too sweetly?"

"I don't know." I stared into the depths of my cup, looking for inspiration. "...but I know a man who might."

5

Daylight, as you can probably imagine, is a problem for me. A problem that meant the arrangements of our next meeting had to be left with Tamara.

Luckily, the girl is nothing if not resourceful, so while I slept the day away, her hard work paid off enough for us to attend an appointment in Blackwood Heights with one of St. Germain's more reclusive residents.

His name was Doctor Kieren Rivers, a man who looked like he'd been carved from the bark of an old walnut tree—all gaunt lines and quiet, time-worn strength.

These days, he wore the title of Head of Palliative Medicine at St. Jude's Infirmary, but that wasn't the reason I'd rung his bell. No, Doc Rivers and I went back to much older, far stranger times.

"I've prepared a French roast," he said as we took our seat, his voice as smooth as velvet and twice as expensive. "Somewhat dark for my taste, but I thought you might appreciate the gesture."

Dressed like Sunday morning lounging with a heavy side of midnight brooding—gray slacks, a shirt open at the throat, a vest that was still buttoned, and a gold watch chain which disappeared into his chest pocket—he waved a long-fingered hand at the pot of coffee on the table and the four bone china cups lined up beside it as if waiting for their cue like he was a magician finishing a trick, rolled up his shirt sleeves and, with practised grace, played mother.

"Not that it isn't a most distinct pleasure to see you again, Ms. Durant," he said, sinking into a high-backed armchair that probably cost more than my office with his own cup. "But judging by the effort expended to reach me," he continued, "might I assume your visit is for reasons more pressing than a late-night coffee?"

He wasn't wrong.

The doctor's Blackwood Heights townhouse, perched atop a steep flight of stone steps which lent it an air of being too good for the street below, came with thick curtains, thicker locks, and the kind of neighbors who knew how not to ask questions. Blackwood Heights meant the kind of money that never needed to be spent and the type of influence that went unspoken. The folks who strolled its maple-lined streets were society's winners —educated, moneyed, connected, and flush with the kind of luck that got handed down with the family crest, the kind of luck I'd turned my back on a long, long time ago.

But it still roused a few too many memories. The air smelled like fresh-cut grass, wisteria, and trust funds, but more than a hint of the past—*my* past lurked beneath. The scent of unearned, privileged, indulgence—bittersweet and bruised, like overripe fruit.

No, Blackwood Heights wasn't a place built for just anyone, but then, Kieren Rivers *wasn't* just anyone.

"Somewhat... yeah," I said in answer to his question as I took the proffered cup. It had, in fact, taken Tamara three tense rounds with Connie, the doctor's gatekeeping secretary, and the dropping of a name I don't lean on anymore, to buy us this slice of midnight in the doctor's own spacious and tastefully apportioned digs.

Steam curled from the rim of my china cup, rich with the aroma of a coffee with both a name and an address, a vapor which rose to meet the muted ghost of the no-longer-smoking incense parked on the mantel, all frankincense and forgotten temples. I let the deliciously bitter liquid sit on my tongue for a moment, set the cup down, and told the doctor everything.

When I finished, he pressed his long fingers together like a man in prayer, bowed his head, and froze like a statue. You could've balanced a nickel on his spine and not seen it tip. Six long seconds later, he spoke.

"I'm afraid, in the case of Ms. Chamberlain's sister, I find myself unable to offer any assistance." His voice came deep and creaking, like a sermon for the damned. "Her affliction lies outside my professional sphere—beyond even my 'extra-professional' remit—and the only place I could escort her to is not a place any of you would care to visit."

That lit a fuse in Rose. She leaned forward, ready to blow, but Tamara's hand found her wrist, and, like that, the spark died. Another resentful pang shot through me like a stiletto-sharp reminder of everything I'd lost but I batted the unwanted emotion aside.

"Unmasking the author of your 'Binding', however," Rivers continued, "presents us with certain... avenues." He melted into the shadows of his high-backed chair. "As Ms. Durant knows, long before I assumed my current role, it was my duty—my *privilege*—to act as guide to a certain kind of traveler. A line on my résumé, which lends me a knack for knowing the *where*, *when*, and, on occasion, even the *who* of particular items and events."

He jabbed a skeletal finger into the arm of the chair, scoring a neat, white line across the old leather with his nail like he was drawing the first points on a map none of us wanted to follow. "All we need do," he continued, "is trace this 'Binding' to the moment it was crafted. But understand this—" he raised a slender hand of admonition "—as your Mr. Hoyte says, the power to weave a spell of this magnitude does not come easy. If we track this *Binding* to its roots, you may find yourself face-to-face with a most formidable foe."

Across from him, Rose, her hands clasped tight enough to bleach bone, was locked in internal debate. When she finally spoke, her voice was a flat sheet of ice laid over a raging sea of fury.

"My sister's in your hospital, Doctor Rivers," she said. "She's in a coma she might never crawl out of—a coma signed, sealed, and delivered by the same bogeyman you're warning us about. The last time I saw her, she woke up and screamed in my face like every demon in hell was flaying her soul, and then slipped away from me again like so much smoke. So you'll forgive me if I don't give a rat's hairy ass how 'formidable' this bastard is, and don't care much for your risks either. I'm not in this for *safe,* Doctor Rivers. I want to find the creep who's tormenting Grace, and make him pay for everything he's done to her, everything he's planning to do to *me*, and make sure he never gets the chance to torment anyone ever again."

I shot Rose a sharp glance. From the little I was learning, she was a woman who wore her heart pinned to her sleeve, but this was new. There was steel hiding behind those wide, tear-wet eyes and an unexpected fire in the words of the girl in the powder-blue sweater. I felt a surge of admiration and unwarranted pride bloom in my empty heart.

"Indeed," Rivers said, his voice as quiet as graveyard dust and as heavy as a headstone. "I commend your spirit, Ms. Chamberlain, I do, but conviction must ever be tempered with caution. For a path, once laid, can be traversed in either direction." He didn't move, but his stare was sharp enough to carve meat. "Tug on this thread, and there's every chance something will tug back —at you, and at you... and, of course, at you." As he spoke, he raised one finger as thin and pale as a sliver of ivory, and pointed it, in turn at Rose, Tamara, and finally, with deliberate care, at me.

There was no menace hidden in his words, but their meaning rang as clear as a bell. We were about to kick a hornet's nest, and these particular hornets had magic. I could take the heat—I'd walked through worse—but Tamara? Rose? I had no right to expect the same from them.

But I needn't have worried. Tamara's jaw tightened. A look

I'd seen before. "Okay," she said. "That's twice in two nights someone's given us the whole 'dire warning' song and dance. I really don't see the use in us rehearsing it again." She shot me a look with a world of weight and history piled up behind it. "If the mystical breadcrumbs we spill leave a trail for this bastard to follow then I say let him. We *have* to know what we're up against, Charlie—we need to."

Rose didn't say a word, but she didn't need to. Her eyes, cool, clear, and full of that same need for answers, said it all.

I gave her, and then Tamara, a long, judicious look and returned my attention to the doctor, setting my cup down with a soft *click*, as final as a revolver's chamber sliding into place.

"Alright, Doc," I said, "where do we start?"

6

Once again, I left it to Tamara to see Rose home.

It was a little late for Callaghan's, and far too early to hit the hay, so instead I did what any self-respecting creature of the night with her own private eye firm would do. I hit the office that sat one flight up from a tailor's shop that never saw a customer and two doors down from a Chinese laundry that was *definitely* just a laundry. Tamara and I had met some 'interesting' characters in our line of work. Friends, fiends, and felons—people and creatures who committed nasty little crimes for nasty little reasons, each their own brand of low-grade evil. Our unknown quarry seemed to be a creature of a different stripe. A man who held magic in one pocket and money in the other. A man with the sense and influence to keep his face out of the spotlight.

Power, money, and anonymity—it wasn't a combination I liked.

As I turned onto Revello, my boots clicking a tired rhythm against the wet sidewalk, I looked up at the single dark window that marked my own particular, peculiar, corner of the world. Nothing stirred behind it, and that was fine by me. I didn't need company. I needed quiet. I needed the time and space to think.

My mind flew to that dingy alleyway where I'd rescued Rose from the clutches of The Weasel. For her, that had been the end of the story, but I'd had another fight to face.

Even with his eyes shut and face as slack and soft as a sleeping choirboy, The Weasel had stunk of petty cruelty. A man who was as sharp and vicious as the blade he'd tried to stick me with, it was as if he was born with a knife in his hand and a grudge against all humanity in his heart. I remembered turning him over using the toe of one boot and nudging him once or twice for good measure before dropping to my haunches to give him his wake-up call. I remembered his scream as I applied ungentle pressure to his injured arm, and the way his eyes bulged as I kept that pressure on. I remembered asking him who The Hand had been working for, what the document I'd seen him try to get Rose to sign was, and the tough-guy grin he'd tried on as he told me to go to hell.

But most of all, I remembered the blood.

Because he'd made a point of showing me the depths of his defiance, underlining the point with a couple of overly descriptive threats and a glob of bloodied saliva spat straight into my face. It was more than enough. I forgot all about my mantra—forgot the promises I'd made to Tamara and the promises I'd made to myself. I felt The Thirst—that deep, clawing need to drink fresh, vital blood—rise up within me, felt my cheeks hollow and my brow drop as my teeth fused and split into a collection of cruel, barbed fangs. I felt the Hunger—the urge to take the human life so obviously at my mercy and, in a frenzy of flesh-ripping destruction, end it as it pleaded with me to let it live.

But I didn't.

And it wasn't because of my mantra, those few lines of memorized platitude I used to remind myself of the humanity hiding behind the monster. It was because of the ghost that Rose Chamberlain—a girl whose name I didn't even know yet—had raised for me.

Trying my best to bury the thought, I trudged up the stairs, unlocked the office, and made straight for the half bottle of overproof brandy hidden in the bottom drawer of the desk. Because, even now, wrapped tight in the dark, I heard the echoing voice of the man with the smoked glass spectacles—the man who'd come to court to damn me. I felt the touch of his hand on my shoulder. I smelled his cologne, expensive and refined, with notes of amber, lavender, carnation, and, buried somewhere beneath it, I smelled the medicinal tang of camphor.

And I saw *her.*

I sank into the chair behind the desk that hadn't been tidy since Prohibition, kicked off my shoes, and poured myself two fingers of false comfort. The past was the past, and if I was going to help Rose, that was exactly where I needed to keep it.

Because Tamara had said this job felt different, and she was right. It wasn't the usual hustle, the kind you could either shake down or lock up. This business held weight and history. It held design. First, there was the approach—a hundred-dollar handshake and an offer of employment that didn't smell like any work I knew of, and then there was the threat Grace Chamberlain, condemned to a coma with a scream stuck in her throat.

No, the curve was too steep—too fast, like two ends of a magic trick missing a middle. Maybe it was old age making me cynical. A couple of hundred years will do that to a girl. But my gut was telling me someone was holding cards I hadn't seen yet, and I didn't like that. Not one damn bit.

I rescued my glass and sauntered into the back room, letting my fingers drift over Tamara's case files. Every perp and patsy she and I had ever locked horns with was in there, row after row of them, standing like stiff-backed soldiers, their sins cross-referenced and color-coded. Tamara might have been a girl fueled by strange obsessions but when it came to organization she was a goddess. My fingertips danced over the labeled spines, past crisp edges of law and lore, and travelled on to the one thing I hadn't counted on Tamara returning to its rightful place.

The Machine.

#

Smoke, crumbling brick, and the damp tobacco of a million discarded cigarettes assaulted my nose as the room around me faded, becoming a scene from the big city night. The sounds... the odors, the... tastes slithered around me. Distant cars. Exhaust fumes. Footsteps. The stink of rotting garbage.

Through it all I ran. Not heading towards anything. Running a*way*. But it was too much. Too hard. Too far. My knees buckled. Cracked asphalt leapt up to greet my fall. The breath flew from my lungs in a long, ragged sob as the rough surface of the road tore into my palms. Rain hammered the back of my neck, soaking through my bloodstained shirt.

Behind me, I heard footsteps, their pace measured and patient. The sound of a predator who knew the chase was over.

I rolled onto my side, the cracked brickwork around me sweating rain, and tried to crawl from my slowly advancing doom. My fingers scrabbled for purchase on the uneven ground. From somewhere overhead a neon sign blinked red and blue across the puddles—Red for blood. Blue for bruises.

The figure that appeared beside me was all angles and shadows beneath the brim of a rain-slick hat.I couldn't see the glint of the figure's cold and hungry smile, but I could *feel* it. The blade in my murderer's hand rose high. My stomach heaved and roiled. My mouth filled with thin rivulets of liquid tin. A coppery taste birthed by my own blood, and sour, salty acids.

There was a flash.

It wasn't lightning or even neon, but a searing burst of unearned memory. Memories of pain, futility, and release. In a puddle I saw a strange woman's face—*my* face—my tears merging with the relentless rain.

And there, lying half-naked and helpless in the storm, I died.

#

It was the slam of the office door that woke me, dragging me from the restless vision-haunted slumber still clinging to me like a second skin.

I peeled my cheek from the desktop, wiped sleep from my eyes, and listened. Two sets of footsteps—one slow and deliberate, the other light and sharp. Easy voices. Laughter. As they neared the door I sprawled behind, the tone of those voices changed, becoming hushed and serious—the kind of serious that kills.

Two more steps, and one terse, whisper-filled conversation drifted to my ear before the door swung open to reveal the figure of Tamara Quinn, her .22 pistol in her right hand, the muzzle aimed at my chest.

"We've moved on from crossbows, I see?" I said, my voice dragging weary.

Tamara let out a sigh sharp enough to slice bread and dropped the gun to her side.

"Charlie! I nearly put one between your eyes! What the hell are you doing here at this hour?"

Over her right shoulder, I caught a glimpse of a sheepish Howard.

"Couldn't sleep," I muttered, scrubbing at my left eye. "We wrapped things up with Rivers sooner than I expected, and my brain was still buzzing so I came here for a drink and a think."

Tamara's gaze flicked to the fridge, where we kept the blood-bags.

"No, not that kind of drink." I raised an eyebrow. "I stuck to the booze—needed it, too." I jerked a thumb towards The Machine. "It talked to me."

"Oh?" Tamara's voice dripped with reluctant curiosity.

"Yeah. Another murder." I smoothed down my shirt and frowned at a small alcoholic stain. "Another girl."

"Like the one it showed me?"

"Take a look." I tossed her the sketch pad.

Tamara studied the pencil shaded record of my too-real experience, flicking between it and her earlier work with a frown.

"Damn near identical. Could almost be the same girl."

"No." I leaned in, pointing at the face of the fallen woman

depicted in graphite. "Even if I botched that visible sliver of cheekbone—and we both know I didn't—the coat's all wrong. And the shoes? No. This is a different woman."

Tamara strode over to The Machine, pad in hand.

"Then, assuming we're chasing the same killer, he's sure got a type—two blondes both with slim builds and small frames —kinda like..."

"Rose?"

"Yeah," she said. "Like our client."

The room hung quiet for a beat. Outside, the rain started up again, tapping impatiently at the window.

"The real question," she went on, her eyes locked on nothing in particular, "is do we really buy Rose's dream guy, with his C-notes and his magical comas, as our St. Germain Ripper? Does a man who hides behind spells and nightmares really step out into the rain with a knife?"

I saw Tamara's point. From everything we'd scraped together about our mystery man he was the kind of customer who let others do his dirty work for him. A guy who kept his hands as clean as his motives were murky. It didn't jibe with the intimate brutality The Machine had shoved so rudely into my head.

"Maybe not," I said, my voice as slow as a hangover. "But the timing? The way these girls look? That's one hell of a coincidence, and you know how I feel about coincidence."

Tamara's expression said she did.

"There's another thing, too," I added, lifting a hand to the nape of my neck to work out a knot that felt like it had been tied by a sailor with a grudge. "Where are the bodies?"

Tamara raised an eyebrow, but I wasn't through walking the thought out. "Let's say The Machine's got the skinny on these killings. Then why don't the cops? Why aren't the papers screaming about it in twenty-point font? Where's the moral outrage, the manhunt, the mayor chewing his cigar down to the label? I mean murders like this don't disappear into the gutters, Tam. They make *noise*."

Tamara's lips pursed. "So?"

"I don't know," I admitted. "Not yet. But either this guy's figured a clean way to disappear people that the local *Gendarmes* haven't worked out, or these deaths haven't happened yet and The Machine's giving us the jump. Either way, we can't let ourselves get caught up chasing shadows when we've already got ourselves too many questions and not enough answers." I took a breath, letting the stale taste of alcohol remind me of a night that wasn't done. "Besides," I added. "even if this backstreet butcher *is* our man, Doc Rivers is still our best chance of getting at him."

"And if he *isn't*?"

"Then the sooner we make Rose safe, the sooner we can start our ripper hunt in earnest."

"I guess." Tamara sounded unconvinced. "On that front, the day's almost done, but sundown's not due until 7:21 so that gives us an hour and change before we can safely head out." She flicked a thumb toward the frosted glass of the door. "The closed sign's been up all day to let Howard and me get some sleep, but even if someone is dumb enough to knock on it post-sundown, I've coached Howard on exactly what to say and exactly how to say it." She fixed me with a knowing look. "Do you need to take on a drop of blood before we pick up our client?"

I risked a glance at the small refrigerator "Yeah," I said. "I really do."

7

The building at 101 Orchard Place squatted between its two slightly taller neighbors like a guilty conscience. Built from broken dreams and cheap rent it was the very definition of function over form. Light leaked from its windows in random patterns of sleep and wakefulness that conjured the picture of some half-drunk, many-eyed titan.

I crossed the street towards its heavy door with a purposeful stride, flashing a nod to the Dvargn guard who leaned against the doorframe. He voiced a throaty grunt in reply, his eyes fixed on Tamara, trailing behind me like a shadow. Inside, the place was about as soulless as yours truly.

#

Not that I'm any kind of an expert on souls, you understand. No, when it comes to the metaphysical I'm happy to let the philosophers and theologians argue out the finer points.

But, according to pretty much all the accepted lore, I lost some quintessential part of the human condition on the day I got turned—the day I became a vampire. I traded in my soul for a shiny set of supernatural gifts and a one-way ticket to damnation—or so they say.

I still *feel*, though. I still know the whole gamut of human emotions—hurt, regret, guilt, and even love. So, either the accepted lore is wrong, or whatever's sitting where my soul used to live is doing a first-rate impersonation of the girl I used to be. A girl who as she walked through the door of 101 Orchard Place, found herself in a wallpapered version of purgatory.

#

The lobby walls were decorated in a hundred shades of cheap cigar and rising damp. It was an oppressive atmosphere that seemed to *suck* the light from the naked bulb that dangled from the ceiling like a hanged man. Even the carpet, frayed at the edges and cursed with a geometric pattern so loud it hurt my eyes was curling up like it wanted to crawl away.

"Nice place." Tamara wrinkled her nose as she inspected a patch of mold growing in the corner by the door.

"Yeah." I hit the elevator button. "Hopefully the rooms upstairs are a little less grim."

The car that arrived was constructed of brass and rosewood—a handsome once-upon-a-time carriage half-wrapped in the scents of beeswax and old grease and set in a wrought-iron skeleton that allowed its occupants to see the heavy chains looped through greased wheels and the oiled gears that seemed to groan with effort. Like the guillotine, it was a mechanical marvel of its age, a wonder of the modern world right until the moment it fell.

"There's no way in hell I'm getting in that!" Tamara planted her feet in the patchy carpet like they were tree roots. "Not for all the tea in China."

"Suit yourself." I nodded to the stairs. "It's four flights, if memory serves. But don't worry. I'll wait for you at the top... probably."

The look she gave me could have cracked diamonds, but it was too late. I was already stepping into the elevator car. I started to slide the gate shut with a metallic clatter and threw her a grin.

"My God, I hate you sometimes, Charlotte Durant," she

stormed past me, moving like an exclamation point. “I do, you know.”

The ride was both smoother and faster than the aged mechanism suggested, with the only ungainly jolt supplied by Tamara’s explosive exit from the confined space. The speed of her egress gave her a head start, but I still made it to the door of Rose's apartment a few paces in front of her.

#

As a disgruntled Tamara pulled up beside me, I rapped a sharp tattoo on the apartment door. The treacle-slow pause that followed was agony. My hands curled into fists at my sides, my thumbs traced the knuckles of my forefingers. With every passing second, my sadistic brain presented image after image of every agonized death and every enduring torture that could have befallen Rose.

A few endless minutes passed before the sound of soft, hesitant footsteps echoed from beyond the door and the latch slid back with a metallic rasp like a dagger being drawn. The door cracked just wide enough for faltering electric light to spill out and Rose’s face to appear.

Relief washed over me like a hot shower. It was the closest I’d been to a heartbeat in a couple of centuries.

“Ready?” I asked, swallowing the emotions.

“As I’ll ever be.” Rose’s voice was firm, but her haunted eyes betrayed it. “I just need to grab my coat and find my clutch. You want to come in?”

I glanced at Tamara, who consulted her watch. “Okay,” she said. “Make it quick, though.”

#

When you boiled it down, there wasn’t a whole lot of apartment to Rose’s apartment.

The front door led to a space-saving combination of lounge and kitchenette decorated in a tired shade of magnolia that had long since given up trying to be cheerful. In keeping with this stark functionality, the lounge area made do with just one thin couch and one coffee table.

A dog-eared paperback—its cover a lurid depiction of a woman in a torn red dress clinging to a guy with a fedora, a gun, and the stare of a man who knew too much and slept too little —lay on the table, face down and abandoned. The only light by which to read the pulp novel dangled from the center of the ceiling, a bare bulb casting uncertain shadows like a faint and faulty star.

In the room's corner, a cardboard box, half-packed with neatly folded clothes, slouched against a door I guessed led to Rose's bedroom. Along with the novel, it supplied just about the only human touches in a place dressed like a waiting room.

“I won't be long, I promise.” Rose's too-bright voice floated from behind the supposed bedroom door.

“I know I should be ready, but I called the hospital a few times. There's no change in Grace's condition… I didn't really expect there would be, but I needed something else to think about besides this ‘ritual’ Doctor Rivers has set up for us.” She hesitated, her voice hitching enough to betray the cracks underneath. "I needed a reminder of why.”

Rose appeared in the doorway, a vision of frightened fragility. “Oh, Charlie,” she breathed. “I'm terrified.”

I stepped forward, fumbling for some words, some warmth, but Tamara was faster. “Hey.” She took hold of Rose's arm, her voice a warm scarf in a cold room. “It's okay. We're all a little spooked. Right, Charlie? I mean who wouldn't be?”

I nodded, trying to make the ache of being outpaced again look something like confidence. “Tamara's right,” I agreed. “We might've danced this number before, but tonight's set to a different rhythm, and that makes us all a touch jumpy.” I let a pause stretch its legs. “Still, I know Doc Rivers, and if he says we're safe, then we're safe.”

Rose's gaze was wide and wary. “You're sure?”

I looked too deep into those warm, brown eyes and tried to

radiate an aura of assured honesty. “Absolutely.”

She held my gaze for a beat and then smiled, a small, almost reluctant tug at the corner of her mouth.

“Alright then," she said. "Let’s do this.”

8

"No Doc," Tamara said, stating the obvious.

We were loitering by the rear entry of St. Jude's Infirmary, our preordained place of meeting, and we'd arrived dead on time, too.

I grabbed a pack of smokes from my coat pocket, lifted it to my lips, and pulled out a cigarette. "Don't worry, if the Doc says he'll show, he'll show." I found a match, blew a cloud of smoke into the cool air, and let the old stone of the hospital's outer wall take my weight. "He's not the kind of man to leave a girl twisting in the breeze."

"So, what kind of man is he then?" Rose's voice creaked as she caved to the temptation to fill the silence. "I mean, I know he runs some big hospital department, but the way you guys defer to him when it comes to magic and power, I'm guessing he's something else, too, something *more*, right?" She looked right at me, waiting for an answer in the same way *she* used to. "So what is he? Some kind of wizard or warlock? Something else?"

I let a plume of smoke drift toward the bruised sky. "'Something else' pretty much covers it," I said. "I first met Kieren Rivers long before I'd even heard of St. Germain but, back then, he went by a different name and a different look. He offered to escort me on a journey I wasn't quite ready to take. When I hit town I discovered he'd got here first and we got... reacquainted." Rose made to ask another question, but I cut her off with the arc of the dying cigarette I pitched against the hospital's wall.

"There are things buried under this town's foundations that'd make a banshee scream for its mother, Rose. Old things... wrong things, but Doc Rivers is different from them. Not better, and not entirely worse, just... different. "I paused, trying to find the right words to dress my thoughts. "He's older for one—more ancient than all the ink in all the holy books in all the world—a guide who, for the right price, will take you where you were always going to go, carrying his lamp to show weary travelers the way to their final rest. Kieren Rivers isn't just another creature torn from the pages of myths and legend—Kieren Rivers *is* legend."

I paused, letting the smoke and the silence round out the talking, and, as Rose's expression stiffened, realized I'd said too much. I looked desperately toward Tamara, silently pleading for help, but before she could say a word, the iron gate that secured St. Jude's creaked open and the man himself stepped out of the shadows.

Doc Rivers smiled, raised one slender finger to his lips, turned toward a small door marked 'Staff Only' and gestured us to follow. But, as we fell into step behind him, I couldn't help but wonder how much of our conversation he'd overheard.

#

St. Jude's Infirmary carried its years with a dignified grace. It was built in what I'd call 'The Empire Style'—a style that's commonly known as 'Federal' in these United States—with tall, arched windows and high ceilings set in pale stone and the reddest brick. Bauhaus propaganda promoting handwashing and vaccinations interrupted the sallow pastel paintwork of its corridors, infecting the aesthetic with a stark modernity. The air practically hummed with the antiseptic reek of camphor, iodine, and the faintest whisper of oxide.

Doc Rivers navigated the empty halls with a stiff grace, each of his footfalls as light as a cat's, and we followed behind, our own steps echoing loud and hollow, until we reached the plain, unmarked doorway I knew guarded the private consultation suites of the hospital's senior physicians.

Here the atmosphere differed. There was no sharp tang of bleach or bite of ammonia. Instead, the air was dressed in something far richer—a trace of leather and hand rolled cigars and a whisper of brandy. The forgotten ghosts of some exclusive gentlemen's club.

Not that I've ever *belonged* enough to be handed a glass of royalty-approved cognac.

No, I never quite earned a seat close enough to the men who talked politics and plotted intrigue over roasted partridge and undeserved privilege for that honour. I held the wrong rank and the wrong gender for the powdered wigs, plotting, and partridge of my younger days to ever mean all that much to me. The closest I ever got to the good stuff was the dirtier buzz of the half-bottle in the back-office bureau.

Perhaps sensing the edges of my reverie, the doctor shot me a glance over his shoulder. I flashed him a smile and we moved on, swiftly passing three near-identical doors that bore the names of the physician-cum-administrator they belonged to. At the fourth—a door on which his own pseudonym dwelt—the doctor silently ushered us in.

#

The room beyond that door had been stripped of any trace of restrained elegance in favor of a scene ripped from the pages of gothic horror. Most of the furniture had been removed, leaving ghostly indentations in the deep pile carpet. The phantom shape of a desk and its trio of attending chairs and impressions of the kind of exam table that had seen cold hands and bad news in equal measures.

But in the center of the cleared room, like the eye of a very private storm, stood a small tripodal pedestal holding a clay bowl that was a dead ringer for the one Rose had described from her dreams. Inside the bowl was a burnt-orange powder that hadn't come from any pharmacy I knew of, and around this centerpiece sat four cushions, each marking one of the cardinal points. It all looked like a séance gone wrong.

"If you ladies would be so kind as to take your places," Doc Rivers said, his voice butter-smooth. "Ms. Chamberlain, I think by the window; and her two guardian angels flanking her."

Almost as if he were preparing for surgery, he removed his jacket, hung it from the coat rack beside the door, placed his gold, square-faced wristwatch in the pocket of his vest, rolled up his shirt sleeves, washed his hands in a small porcelain bowl, and then lowered himself onto the last cushion, closing the circle. Candlelight threw sharp shadows across his cheekbones and jaw as he drew two silver *obols* from his vest pocket and buried the coins beneath the orange powder with the reverence of a priest at Mass.

"In the box at your feet, you will find a knife." Rivers didn't raise his voice, but then he didn't need to. "In a moment, I will ask each of you..." Without so much as a twitch of his neck, he swept his gaze across us all in turn. "to hold your left hand above the bowl, draw the blade across your palm, and let three drops of blood fall. Three. No more. No less."

I popped the lid off the indicated box and the candlelight glinted along the metallic edge of a scalpel—a tool with neither heft nor reach but which, in the right hands, could undoubtedly kill. My gaze slid over to Doc Rivers, looking for assurance, a hint this wasn't the kind of ritual people didn't come back from, but my attention was caught instead by Rose. The small girl's face was pale and strung as tight as piano wire, and whatever nagging doubt I might have been feeling was written in her eyes with far more emphasis.

"You need not worry," Doc Rivers said, as if reading minds. "While it is true the ritual calls for the spilling of blood—" He nearly pinned me to my seat with a look hot enough to light the cigarette I wished was in my lips. "—it should be nowhere near enough to cause any unwarranted distress."

He turned his attention to the bowl, his fingers drawing shapes older than language in the orange powder. For a moment, I fancied his face changed, becoming strange and distant—becoming less doctor and more... *more*.

"Ms. Chamberlain," he said without looking up, his voice as solemn as a tolling funeral bell. "As the Binding was presented to yourself, it is for you to begin the ritual. We will then proceed counterclockwise. Once your offerings are made, each of you will find adhesive dressings in your box." He flashed a rictus-tight grin. "It does behoove us to be wary of infection."

"Do we need to?" If the doctor's words were some dry attempt at humor, Rose wasn't laughing. "Not the dressing. The blood, I mean. The ritual. It all seems—"

"—If you wish my help in unmasking your adversary, I'm afraid so, Ms. Chamberlain," Rivers interrupted, his voice soft but final. "I understand how this ceremony may appear to you, but as Ms. Durant may have mentioned, I possess some small expertise in these matters."

"Right." Rose bobbed her head, a gesture aimed not at Doc Rivers so much as the swarm of doubts buzzing behind her eyes. I couldn't blame her. This ritual, with its incense, its sacrament, and its blood, had a way of curling under your skin and whispering things you didn't want to hear. Things that set my teeth on edge.

With a deep inhalation of courage, Rose leaned toward the bowl, scalpel in her right hand, her left hovering uncertainly above the powder. Tension coiled in me like a spring. I could practically taste Rose's fear. The whole room felt smaller than it should.

Hot wax dripped down the candles in lazy trails, as smoke curled away from the flickering flame—and I could *smell* it.

The breath of the women sitting either side of me came shallow and ragged, mirroring the unsteady rhythm of their frightened hearts, and I could *hear* it.

The bitter, herbal tickle of the powder in the bowl scratched the back of my throat and I could *taste* it.

Rose lowered the blade to her skin, but the cut I was dreading didn't arrive.

"And then what?" she asked, her paper-thin voice trying for bold. "I mean, you say this will track down the guy from my dreams, but how?"

"I apologize." The doctor lifted his head and the candlelight flickered once more across his face. "I should, perhaps, explain. The blood, the... *offering*, is the toll you pay to cross the bridge between you and that you seek" His voice was as smooth and rich as spiced brandy. "This ritual is designed to aid that progress."

Rose's eyes narrowed, suspicion coiled up in them like a snake under a porch light. "How?"

"The Binding is the link between you and its creator," Doc Rivers replied with remarkable patience. "You and your designated protectors will traverse that link, moving like smoke through a keyhole, to the place—perhaps even the moment—that the Binding was devised."

Rose chewed on the knuckle of her thumb, her brow furrowed. Her eyes searched for mine, asking questions I couldn't answer, but I met her gaze and let my silence tell a gentle lie. It wasn't much, but it was enough.

She leaned forward again and unleashed a single clean stroke across her palm. The shock of the pain lit up her face like a flashbulb and three drops of her life's blood hit the powder in the bowl with a wet smack.

And inside me The Thirst stirred. Restless and needy.

"My turn," Tamara's voice rang out, bright and sharp enough to yank me out of the trance I'd been falling into.

My eyes slid from the blood bubbling on the powder in a slow, sensual Argentine Tango to her face with a silent thank you that received only the faintest twitch of her lips in reply. I caught the worry lurking behind that smile.

Turning away from me, she picked up her scalpel and got to work.

For most people the sound of a blade on skin is only a

whisper, but to me, it screams. I turned away and let my gaze drift to the painting hanging on the wall behind her. A sluggish black river, captured in oil, that wound through a narrow, stygian cave so dark it might've contained the world's first grave.In my periphery I caught an odd expression flash like lightning across Rose's face.

"Okay, I guess that's me done," Tamara said, the words once more underscored with contrived intensity. "Just you to go, Charlie."

I didn't say a word. I simply shut my eyes, took a needless breath that scraped the inside of my throat, and raised my hand over the bowl. My lips felt like they'd been filed down and left to crack. The Thirst stirred like a dog kept too long in the kennel. The scalpel in my hand was a millstone as the blade slid across my skin, and a thick drop of blood all logic said shouldn't be flowing through my shriveled veins fell into the powder with a sound I could feel in my teeth. Another drop fell. Then another.

And, as that third drop hit, Kieren Rivers started to chant.

There was no hesitation, no showmanship, just a stream of guttural syllables that didn't belong to any language I'd ever heard. His eyes clamped shut almost like he was afraid of what might look back at him.

And then the lights went out.

Not the switch-flipping kind of light. No, this was the rise of an unnatural darkness that blotted out everything. A darkness that was somehow heavier and hungrier than mother night.

In the bowl, the blood bubbled and hissed, spitting like bacon on a skillet, although it didn't smell too much like breakfast. This seething, boiling mass melted into the orange powder, turning thick and sludgy, becoming a soupy brew the color of mud and old bruises cut through with thin veins of silver that I guessed were the remnants of the two coins.

And then it got angry.

The raging slurry thrashed and jerked like it was trying to escape and, as if answering the silent cry, a cloud of dark oily smoke erupted from the bowl. Smoke that didn't rise, but *sank*. The miasma oozed over the edge of the pedestal like a nest of snakes, spreading as it spilled onto the rug and crawled across the floor. The walls disappeared. There were no corners any more. No ceiling. No floor. Only thick clouds of constantly shifting shadow where the architecture used to live.

I fancied myself a woman set adrift in this featureless landscape. A woman lost in a place that had neither reference points nor signposts. A woman totally unchained from the mundane world of linoleum floors and reliable lighting. Tamara and Rose, even the doc, all had disappeared. Only the murky void persisted, humming, low and mean in a minor key.

But, within this oppressive haze, shifting images started to bloom. Vignettes that were stitched from both memory and madness. I saw a young woman, her skin pale as moonbeams, her blonde hair a halo, sprawled on a bed that looked too grand to die in. I saw an ornate desk, in an elegant room and a glass vial whose contents glinted darkly.

I saw the face of its creator.

His face.

Dark and passionless eyes peered at me through octagonal, smoked-glass spectacles like I was some caged curiosity. The eyes of a man who only ever appears in your dreams to rearrange the furniture and ask you if you're still afraid of drowning. The eyes of the man who came to court to take my Marie-Thérese away from me. The man who damned us both.

I turned away, the beginnings of a scream rising in my throat, but before I could give my torment voice, a dark crack opened before me and something else pushed through. Not light exactly, but more the *idea* of light. The syrupy glow, a pale green incandescence born from somewhere deep and still, bled through the haze like an autumn sun shining through brackish water. As I squinted into this dismal glow it gathered itself into a figure, its limbs and contours forming like a ghost trying on flesh for the very first time.

But not the figure I was expecting.

#

In the spot Doctor Kieren Rivers, with his quietly expensive wardrobe and his clipped elegant style, had been sitting was a hunched and skeletal creature wearing tattered funereal robes of the deepest, darkest gray, cinched at the waist with a rope so rough it could've been torn down from a gallows. From beneath its deep cowl, a ragged beard, soaked through with the swampy detritus of some drowned world, spilled out in thin and tangled knots. Even the air itself seemed to curl away from this spectral figure and as it did it carried the retreating brume, now redolent with the smell of old tombs and dead water, along with it.

An arm that was little more than bone pressing against leathery skin stretched out toward me, the hand open as if presenting me with a gift and from beneath the dark hood, sunken eyes, filled in equal measure with ancient wisdom and endless grief, surveyed me with unexpected compassion.

Whispered words that carried not a shred of sound echoed in the catacombs of my mind.

I know,

I understand.

I'm sorry.

And, as the tenebrous clouds around me shifted and shimmered anew, the deep hood fell away to reveal a dread figure that I'd known for so very, very long. Its gaze raised to meet mine in full.

And it winked.

#

The quiet, refined taste of Doctor Rivers' office and the creeping fog which had possessed it melted away like a midnight promise, leaving me in a much larger room.

On my right, floor-to-ceiling windows stretched tall and smug either side of a pair of French doors that opened onto gardens so spacious there were grounds to call them Grounds—the kind that probably needed a full-time staff and a ride-on mower to maintain. On either side of the doors two Romanesque busts glowered like tuxedo joint goons.

The other three walls of the room, a study or office of some kind, were half-paneled in a dark walnut, that was varnished in new money and polished with aspirations. A thick, biscuit-colored wallpaper lurked above. Against the fourth wall, the one directly opposite me stood a bookcase whose shelves were stuffed with leather-bound volumes that had never once seen daylight, interspersed here and there with enough arcane *objet* to make any museum curator jealous.

In front of this bookcase sat a pedestal desk big enough to hold court, and behind the desk sat a man who made my teeth itch.

His hair was jet black, slick, and scented with a restrained oil that smelled of oranges. His suit was bespoke, and equipped with just enough flash in the cufflinks, pocket square, and tie pin to say *expensive* without having to raise its voice.

His face was a sculpted lie stained with a flawless sea-salt tan that had probably been exfoliated by someone with a Scandinavian accent.

The body under the bespoke threads looked lean and coiled—like a man who trained daily in a room with a mirror on every wall.

The stink of money hung off him like some kind of tarnished aura.

As I completed my assessment the man looked up at a sound from behind me. His narrow eyes, brown with a flicker of amber, were predatory and calculated. The eyes of a well-dressed wolf.

And they looked right through me.

Rose appeared at my shoulder, Tamara a wary shadow in her wake. “That’s the guy!" Rose said. "The guy from my dreams!”

I nodded once, my eyes not moving. The suit, the desk, the eyes—it all added up to the kind of guy who could buy whatever the hell he wanted without thought and without hesitation. The kind of guy who could *own* you and let you know it, too.

"Excuse me, Mr. Drake."

I turned toward the voice to see a gray-haired woman enter through the same door that had stolen the sharp-dressed man's attention. Closing the door on the smaller and far less luxurious office space behind her, she entered the room with brisk efficiency, entirely uninterested in the three uninvited guests in her way. I had half a mind to step directly into her path and see if she'd pass straight through me.

"I have the latest batch of Bindings ready for you to sign."

The man she'd called Drake looked up and hit her with a smile that gleamed white, symmetrical, and absolutely soulless. "Ah, Ms. Barrett. I was just admiring your work on the Judd file. Your attention to detail really is immaculate."

Barrett allowed a modest blush to tinge her cheeks. "Why, thank you, Mr. Drake. It was an intricate Binding to prepare, but I believe it to be iron-clad, and, with a little luck, it could even generate some repeat business."

"So I see." Drake let his wolfish smile linger. "You know, if your work keeps hitting this standard, we may have to revisit our discussions about a raise." He nodded toward the stack of papers in her hand. "Anything of interest?"

Ms. Barrett shuffled the pages with a deliberate concentration that reminded me of Tamara. "Nothing much. There's the Osborne woman of course, but I have a feeling that account has all but run its course—other than her, it's just the usual collection of worn-out actors and self-obsessed socialites. Oh, and we've been contacted by the representatives of an up-and-coming politician eager to smooth the road ahead." She gave a wry little twist of her mouth. "Image is so very important to those types. I've taken the liberty of booking the gentleman in."

Drake rose, fastening a button on his jacket, and strolled toward the tall French windows. The bright morning sun that should by all rights be cremating me painted a broad swath across his face. "Very good." The words emerged a breath this side of tired. "Leave the rest on my desk. I'll handle them later."

Then he paused, not quite looking back. "On second thoughts, I might use this new client to aid Miss Pell's development. That girl has such potential, such talent, such... *drive.*"

Ms. Barrett's smile turned as sharp as a snapped mousetrap. "As you wish, Mr. Drake." She placed the paperwork on the desk, turned on her no-nonsense heels and strode out the room, leaving behind nothing in her wake but dry paper and discipline.

I turned to watch her exit, but as I moved, the view once more dissolved into sickly clouds that shimmered with a greasy, yellow-green light like a fever dream rolling over a frozen swamp. When the fog parted again, I found myself sitting on a cushion in the consulting rooms of Doctor Kieren Rivers, looking once more into the grave, curious eyes of the physician himself.

9

"So it's definite then? Our guy is this 'Drake' character?"

It was the night after our trip through the looking glass and Tamara and I were holed up in the bosom of Charlie Durant Investigations, briefing Howard, who sat across from us with the wide-eyed reverence of a kid at the moving pictures.

"Looks like." Tamara conceded. Her voice walked the highwire between exhaustion and resolve. "Rose tagged him as her 'dream' guy the moment she saw him."

"That she did." I peeled myself away from the neon reds and sodium yellows of the city traffic and fished out a cigarette. "And between that and the Binding-mill he's running, I'd lay good money we've got our man— or his name, at least."

"Drake." Tamara tasted the word. "It's not a lot to go on."

"No," I agreed, striking a match and pulling deep on a fresh cigarette. "And that's why I was hoping Howard might help us out."

"Me?" Surprise bloomed on the big man's handsome face.

"You." I jabbed my cigarette toward Howard like a cue stick. "When Drake's assistant, or secretary, or whatever, rattled off that list of clients, she said some of them were actors, and since you already rub elbows with that crowd..."

The big man's brow knitted, his eyes narrowing as he followed the thread I'd left dangling. "I know my way around the agencies and a couple of the studios, sure, but I can't say I've ever heard the name 'Drake'. What, exactly, does this character do with his 'clients'?"

"From the information gleaned from Mackenzie and Rivers and everything we saw last night, he's running a version of the fairy godmother hustle." I inspected the glowing tip of my cigarette. "Wishes —youth, beauty, fame, and anything else you might want—all granted by a Binding and a signature."

Tamara cocked an eyebrow. "And I'll bet my last pair of heels those wishes don't come cheap."

"No bet," I said, exhaling a ribbon of smoke that curled toward the ceiling like it was trying to leave the room. "But if Mackenzie's right, it's more than cold hard cash these folks are handing over." I shot Howard a glance. "Any of this sound familiar?"

Howard didn't answer right away. He simply rose from his chair, six feet and change of surface-level grit, and paced toward the door. For a second, I thought he might leave us. But, just before the threshold, he turned and leaned against the frame, his arms crossed and his eyes shadowed.

"There *is* something," he said. "A rumor I've heard at certain parties and certain casting calls. They call it *The Treatment* —with a capital 'T'—I never heard any details, mind, only whispers, but a couple of folks disappeared for a few weeks and came back looking better than they had in years. I figured it was some kind of surgery or a new miracle cream, but this..."

"Yeah." I stubbed out the butt of my smoke with a slow grind. "It fits all right—fits like a glove."

Tamara looked at me, a familiar fire crackling beneath her lashes. "Then I guess we should pay this 'Mr. Drake' a visit."

"Maybe," I said, weariness putting an edge to my own voice, "but let's not forget what Doc Rivers told us. Last night's séance might've lit up Drake's radar like a bar sign, and if this *is* Caster business, we wouldn't just be crossing lines, we'd be stepping into someone else's backyard—a someone whose dogs bite." I let my arm curl across my ribs in a wasted crumb of self-comfort. “No, our first order of business has to be reconnaissance. We might have had our first peek behind Drake’s curtains, but we still need to know more— Howard, are you still in contact with anyone who underwent this ‘*Treatment*?’”

Howard shrugged. “I guess. It’s been a while, but I can dig out the little black book. Make a few calls. See who picks up.”

“Good. Then we start there. Meanwhile…” I reached for my coat. “*Someone* needs to check in on Rose. Last night’s mystical matinee was pretty intense and I want to know if she’s dealing.”

Tamara started to rise, but I sat her down with a raised hand. “No, not you, Tam. Last night hit us both harder than we'd like to admit, and you were pretty much running on fumes and stubbornness before we left. No, you grab the sofa bed for what’s left of the night. I’ll take this one.”

Tamara opened her mouth to protest, but before she could I pushed past her and headed into the night.

#

When trouble arrives, it nearly always brings a calling card. Sometimes, these warnings whisper and sometimes they shout. As Orchard Place loomed into view that night, they screamed.

The stocky body of Tamara’s Dvargn guard sprawled like a broken puppet against the doorway of Rose Chamberlain’s apartment block. I sprinted to the fallen man’s side, a shiver of something sharp and cold crawling down my spine, but the squat man’s chest still rose and fell in a jagged, rattling rhythm, that was more crackle than breath. It meant he was alive, but the livid purple welt on the side of his head said someone had recently tried to cure him of that condition. Thankfully, his assailant hadn’t drawn blood.

I laid a hand on the squat man’s shoulder and gave him a cautious shake. “Charlie! What the… What happened?” he slurred.

“I was hoping you might be able to tell me.” I tried to

remember the Dvargn's name, but came up blank. "It looks like someone jumped you. Did you see who?"

"No," the stocky man made a brave show of propping himself up on his elbow, the wince the motion drew from him holding the kind of honesty you can't fake. "The honorless curs jumped me." He collapsed again with a grunt and a curse. His lip curled into a sneer. "I turned from the wind to light a smoke and *bam!* A lightning bolt erupted behind my ear. The pavement was in my face, and I'm swimming in stars. I hear boots— three pairs, maybe four—charge the door." He shook his head, as if to dislodge the memory. "And that's all. I couldn't stop them, Charlie. I'm sorry, I failed you."

I rocked on my heels, my fingers brushing my chin. A hard knot of unease formed in my gut as my thoughts turned to Rose Chamberlain. If Drake *had* been spooked by our magical intrusion, then this could be his next move, a midnight delegation of Hand goons sent to deliver a message, something I should have maybe anticipated.

I rose slow, the worry inside me settling into something hot and solid. "Don't fret," I said to my fallen friend, my voice grating like gravel stirred up with regret. "You did everything you could."

No, this one was on *me*.

I tore my eyes from the doorway to meet the Dvargn's unfocused gaze, concern fighting a losing battle with keener, more vibrant emotions."You sure you're going to be okay?"

The look the Dvargn shot me was withering.

"Just go, Charlie."

#

This time, I didn't even consider the elevator. Instead I hurtled up the stairs three at a time. My boots beat out the rhythm of a funeral drum as I raced across each narrow landing until I reached Rose's floor, pushed through the heavy door that led to the square of adjoining corridors, and raced on to apartment 413.

As I neared my destination, a fresh jolt of alarm surged through me. Because the door to the apartment, or what was left of it, hung halfway out of the frame like a lonely drunk. Its lower panel had been kicked in with the kind of force that said the kicker didn't much care what was on the other side and through the jagged remains the stale stink of bad men doing worse things reached out to me. The stench of sweat and desperation.

I stopped, leaned against the wall, and listened. My hearing is sharp—supernaturally so—but the coarse voices inside the apartment were clear enough for even the weakest human ear. And one voice, all nasal and greasy, sang out high above the rest. A voice I could never, ever forget.

"You know we're gonna find it, so why not save us the time, and tell me where it is?" The sneer riding The Weasel's words was unmistakable. It seemed like the creep was enjoying himself, but a quiet, desperate sob told me Rose wasn't. "And don't think you're going to get any more of those sly little kicks in, either. We're wise to your tricks now, sweetheart, and this time there's no freak of a friend on hand to save you. So stop your goddamn whimpering and tell me where the damn thing is."

Silence was his only reply.

"Okay, boys, toss the joint."

The sound of a room being torn apart by men with thick hands and thin patience erupted. Kitchen drawers hit the floor, cabinets spilled their contents in a cacophony of clangs and thuds.

And that was enough for me. I stepped away from the ruined door, took a wasted breath that tasted like ash and faded out.

#

It's nothing quite as flashy as invisibility. Think of it more like stepping sideways through the cracks in people's perception. A trick of the eye and a twist of the mind. I simply allow myself to fade into the wallpaper of the world. The exact same trick I'd pulled back in the stinking alleyway on the first night I'd danced with The Weasel.

Most folks are wired to ignore things they can't understand, you see. A stray sound. A subtle movement. All of it can too easily be attributed to a cat, a shifting shadow, or a gust of wind. People might have their primal fears, but that doesn't mean they want to face them. No, the only thing they really want is an explanation they can understand.

Which meant as I slipped past the broken door into Rose's apartment, I might as well have been a ghost. Nobody saw me. Nobody ever does.

Not until it's too late.

#

The apartment was like a war zone.

In the kitchenette, two thick-necked gorillas were busy tearing through drawers like they were hunting for hidden gold. A crash and a curse told me someone else was redecorating Rose's bedroom in twenty shades of blunt force.

But the real prize stood in the living room.

The Weasel loomed over a hog-tied and hooded Rose Chamberlain like a vulture assessing its dinner. His good arm hung by his side. The other was strapped to his chest in a sling made from what used to be a reasonably nice scarf. His face—a mosaic of scrapes and bruises capped with a nose that had taken a hard left and hadn't come back—looked like it had been run through a concrete mixer.

It meant alongside at least three hired lumps of muscle I had one broken-nosed sadist holding a grudge and a switchblade to consider. One-on-one, I could take apart each goon like bad wiring, but all together? Well, that was another story, because given the chance to team up, they could pull the rug right out from under me.

I need space to fight my fight, you see—space *and* time.

Not just to win, but to win *clean*.

Because the truth of it is, the real fight is never against *them*. It's against *me*. To keep the monster I really am locked firmly behind bars, my strikes need to be measured, my movement tight, and my aggression disciplined. These are the self-imposed rules I have. Rules that call for precision. No flailing, and definitely no blood. Not unless I want something else to come out to play.

If that were to happen—if I were to surrender the wheel to the vampire—the Weasel and his boys would go down hard, fast, and permanent, leaving a helpless, hog-tied girl alone with a raging, bloodthirsty monster. Of course there was always a chance I could hold it off, after all, I'd done it before, but that "before" had taken every ounce of my will and more than a little outside help. No, once The Thirst starts screaming and the taste hits my tongue, it's very nearly impossible for me to stop. The Hunger howls even as The Thirst for blood rises, and mercy is the first thing it destroys.

All of which meant direct conflict, however tempting, was off the menu.

Luckily, I still had an edge I could push because, to all extents, I was unseen, and unseeable. As soft and quick as a rumor I moved past The Weasel. The sharp-faced goon, bless his broken nose, was far too busy basking in his petty cruelty to notice me drift on by, so I slipped on, moving toward the bedroom, where a tall mug with thinning hair and a nasty scar was searching for secrets in Rose's underwear drawer.

A sharp strike to the side of the neck, and the ransacker folded like a card table.

One down.

I left the perverted heavy dreaming of better days and crept back toward The Weasel.

He was still trying to intimidate Rose, leering at her with hard eyes she couldn't see but a kick to the back of his knee and a boot to the side of his head was enough to remind him of his manners and send whatever loose screws still remained rattling free.

And two to go.

But that's when the game shifted away from me, because as The Weasel hit ground, he let out a sharp yelp, more of surprise than pain, but plenty loud enough to turn heads.

In the kitchenette a slab of meat with a chest like a beer keg and mile wide shoulders spun around and spotted his fallen boss. He called out the alarm with a short, sharp yelp of surprise he aimed at his buddy, a shorter, meaner punk with a face that looked to have been earned in the ring.

Shoulders and Slugger didn't know what they were looking for—not yet, but they at least knew *something* was wrong, and that meant at least half the battle with myself was lost—because once they started to look they'd start to *see*. There was no way out of the room, and, this time, no clever way to disappear into the wallpaper. There were just two slow-witted killers, one defenseless girl, and one morally hamstrung vampire about to make her unplanned appearance.

I wasn't thrilled with the odds, but luckily for me, I still had one last card left to play.

#

It's not quite the same as the invisibility schtick—well, not exactly.

That trick leans on convincing the eye it saw nothing that the brain would care to admit to, but this was the exact opposite. Instead of ducking *away* from perception I force the mind to see something it can't possibly hold without breaking.

I don't fade *out*. I fade *in*.

You see, most times, I make myself *less*. I become forgettable, ignorable, but imagine if I could do the reverse. Imagine I could become *more*, that I could allow every nightmare and irrational fear my adversaries have to crystallize into pure, focused terror.

It's an effect I can only make last for a few seconds, and

God how those seconds *burn*. The Hunger screams for release and The Thirst claws at my throat until it would take just one careless slip to turn me from the woman trying to save Rose into the monster she needs saving *from*.

But I guess needs must when the devil drives and Old Nick was most definitely at the wheel.

So I let the full force of my concentrated presence hit home, turning up the color, the sound, the *reality* of what I am until I became something *more* than real. Something that breaks minds.

Slugger screamed—a high, keening cry that was the antithesis of his oh-so macho image. His buddy simply went sheet-white and strangely still, the tire iron slipping from his fingers with a sad little clatter and a liquid stain spreading across his crotch.

As I took another step into the spotlight of their horror, The Hunger bayed and The Thirst sang out. Every ounce of me screamed to *take*, to *kill*, to *drink*. I held on tight, clinging to the memory of the innocent girl I once was and the woman she had become. A woman who cared. A woman who'd learned to say *no*.

The screamer went first. My fist cracked across his jaw in a single, clean strike, dumping him into the kitchen cupboards with a crash and putting an end to his noise. As he fell he tried to save himself but only managed to catch hold of Rose's coffee pot which shattered in an explosion of glass to lie broken and useless on the linoleum beside him.

The other goon—the one with the shoulders and the unfortunately stained trousers, finally caught up with his own balled-up brain and the illusion of my reality cracked just enough for him to see past the fangs and the fury to the skinny five foot four dame in scuffed boots who lurked underneath—a girl any torpedo worth his salt would see as easy meat.

And that was his mistake.

He roared something stupid and charged me, moving like a man late for his own funeral but I didn't run or sidestep. No, I moved *toward* him and, with a Matador twist of my hips and a hard shove sent him stumbling right past me to collide with the table I'd noticed on my earlier visit—a table which had been flung aside during the search of the apartment, and now lay upside down like it knew the script.

As the bruiser collided with the fallen furniture like the last train to Regretsville, the wood snapped underneath him. Air fled from his lungs in a whistling grunt, earning a startled gasp from behind Rose's gag as the violent sounds reached her ear.

She was still with us, and that meant I needed to remain present too. Because the fight wasn't over yet.

Shoulders hauled himself upright, coughing like he'd just downed his last paycheck and his glassy, furious eyes scanned the wreckage for a weapon—any weapon. A length of splintered table leg almost leapt into his hand. It was a weapon born from pure chance and flailing desperation, but one that lent our fight an aspect ripped from the pages of every penny dreadful Dracula pastiche ever printed.

Vampire against stake. The stuff of legend.

#

Not that sharpened wood holds any mystical power over the undead. It is only wood, after all. It can no more differentiate between your heart and mine than a bullet can choose which target to hit. A jagged foot and a half of broken table leg through the chest will still do a little more than leave a mark, though, and this particular foot and a half of table leg was heading my way.

I stepped back, my weight on my left heel, and once again let him rush empty air. The scent of his barbershop cologne and a fondness for peppermint humbugs drifted in his wake. The situation felt a little too like my fight with The Weasel back in the rain-soaked Warren. The bricks might have been traded for drywall and the blade replaced by a length of splintered wood, but the lump of frustrated testosterone charging at me? Well that was pure *déjà vu*.

In the kitchenette, Shoulders' pal let out a groan—a soft

reminder that there was a clock that was ticking. Because the moment Slugger got back in the game, things would get crowded again. It meant I had to end this dance, and end it now.

Shoulders charged me again, moving full steam ahead, without a single thought of brakes. Once again I dipped his lunge, slipping past him like smoke, but this time, as he passed me, I drove an elbow into the sweet spot at the base of his spine. The goon jerked forward with a yelp, his balance teetering. Pivoting on my heel, I made hard contact with the side of his head, buying him a one-way ticket for the midnight express to oblivion. He crashed into his slowly rising partner with a sound like a wardrobe collapsing. The improvised stake skittered across the floor, and, with a last weary twitch that said their fight was done, both men finally went still.

But I still needed to move.

I rushed to Rose's side and knelt, my fingers already tugging at her thick bonds—stockhouse-grade rope, tied with the kind of conviction that doesn't loosen easy—not even for a gal of my supernatural strength. Admitting temporary defeat I sat on my heels and tried to quiet the passions still surging inside me for long enough to give it some thought.

The Weasel!

He was a knife man, that much I knew. The first time we danced, he'd brought steel to the party—a long, slim stiletto he probably called Katy or something. The kind of blade a guy like The Weasel doesn't go long without replacing. A quick pat-down proved me right. He'd tucked his new piece unimaginatively down his left sock.

The new knife's blade was narrow, clean, and almost pretty but the ropes securing Rose were neither pretty nor narrow and they weren't about to yield to Katy either. I glanced toward the kitchen where a storm of cookware and cutlery still lay scattered and there, half-buried in the mess. I spotted my—no, *Rose's*—salvation. A serrated bread knife, forged from the finest stainless steel. It wasn't a delicate tool, but its toothed edge chewed through the rope in a dozen or so rasps.

Rose sat up slow and rubbed her wrists.

"No," I said. "Don't ask questions, just move." I hoisted her off the floor and steered her toward the wrecked doorway, the burden light, her steps uncertain.

"You need to go," I continued. "Now! Head for the office. Don't stop. Don't look back. *Go*!"

Rose's eyes dilated with fear and confusion. "But what about you?"

I cracked the door, gave the hallway a once-over, and tried on a smile I didn't feel. "Never mind me. Find Tamara. Tell her everything that happened here and tell her you both need to stay put until I get back."

Rose's expression said she wanted to say more, but a heavy sigh was about all she managed. With a frustrated shake of her head she jogged away, limping ever so slightly. I watched until she reached the corridor's end, closed what was left of the door, and shut my eyes.

Because I had work to do.

10

"Okay, once more, and with just a little more feeling this time. No, I didn't bite anyone. No, I didn't drain anyone. And no, I sure as hell didn't kill anyone. Okay?" It was three hours after the fight at Rose's apartment. I was parked on the corner of the desk in Charlie Durant Investigations, and Tamara Quinn was holding court.

"Then why are you so high on the bloody side?" She fired the question my way in a flat, emotionless tone that was as pointed as any stake. "And don't even think about denying it, Charlie. You're lit up like a neon sign in a blackout."

I slid toward the back room, where, if the world had any mercy left, Rose was still catching some well-deserved shut-eye.I knew I'd shut the door, but I checked it again anyway. She didn't need to hear any of this.

"Look," I said, dragging a hand down my face like I could scrape away the weariness. "A couple of The Weasel's guys caught a peek beneath my mask. I'd already bounced one of the gorilla's heads off the linoleum hard enough to make him see stars, so the odds are any 'exotic' descriptions from him will get chalked up to post-concussion fairy tales—but his pal was made of sturdier stuff. When I doubled back to make sure everyone was nicely asleep, he was already blinking. I tucked him in again, but his lip was bust up pretty good, so, I..."

"...had yourself a taste?"

"Yeah," I muttered, hoping the confession might sting less if I didn't meet her eyes.

"Look, Tam, a bunch of goons were attacking our client. I asked them to stop, and in the process of asking broke one arm, two legs, and cracked a few skulls. I made some god-awful choices and a whole laundry list of mistakes along the way, like I almost always do, but dissecting every fight like this is getting old. It's done, Tam. *Un accord conclu.* What's the point in tearing it to pieces?"

That got Tamara to her feet. "The point," she snapped, her voice a shade under a shout, "is to keep you safe. And I don't mean safe from The Hand or any other member of the growing chorus line of creeps and killers that want us both dead, I mean safe from *you.* You know what you are, Charlie. You know the devil you carry around in that pretty frame of yours. So, if I have to play inquisitor each time you stumble in bruised and blood-drunk, then guess what? I will!" She flopped into The Client's Chair and flung a hand toward the back room. "In there, next to the sofa-bed where your distressed damsel is recovering, there's a fridge full of blood bags awaiting your non-violent consumption. You might want to remember who put them there."

It was true. Before I met Tamara, my life had been, well, '*messy*', as Patrick Callaghan might say. See, blood isn't simply a need for me. It's not some neat little biological requirement you can check off like a snack or a nap. It's a craving. A gnawing, sleepless ache that hums under my skin like a live wire—and it's not just the blood itself—it's the act of *taking* it. That's the part nobody talks about in those two-bit pulp rags, with their silk-lined coffins and hypnotic eyes. The violence that rides shotgun with the bloodlust. The Hunger that sits beside The Thirst.

Long before I ever heard the name St. Germain, back in the days Napoleon was just an enthusiastic revolutionary and the steam locomotive a novelty that would never last, I tore through Western Europe like a plague. I painted every corner of the map red as I fed my twin passions, leaving whole cities trembling in my wake. Mobs hunted me with their burning torches. Militias tried to kill me with their rifles. But I always managed to disappear before the hammer dropped. I guess even monsters have their survival instincts.

As a result of these too-close escapes, I learned to hone my indiscretions. I got clever. I became quiet. I started picking victims nobody would miss—killers, predators, the guilty, the feared and the gleefully unmissed—I fed the beast inside me and dressed it up in something close to justice.Eventually, even England, the place where I sought refuge after exhausting mainland Europe, grew too small. So I curled up next to crates of sugar and rum in the belly of a tall cargo ship bound for The New World. A world in which I found St. Germain and Tamara Quinn.

Even the most righteous of my late-night hunts came to an end the day Tamara stepped into my life. She pulled the brakes, stocked the fridge with blood bags, and tracked my intake as keenly as any prohibition agent. Tamara didn't just keep me fed; she kept me *contained*, and thanks to her I managed to stay about as human as a vampire ever can.

I suppose it gave her a right to be pissed.

"Alright, Tamara," I said, holding my hands up as I surrendered to common sense. "I know what I owe you. Don't think for a second I don't. But I need you to let this go, because while we sit here picking through every thrown punch and every stolen drop of blood, we've got a client sleeping off the latest chapter of a nightmare in our back room, and if we're gonna have any chance of dragging her out of that I'm going to need you pulling right beside me."

Tamara took a deep breath, sucking down frustrations and exhaling hard. "I *had* a point," she said, her sullen voice softening at the edges. "A real one, too. And I'd make the same point again—a hundred times over, if I thought there was any chance you'd listen—but no, instead you have to roll out another of those noble Goddamn speeches you know I hate so much." She screwed up her mouth as if she could taste the simmering vexation. "And before you ask, yes, of course it worked—just like you *knew* it would." She shook her head as her irritation slowly gave way to resignation."You have a plan?"

"I'm working on it."

"That's a 'no', then."

"Kinda." I dropped into my seat, stretched out my legs, and tried to work the tightness out of my calves.

It felt like I'd been dancing on broken glass for most of the night, and the comedown was starting to settle in. I pressed my lips tight, chewing on the thoughts rattling around my brain. "We've got the Binding," I mused. "And we've got Rose, too. That's two game pieces that Drake and his Hand lapdogs seem kinda eager to get their mitts on. Thanks to Doc Rivers we've also got a name and a face to hang on our dream guy. So, if Howard's little black book can shed a little light on this 'Drake', that might hold the key to this whole rotten mess."

Tamara nodded her dubious acceptance. "And if Howard draws a blank?"

Before I could give her an answer, a shrill, unearthly scream ripped through the office.

#

I hit the back room door a half-second before Tamara, adrenaline snapping through me like somebody had fitted jumper cables to my cold, dead heart. We'd left Rose to sleep off her demons on the sofa-bed, but it was plain she wasn't sleeping any more. I kicked through the door, expecting trouble. Drake, or a couple of his black-suited choirboys, maybe even our mysterious back-alley killer, but there were no assassins, and no knives.

Just Rose.

She was standing by the pedestal next to the bureau, a bedsheet clutched tight across her chest the only thing saving her fragile modesty. Her eyes were wide, but her lips were sealed tight. The scream we'd heard, the scream we were *still* hearing, didn't belong to her.

It belonged to The Machine.

"I barely touched it." Rose's eyes never left the mahogany

box her fingers rested on. The breathy tremor in her voice underlined her obvious distress. "Did I hurt it somehow? Is it in pain?"

"I don't know," the words dropped from me like loose change on a cold countertop. "But maybe you should take your hand away."

She looked at her hand like it belonged to someone else and yanked it to her chest where it joined the hopeless fight for her virtue and The Machine fell silent. A lifeless construct of wood and copper once more.

"I'm sorry." Rose's face was ashen. "I only wanted to look."

Once again, Tamara moved first. She strode over to the sobbing girl, threw an arm around her shoulders and sat her gently on the sofa-bed. As in the café, a surge of unwelcome jealousy rose in my breast.

"It's okay." Tamara's hand brushed Rose's shoulder like she was made of glass. "You couldn't have known." She glanced at me, her eyes sharp. "What you touched... we call it 'The Machine'. It can make you see things, make you *feel* things. Is that what happened? Did you see something?"

Rose's head bobbed twice. "I think it showed me the future —*my* future," she gobbled down a frantic breath. Her eyes held the kind of terror that can make a person forget how their legs work.

"I'm going to die, Charlie." Those liquid eyes searched for mine. "I'm going to be killed in the bloodiest, most painful way you can imagine—and there's nothing anyone can do to stop it."

#

It took time, and the liberal application of some of my 'emergency' brandy, to halt Rose's tears. Tamara did the rest. Her quiet words eased the panic out of the girl like steam escaping a cracked kettle. For my part, I kept my distance, a silent and vaguely ashamed spectator nursing a bottle of misplaced guilt.

As the overproof liquor worked its mundane magic, Tamara circled gently round to practicalities. Things like getting Rose into something other than a bed sheet. In order to give the still shaking girl some privacy she shooed me out the room with an arched brow, and, like a good little bloodsucker, I wandered to my usual station at the window, watching the traffic slouch past and listing all the ways I'd failed to be the woman I pretend to be.

Five minutes later, the door reopened and Tamara strode over to the desk, a sheepish but fully clothed Rose trailing in her wake.

"All okay?"

"She's had a fright, is all." Tamara helped Rose into the client's chair, her expression guarded, the words yet another gentle lie. "You know The Machine."

I knew alright. Even with my far-too colorful past, the heady cocktail of emotion and sensation the Caster artifact threw into my brain wasn't something I'd ever truly get used to. It sure as hell wasn't anything Rose should ever *have* to.

"So, 'The Machine'." I brushed my lower lip with my thumb while I worked out the next sentence. "Like Tamara said, it grants visions... or maybe *impressions* is a better word. You might get a glimpse of a face, or the feel of a location, but, in the main, it's the feeling of a person or the events that person is undergoing it shares with you—feelings that can seem so real, so... harrowing." I looked at her face, as pale as porcelain, to see if any of this was hitting home. "I'm guessing whatever it showed you was especially so."

Rose's expression told me more than any words ever could.

"Alright," I said. "Then, if you feel up to it, maybe you can show us what that was. Details are important so give us everything you remember." I reached over to the table and laid the sketchpad and pencil in front of her.

"And what, exactly, am I meant to do with those?"

It wasn't sarcasm or aggression, just the kind of blunt talk people often use to hide their own fear and uncertainty, but it gave me hope. It meant a spark of defiance still shone behind those baby browns.

"We've found the best way to manage The Machine's messages is to sketch what it shows you." Tamara's tone contained more reassurance than I could ever conjure. "I know it sounds stupid, but it gets what you've experienced out of your head and puts a little distance between you and the nightmare you've experienced. Don't worry if you're no Da Vinci, The Machine will guide your hand. With a little luck, we might even use what you draw to prevent your vision from coming to pass."

Rose stared down at the pad and pencil like they might bite. "I don't think I can." Her shell-shocked eyes latched onto mine, looking for any kind of help. "Can't I tell you?"

A surge of sympathy bloomed in my undead heart. Rose Chamberlain had been through hell, and the part of me that hadn't shriveled to dust wanted so much to close the distance between us and tell her everything was going to be okay—that we were going to *make* it okay. But images of a sickbed and dark eyes hidden behind octagonal, smoked glass spectacles reared up in my mind and the moment passed like last night's warmth.

"I guess," I conceded. "But we'll need *everything*. Feelings. Smells. Sounds. Even the bits that don't make sense—*especially* the bits that don't make sense."

Rose wiped her nose on the cuff of her blouse, her gaze fixated on her left foot.

"It's dark," she began, slow and shaky. "And not just lights-out dark. I mean *dark*. There's a window behind me, but it's been covered up with thick curtains, like in a darkroom. I hear a door open, and slow, deliberate footsteps." She paused to gulp down some air. "I can smell hand cream... old leather... amber... oranges. And then I see *him*. The man from my dreams. Only he's upside down, like suddenly the whole world's flipped. And then I hear chanting... the same nonsense from my nightmares." Her voice cracked like an eggshell. I could see her pulse flutter in her neck. "A knife appears before me." She shivered, her hand creeping to her throat. "Only, it's... wrong. Not a knife that's made for cutting or even stabbing. A knife that's a collection of barbs and hooks. A knife that's made for *ripping*. And it's coming toward me… toward my neck, and…"

Her hand slapped over her mouth as if to hold the memory back. Tears started trailing down those flawless cheeks.

"It's okay," I said. "Take your time."

Rose flashed me a tiny nod, her eyes red and shining with the horror. She made to blot them with her already abused sleeve, and Tamara dug through her coat pockets for a handkerchief.

"There isn't a whole lot more," she managed after a moment, her voice thin and tired. "Just the taste of blood in my mouth, all metallic and sharp, and the sticky warmth of it on my face. And then pain, a white fire that tears through my throat, and then … nothing. Just a darkness I knew was death… My death."

I let my attention wander to the window and the long black sedan that slid down the road outside the office like a shark cruising a reef. According to Mackenzie this whole sick game had one goal—to make Rose sign that damn Binding and each threat, each torture Drake visited upon her, was designed to get her to become exactly what she described, a willing, bloody sacrifice to whatever evil forces he served—strung up and butchered like a side of beef.

"No."

My voice didn't rise. Not in volume and not in pitch, but the word fell from my lips like a coffin lid.

"But it was real," Rose whispered, desperation clawing at every word. "I saw it—I *felt* it—it happened."

I turned away from the window and met her gaze head-on. "No," I repeated. "It didn't… it hasn't… not yet. The Machine showed you one possible future, but there's nothing to say we can't change it—nothing to say we can't *try*."

"So?" Tamara's eyes narrowed.

"We move her." My words were meant for Tamara but aimed squarely toward Rose. "Her apartment's blown, and if

Drake's on our trail, this place won't hold up for long, either, so, I'll take her somewhere safe. Somewhere that only one person outside this room knows exists."

"Your place?" Tamara asked.

I nodded. "Exactly. And if Drake finds us there, fine, because I know every shadow, and every creak of every floorboard. I know I can hold it. I know I can protect her."

Rose shook her head, a diamond-hard certainty in her eyes. "But it won't be enough. Nothing ever *can* be. Whatever you do, wherever you take me, he'll get to me. He *always* gets to me."

Tamara pursed her lips. "She's got a point, you know."

"I don't care." My voice slammed the door on the discussion. "We move her, and we move her tonight. We can worry about tomorrow, tomorrow."

Rose started to speak, but I got there first.

"We *can* beat this 'Drake', Rose, but first, I need you safe. You can stay here until nightfall, but at first dark, we go and only when you're properly protected do we start to think about taking the fight to him." I glanced at Tamara, my mouth dry and my body aching but my mind clear. "Because now, I really do have a plan."

11

"And this place really is all yours?" Rose made a show of inspecting the room. "Nice."

"It was a gift." I kept my eyes from her face and the rest of the story to myself.

"Generous," she said in a voice that carried undertones of reluctant admiration. She wasn't wrong. My Lawrence Street apartment, a penthouse sat atop a five-story walk-up three blocks from the office, had been a flamboyant thank-you from a certain Irish mob boss after I helped him keep his nephew out of prison. It might have lacked the expensive minimalism of Kieren Rivers' Blackwood Heights brownstone, but it still had its comforts, and, more importantly, it was mine—my tether to the pulsing heartbeat of the city I called home and a fortress where I could escape from it.

Three nights ago, on the first night I'd opened the door and let Rose in, I'd completed a comprehensive sweep of its many security features, leaving her in the doorway while I made sure the blackout blinds were sealed tight enough for every inch of sunlight to stay locked out, switched on enough electric lights for Rose to feel comfortable, and thought up a hasty lie about new high-rise builds and reflected glare. It was an awkward untruth but a sadly necessary one, because for a girl like me, natural light isn't some mere photogenic inconvenience, it's a cremation.

But, as it turned out, my hasty deception was unnecessary.

Rose didn't once ask the reason for the tight-fitted blinds or even mention the thick drapes. She simply settled in.

"I am okay, you know." It was almost as if she'd read my thoughts. "

I mean I'm not skipping-out-in-the-park okay, but I'm not about to fall to pieces, here, either. I know I've been quiet these past couple of days, and I think you can understand why, but the way I figure, this Drake character wants me scared. He wants me worn out, worn thin, and hanging from my very last nerve." She rescued the breakfast sandwich I'd picked up from one of the city's numerous all-night eateries on my way from the office and inspected it. "But, like you said, The Machine only showed me one possibility...and I *have* to believe there's another—I have to put my trust in you, Tamara, and Howard."

I fell onto the two-seater couch and yanked off my boots.

"And we have to do our damndest to deserve it, too," I said. "Right now we're working round the clock to dig out any leads on our mysterious Mr. Drake—Tamara and Howard on the dayshift, yours truly pulling the nights. It might not be bearing much fruit right now, but it will, with time."

"And until then I'm stuck here all alone, right? I'm doomed to spend my days watching over you as you get your well-deserved rest and my nights trying to ignore the echoing silence and get some rest myself."

I glanced up at her, watching as her bravado faded into restless frustration. I was only beginning to get to know this small, delicate-looking woman, but the fire she'd displayed at Doc Rivers' place coupled with the odd moment of unintentionally spiky humor told me she was a girl who was used to looking after herself. A quality I recognized in myself, and one I remembered from my time with...

"And on the subject of sleep," I said, interrupting my own thoughts. "If I'm going to be of any use at all tomorrow night, I need to be turning in pretty soon. Don't worry about being hungry for company, though. I've asked Tamara to call in around lunchtime with some food."

"Another sandwich?"

I flashed her a weary smile. "Who knows. Maybe this time It'll be a burger, or, if you're really lucky, some soup."

"Lucky, right." She returned my smile with twice the fatigue. "Well, you have yourself a good day's sleep and I guess I'll see you tonight."

But the day's sleep was a world away from good.

#

Versailles. It was unmistakably Versailles. *La Galerie des Glaces* or The Hall of Mirrors, to be precise. A hundred candles or more burned in their sconces and candelabra, supplementing the reflected moonlight that streamed through the tall windows leading to the manicured gardens to my right. A wall of tiled mirrors set opposite those windows duplicated the effect, reflecting and refracting the lights until it almost appeared as if I was standing inside some gleaming diamond.

I remembered the first time I stepped into this glorious radiance as an awestruck child pulling at my mother's hand, and now, over two hundred years later I was a child once more. I wheeled around in joy, lifting my eyes to the ceiling fresco dedicated to the triumphant glory and opulent works of Louis XIV, The Sun King and laughed, a strange, musical sound I'd grown unused to.

In the mirrored walls, a twenty-four-year-old woman copied my movements. An impossible reflection that as I reached toward it, reached back to me. I stared at her gray and beige clothing, so modern, so serviceable, but so out of place. I stared at the shaggy bob her chestnut hair had been styled into, and stared most of all at a face I hadn't seen in over two centuries.

My face.

But even as I marveled at the girl in the mirror, the scene around me changed. A cloud drew across the moon. A spectral wind, blowing from nowhere in particular, rushed through the already darkened hall, extinguishing every single light in its path. Suddenly I was cold. Suddenly I wasn't smiling. Suddenly there was movement behind me.

A pair of dancers, her small and blonde, him compact and precise behind his octagonal, smoked-glass spectacles, whirled in perfect silence, their faces split in soundless mirth. I turned away from the mirror image to look behind me, but the pair, along with the mirrors and the hall were all gone leaving me alone once again.

#

I woke in a cold sweat, my lips dry, and sat up letting the cool air of my penthouse apartment calm the torrent of raw emotions that churned in the pit of my stomach. It was far too soon to head out. Even through the walls and shuttered windows I could *feel* the accursed day and its deadly light. Sundown couldn't be more than an hour or two away, but that was still distant enough.

I debated the wisdom of getting a little more sleep and decided against it. Caffeine and nicotine, that's what I needed—caffeine, nicotine, and the one drug that was out of reach until I got to the office and the little fridge in its back room.

Rising from my bed, I shrugged on my clothes, ran a hand through my hair, opened the bedroom door, and made for the kitchen.

"Wow, you're up early." The voice, of course, belonged to Rose. The blonde girl was curled up on the sofa, a burger wrapper at her feet and a lurid paperback in her hands.

"Couldn't sleep," I said. "So I thought I'd grab a cup of Joe and have a smoke before I head out."

"And finally spend some time with me, eh?" She set down her novel, her smile just this side of arch. "You know, it's funny," she continued. "I mean, here I am with my life in your hands, and these last couple of days have been my first glance behind the trench coat. My first look at the real, relaxed Charlie Durant." Her eyes held mine long enough to make me want to look elsewhere. "Why don't you tell me who that is?"

"There's not a whole lot to tell." I smoothed a stray lock of hair, found a mug and started to pour, doing my best to hide the tight screech of anxiety that ripped through me.

"No?" she said. "A female detective, in a city full of big, strong men and unknown magical menaces? A woman who takes down back-alley thugs and home invaders without breaking a sweat? A gal with an eye for the fellas and another for the dames?"

I stared at her like she'd pulled a gun on me. My eyes narrowed. My jaw went slack.

"How...?"

"Your old pal Kenny the bartender." Her grin spread wide and kinda smug as I took a seat on the other side of the couch. "The guy's about as sore as a two-day hangover, but he was more than happy to share your dirt when I revisited Callaghan's—not that I found anything he told me bothersome." Rose's voice was a purr. "As far as I'm concerned, we like who we like, love who we love, and so long as everyone's up front and honest, and no one's getting hurt, unless they *want* to be, then who ends up in whose bed is nobody's business but their own.

She shifted a fraction closer to me and I shifted a fraction away.

"Yeah, that's always been more or less my take," I said, my gaze doing everything it could to avoid hers. Fleeing to the floorboards and the bare bulb hanging from the ceiling like a waiting noose. "But even then, getting close is... well, there's... risks."

"The law?" she asked, leaning in again, voice sugar-smooth. "Okay, but if nobody tells, nobody knows, right?" she paused. Her head tilted, her eyes keen. "Wait. No... that's not what you mean, is it?"

A spike of unwise desire hit me, a thrill of attraction in a barbed wire coat. My undead heart may not know how to beat, but right then it sure knew how to ache.

She was edging close now. A little too close. I could feel the warmth of her body, could smell the dry, floral breath of her perfume. I could...

"No!" I broke away, pushing myself from the couch like it was on fire and rushed for the sanctuary of the kitchenette. "No, I mean... at least... look I don't know. Every liaison comes with its own set of baggage, Rose, its own risks and responsibilities. Some of them more than others. Maintaining safe, professional lines, for instance, keeping a head clear enough to make the hard calls and enough distance to protect a client in trouble."

Rose vented an arch sigh about half challenge and all charm.

"I suppose," she said. "But, if things were different...?"

"Then they'd be different," I said. "But they're not."

Her smile wilted into something crooked and sad. "Then I guess I'll have to keep my 'safe', 'professional' distance until you've dealt with this Drake character. I can't pretend I like sitting on my hands while you, Tamara, and Howard head off to play hero, and yeah, that isn't my *only* frustration. But I get it. I do. I understand... on both fronts."

Her words landed like a push dagger to the ribs. In my mind's eye, I once again saw two figures twirling across a midnight ballroom. I'd never been a girl who went in for the whole damsel in distress routine—not back when I was a fresh-faced *ingénue* in Versailles' snake pit, and as sure as hell not now. It seemed Rose carried a similar fire. It was too bad she didn't have any choice in the matter.

"Don't worry," I said, stretching out my fingers to bleed off some of the tension she'd stirred up inside me. "You're not missing a whole bunch, Tamara and Howard are probably out there right now, shaking trees for any loose information, an activity that trades long hours for slow returns. It's the side of the job your paperbacks leave out. The grind that gets swapped out for bullets and bar brawls."

"And there's really nothing I can do?"

I pursed my lips. "Well, it might be useful to have some idea why Drake chose *you*. Anything spring to mind?"

Rose looked away, her eyes fixed on a fold of curtain like

it might supply her some answers. “No… I’m just one more nobody, Charlie. Just another girl lost in the stardust shuffle—living day by day and paycheck to paycheck. There wasn’t one damn thing about me you could call special until… ”Her breath caught. “The dreams,” she whispered. “I mean they started everything. What if that’s how Drake found me? How he chose me?”

I ran a thumb across my lower lip, testing the idea like a bad tooth. It was a thin lead, but it was the best we had. “Alright,” I said slowly. “I’ll ask Tamara to put the theory to Mackenzie and see if it flies.” I paused. Reconsidered. “On second thoughts, maybe I’ll ask Howard to put it to him.”

“All while I sit here and hope?”

“Don’t worry.” I wandered over to her, extended a hand and quickly snatched it back before skin could meet skin. “We’ve got a plan, remember. We keep the Binding in the office and we keep you here. Both secure. Both separate. Both safe. Then, when we've got a little more information on our Mr. Drake, we work out how we can get to *him* without endangering *you*. We get the lowdown, work the angles, and only once we’re forewarned and forearmed, do we even *think* of paying our Mr. Drake a visit.”

“To kill him?”

I blinked. “No! God, no! I don’t kill, Rose. It’s the one rule I never, *ever* break. I might bluff or scare—I might even resort to a little violence when the need arises, but killing only ever leads to more killing, and I’ve seen enough of that to last me a lifetime.”

She didn’t look away and, this time, neither did I. Eventually, she folded and nodded her reluctant understanding.

“Good. Now, what do you say to a proper drink? Because that I could murder.” I caught myself and shook my head in mock despair as I returned to the kitchen. "Maybe this Drake character has earned himself a one-way ticket to the mortuary, but I don't know what could possibly make you think I'd be the person to buy it for him."

Rose blinked. “I don’t know. I guess I just thought that’s what vampires do.”

12

“So, she figured it out, huh?” Tamara’s tone was ripe with incredulity. “Got there all on her lonesome.”

We were huddled around a secluded table in Callaghan’s. Thanks to my sudden need for alcohol, four different walls, and an understanding ear it was the least worst place I could be. I blew an unsuccessful smoke ring into the already tainted air and let my gaze settle on hers for a moment. “Yeah, that’s about the size of it.”

“Then she’s got one hell of a steep learning curve." Tamara pulled a face. "I guess Drake pried her mind open a little wider than we thought. Was she super-spooked?”

I shrugged, staring up into the thinning smoke. “That’s not the word I’d use, no.”

#

Truth be told, it went the other way. The second Rose dropped the V-word I nearly let both highballs hit the floor. I managed to save the glassware, but my composure? Well, that was left in shards.

“Oh, don’t bother denying it.” Rose’s eyes twinkled with mischief. “You’re one of those ‘immigrants’ you mentioned back at the diner—a supernatural creature who got drawn to St. Germain like a moth to a bonfire.” The gaze she fired my way brimmed with a little too much triumphant amusement. “What? Did you think I didn’t see how neatly you folded our greasy friend in The Warren? Did you think I didn’t at least *hear* you rip through the same sleazeball and three of his trained monkeys at my apartment last night. They were trained men who get paid well to not scare easy, each of them meaner than a gorilla with a toothache, but even under that burlap hood I could hear their screams.”

I pulled out the good bottle—the stuff I keep in reserve, and with unsteady hands, poured us both a healthy splash of relaxation. A long hiss of soda, three cubes, and a quick stir of the bar spoon I “borrowed” from Callaghan’s made it respectable.

“Fine,” I said, capping the bottle. “Let’s say, just for the sake of argument, that a drop of magic does run through these veins. Why jump to ‘vampire’? Why, out of every monster-movie cliché on offer, would you possibly pick that one?”

Rose raised her chin, provocative amusement dancing on her lips. “Because it fits,” she said. “We always, *always* meet after dark, and if there’s any daylight business to attend to, you always send Tamara. Even today—the first day I’ve had you all to myself—you spent most of it ‘resting’. Basically, if the sun’s up, you’re not.”

I carried the glasses over and passed one to her. “And that’s it?”

“No, that’s only the start.” She took a thin sip, never once breaking eye contact. “There’s also the fact that there's not a single mirror in either your office *or* your home—and then there’s the guy you call 'The Weasel', with his greasy hair and his bruised ego. He was wearing a busted nose, a broken arm, and enough fresh bruises to form a brand-new rainbow in shades of purple when he and his men hog-tied me. Bruises he collected on the night we so nearly met. I know I missed the end of that show, but, as I was a captive audience, he made sure I got the full highlight reel.

She took another sip, the brandy burn smoothing the raw edges in her voice. "He spouted a whole bunch of justifications, and rationalizations—anything to patch the holes in his pride. His *pièce de résistance* was a tale of some red-eyed she-devil who licked the blood off his face. A she-devil who, it turned out, was *you*."

"Which proves what, exactly?" I slid my glass across the table. "That I'm good enough in a fight to rattle a few rent-a-thugs and one delirious, self-rationalizing greaseball with a colorful imagination? That's what makes me Bela Lugosi? I think what you have there is the dictionary definition of the kind of evidence the boys down at the courthouse call 'circumstantial.'"

I sipped my drink, studying her face. A stare she returned in spades.

"Fine," she said. "So the case is a thin one. I'm right, though. I know I am." She fished in her purse for a moment. "You see, back at that coffee shop, as you were telling me all about St. Germain, and magic, and Bindings, I caught our reflections in the plate glass window. The waitress, Tamara, me—we were all there, but where you were sitting—where I *knew* you were sitting, there was only an empty chair. I chalked it up to bad lighting, or a trick of my increasingly fractured mind, but after last night? With everything else?" Her hand dove back into her purse and emerged with a silver compact. "Of course, there is *one* way to be sure. A test that should prove pretty conclusive one way or the other." She snapped it open.

"On reflection."

#

I ran through each and every option at my disposal. It didn't take long. If Rose saw me in the mirror, or rather, if she *didn't,* then there'd be nowhere left to hide and little way to talk my way out of a bad situation. I could always refuse to take her little test, of course, but why would I do that unless she was right?

"I think you forgot something," I took the compact from her hand and snapped it shut with a click that cut through the room like a switchblade. "If I am what you think I am, then wouldn't calling me out on that fact in the dead of night, in a locked room, with no witnesses and no weapon, be kinda suicidal? If I *am* the kind of monster you think I am, shouldn't you be running for your life about now?"

Rose didn't flinch. She just flashed me a slow, knowing smile, like she'd read the final chapter of one of her dime store mysteries. "Now, why on earth would I run?" she asked. "I mean you've already had half a dozen opportunities to finish me off... maybe more, but you didn't. Not when I was so scared and helpless in the alleyway, and not when I was trussed up like a turkey in my apartment. No, whatever else Charlie Durant is, she's not anyone I need to fear. I don't think you'd ever hurt me. I'm not even sure you could." She set down her glass with a gentle thunk, brushed her hair from her neck, and tilted her head like an offering. "But if I'm wrong," she whispered, "go right ahead and prove it."

This close, I could see the flex of the tendons in her throat and way her pulse—sharp and insistent—hammered out a familiar rhythm. The scent of her skin, rich with sweat and lingering traces of perfume, drifted up from her naked neck and hit me like a sucker punch. I leaned in, without thought and without choice, until I was close enough to touch her. To taste her. To...

"No!"

I flew away from her and crashed into the kitchen like a blind woman. One hand clamped the back of my neck, the other caged the hunger clawing its way up my throat.

But behind me, Rose hadn't moved an inch. "Intense," she said. "Kinda proves my point, too. Wouldn't you say?" She patted the vacant seat next to her. "So, if we're done here, why don't you stop playing dumb, and tell me all about yourself?"

"No." I took a chance and faced her. "You're right, okay? About me. About *everything.* I'm sorry, I... I can't do this. Not now. I... have to go, but you'll be safe here." I tossed her the only key to the apartment's only door. "Just, lock up behind me and don't open up for anyone you don't know."

She opened her mouth to speak, but I shut the words down with a raised hand, grabbed for my coat, and bolted out my own front door, tears rolling freely down my cheeks.

#

"And came straight to me, I take it?" Tamara swirled her gin and orange like it held the secrets of the universe. "Scares you a little, doesn't it?"

"What does?"

She pushed her glass aside and leaned in enough for her smirk to land. "That she saw through you so well. That she still doesn't want to run."

I stared at the ice in my glass like it owed me answers. "Maybe. A little."

"Do you *want* her scared of you?"

"No," I said, fast enough that I needed to take a moment to compose myself before I could continue. "Maybe... Look I don't know. It would probably be safer. For her... for me." I risked a glance into the eyes of my oldest, dearest friend. "You know what I am, Tamara. You know what it costs me to stay in control—but she doesn't. She can't."

"And yet..." Tamara said, the words as cool as the gin she wasn't drinking, "The girl trusts you, Charlie," she continued. "She sees past the monster to the woman underneath. The way I see it, *that's* what's really got you rattled."

I set the glass down, my jaw tight. "That obvious?"

"To me, yeah. You see, I've known you a long time, Charlie. And in all that time you've never had anyone you know... *close*."

I cocked an eyebrow, and allowed a hint of amusement I wasn't really feeling play on my lips. "I think your count might be a little out."

"Sex? Sure, you do fine on that front. Better than me, anyway. But how many of those opening nights get an encore? How many make it through breakfast?"

I let silence cling to me like the condensation on my glass

as the ice it held melted along with my appetite for the conversation.

"You collect birds with broken wings," Tamara went on, her words considered. "Waifs and strays. Drifters... girls that are looking to *feel* something. And I think, deep down, you're trying to feel that something too." She sipped her drink and used the gin to moisten her lips. "But you never have. Nothing *real*, anyways. Nothing with a chance to *last.* Not until..."

"Until?"

I looked up, knowing exactly where she was headed.

Rose." Her eyes never left mine. "I've heard the way your voice changes when you say her name, and I've seen the way your eyes follow her across the room. Rose Chamberlain has got her hooks into you, Charlie." She tapped her chest. "Here. But tonight you've found out she's taken a peek behind those walls you put up and still likes what she sees... and you don't have the first clue how to deal with that."

I set the glass down, a little harder than I meant to.

As always, Tamara saw right through me. Not that it mattered.

"So what do I do?" I muttered. "She's what—twenty three? Twenty-five? I'm closer to three hundred than thirty, and I don't age—but she will. So, even if I somehow manage not to kill her, I'll still get to watch her die. I'll still get to bury her."

Tamara's face dropped. "I never thought..."

"Well, I have," I cut in. "I still do. Every day. I watch the love of hand-holding couples bloom like roses through sidewalk cracks. I see old timers swapping stories over stale coffee—and I know I'll never get that." I lit a cigarette, mostly for something to do with my hands. "One by one, everyone I care about will either walk away from me or get carried out of my life in a box. Lovers. Friends... even you. You're the truest friend I've ever had, Tam, but I know someday you'll be just one more memory walking beside me with all the rest of my ghosts."

I took a long drag of nicotine and let the thought settle and my eyes find hers. "That's why I'm going to leave before you, or anyone else I care for, gets the chance to die on me." I continued. "I'll quit St. Germain, find a new town and a new name—a fresh start. And no, you won't find me, because any trail you can follow will peter away before you make it to the city limits."

I risked another glance. "But don't worry, I've made my plans—some of them for you. The agency, the apartment, the keys to the kingdom—it'll all become yours. A parting gift to show the world what Tamara Quinn can *really* do. And you'll have Howard beside you, too. Don't write him off, Tam, and don't overlook him, either. Howard's a good man with a good heart."

I swirled what was left of my drink, swallowed it down, and wished to holy hell there was more. "Walking away from you will be one of the hardest things I've ever done, but it's pain I've budgeted for... if I let things escalate with Rose. If I open that door even a crack..."

"It'll destroy you." Tamara's face was ashen.

"Yeah," I said. "It will."

The damned glass was still empty.

"You see, Rose and this whole mess she's in carries echoes of things that happened to me a long, long time ago. It was a different place and a different time, but it was damn near the same story. A story that sent me down a dark road I never want to find myself treading again."

"You lost someone?"

"Killed someone." The two words landed on the conversation like the last handful of dirt. "That's the part you don't get, Tamara. I'm not the hero of the piece, but I might just be the villain. I'm the kind of monster who's always managed to turn everything she's ever touched to ruin, the kind of story parents tell to keep their kids away from darkened streets and bad choices in equal measure. You think it's Rose I'm afraid of? No, I'm afraid of *me*."

Tamara's expression softened a touch. "So, what are you going to do?"

I exhaled the last of my smoke and glared up at the crack running across the low ceiling like it was the fault line of my life.

"The job," I said. "We made a promise to Rose, and it's a promise I intend to make good on. We'll keep her safe, no matter what it costs, and then, when I know that's done, I'll hunt down this 'Drake' and put a stop to this whole 'Binding' business." I stood, glass dangling from my fingers like a spent bullet casing. "But first of all I'm going to get myself another drink."

"You know that's not what I meant."

"I know. But right now that's all you're going to get."

13

That second drink was needed, and, if I was gonna make good on my promise to Rose and do the job right, sorely so. Because waiting ahead of me was a spectacularly unappetizing conversation.

I hovered before the door of the apartment I kept on Lawrence Street—a place about as close to Fort Knox as magic and modern engineering could manage, thanks to a certain mobster's understandable paranoia. Dvargn Glass, bulletproof, hexproof, and quietly smug about it, graced the windows. The front door was steel-reinforced, rune-scribed, and only reachable by a narrow staircase lined with enough magical alarms to make any demon think twice.There was no fire escape, no rooftop, and no neighboring buildings tall enough to afford a line of sight. It all meant that, for now at least, our client was safe.

But me? I felt as exposed and uncertain as a cold-footed debutante.

I checked my pockets again for the apartment key I knew I'd flung at Rose like a party favor as I made my grand exit, and, once again, came up understandably dry.

Giving my cracked lips a lick, I gathered what remained of my emotional fortitude and rapped twice on my own front door. "Rose, it's Charlie. Can you let me in? Please?"

I stood there, playing a dozen versions of the talk that was waiting for me in my head, each one worse than the last, until the thoughts were interrupted by the click of a lock and the sound of several bolts drawing back. Rose's face appeared in the crack of light that opened between door and jamb; her red-rimmed eyes still beautiful enough to knock the redundant wind out of me.

"Charlie! I thought... Listen, I never meant..."

I raised a conciliatory hand. "It doesn't matter... Can I come in?"

"Can you...?" She blushed and stepped away from the door. "Right. Sorry. The invite thing. Okay, yes, I invite you in... It is your place, after all."

My vampiric nature wasn't the reason I needed an invite from her but I let her point stand, brushed past her and waited until the door closed to say what I really needed to say.

"Look, Rose, I never meant to run out on you like that, I swear I didn't." I smoothed a lock of hair behind one ear, my fingers lingering over my neck where the tension was starting to bite. "It's just... it's been a long time since anyone got quite so close to seeing who... to seeing *what* I am. I guess it was a lot."

Rose edged toward me, some well-meaning platitude forming on her lips but I stopped both the words and the motion with another flat palm.

"No," I said, low but firm. "You think you're okay with this, Rose. More okay than I could've ever hoped, but you've got no idea how dangerous that thought is."

Those too-wide, tobacco-brown eyes looked up. Her chin dipped and her shoulders drew tight like she was bracing for a punch. Something fraught but surprisingly deep crossed her face—fear, sure, but something else, too, something worse. Concern, maybe? A glimmer of pity?

"You throw the word 'vampire' around like it's a nickname," I continued. "Something ripped from the pages of a comic book or some Goddamn awful novel, but you don't know what the word means, or how lucky you are to still be breathing."

She opened her mouth again and then, when the words wouldn't come, shut it. I barreled on.

"I spoke to Tamara," I said, pushing past the knot in my throat. "And she agrees. So if you still want us, then we're still on the case."

Rose stepped forward a fraction. An advance I matched with a half-pace backwards. Like we were dancing a dance we didn't know the music to.

"But before we get to anything else, we need to talk," I said. "Not now. I need the daylight hours to rest up. You'll get your answers, I swear—as many as you want—just... not yet."

"Okay, Charlie, whatever you need. I just want you and me to be..." She looked up, the brass-tacks bravado she'd shown earlier tucked behind something smaller and quieter.

"I know." The smile I gave her held all the warmth of a neon sign at closing time. "Me too."

"I guess I'll say goodnight, then." She turned toward the guest room, stopping shy of its threshold to toss one last smile—about half acceptance and half apology—over her shoulder.

"Yeah," I said, forcing my voice to sound a whole lot steadier than I felt. "Goodnight." I reached out, summoning every ounce of my courage and laid a hand on her arm. "If you need anything during daylight, Tamara's number's in the book next to the phone. I'll be with you as soon as I can."

Rose nodded once, and disappeared into the second bedroom. I stood there for a second longer, the relief I felt at the conversation's conclusion battling against fresh waves of doubt, and then turned toward my own room. The next night promised much and I needed to silence the voices clamoring inside me. I needed rest.

It was just a shame I didn't get much.

#

A baroque melody, played on flute, violin, and clarinet, rose into the air and a procession of revelers answered the call like they'd been waiting a couple of centuries for their cue. Rose, orange blossom. Sorrentine lemon, smoky incense, and exotic

Sumatran patchouli clung to the air like old promises, the exotic scents underpinned with cold marble and the heat of intrigue as a procession of satin whispers and Masquerade masks drifted past me. It was a heady atmosphere. One that summoned a hundred memories I desperately needed to forget.

I stood, frozen in this palace of personal history, the weight of my past pressing on my shoulders like a velvet shroud. But why? Why here? Why now?

"Because it's another dream," Tamara said.

I spun on my heel, and there she was, a pace to my left and a couple of centuries out of uniform.

The blue silk of her dress was trimmed with bows. Her sleeves were a mess of ruffles. Her hair was stacked high and pierced through with a single peacock feather like an aristocratic exclamation point. A marvel of hoops and panniers gave her a silhouette I recognized as belonging to the *Robe à la Français* style. It was a far cry from the slacks and throat-opened shirt she'd worn for our rendezvous at Callaghan's.

"You don't say," I muttered in answer to her observation.

Tamara twirled, all teeth and mischief, sending silk and shadow spinning. "What's wrong? Don't you like the new look?"

My eyes drifted from the flare of her skirt to the ceiling fresco in an attempt to swallow the frustrated retort balancing on the tip of my tongue. It was Howard who beat me to the punch.

"I do," the big man said. "A hell of a lot more than I like *this* get-up, anyhow."

If Tamara had dived headfirst into the powdered wigs and peacock feather fantasy, Dream-Howard's outfit still clung to reality—but only by a thread. He wore the powdered face, painted beauty mark, and curled wig of a man-at-court, accessorized with an elegant silver-tipped cane that said Monsieur *could* duel but would much rather stick to the nonchalant elegance for now. The rest of the outfit was pure Howard—a rumpled suit, a tie worn loose around the neck, and a dog-end cigarette burned down to its dying gasp—the latter pinched between two gloved fingers.

"Oh, I don't know." Tamara simpered in a very un-Tamara way. "I think you look kinda dashing."

"'Dashing... right.' Howard had the good grace to blush. "Want to tell us what we're doing here, boss?" He turned away from Tamara and fixed me with a look that wanted answers but I opened my mouth to find the words missing in action.

Because, the truth was, I didn't have a clue. This wasn't some sleep-borne rerun, dredged from the recesses of a too-old mind. This was something more. Something new.

But, as I started to share the thought with my colleagues, the music died. As if someone had pulled the needle off a record, the unseen orchestra simply stopped mid-phrase and a perfect awed silence fell across the room as every masked reveler turned toward the far end of the hall and voiced a collective, silent gasp.

I followed the gaze of the long-dead celebrants, and there she was, framed in candlelight and history and wearing enough grace to shame the gods themselves.

Rose Chamberlain.

She glowed, and I don't mean that metaphorically.

The mirrors. The moonlight. The flickering flames. All conspired to catch every sequin upon her shoulder and the jeweled hem of her gown. Even the gleaming white of her smile conspired to gleam in a way that transformed her into something divine—a beauty that felt like a punishment.

And all of a sudden, I wasn't sure if I was dreaming or remembering.

#

She paused in the doorway to the War Salon like a ghost who had yet to make her peace with the afterlife.

Whereas Tamara had chosen Versailles blue, Rose's gown was pure white embroidered with blood-red roses, a reminder of the dress she'd worn on that first night at Callaghan's. Her honey-blonde hair, decorated with ribbons as red as blood and pinned fast with long silver needles, was arranged with an iron control disguised as elegance. Her lips and cheeks were painted in shades of heartbreak just rich enough to hint at impropriety and the beauty mark on her cheek served as the period to a dangerous sentence.

As she slid past the swirling courtiers, her bearing straight-backed and sovereign, a lone flute picked up a soft and weeping air to accompany the high-pitched trill of some hidden bell. She didn't look to her left nor to her right as she glided toward the silver chair that had been posted by the door to The King's Chambers and took up a station by its left arm, but simply stared straight ahead, her head held high. She was a consort-queen summoned to the court of fate.

And one of a pair.

Because all of a sudden there was a man standing to the silver chair's right—a man I was beginning to know far too well.

He wore a *habit à la française* in deepest black with a silver trim as crisp as a sealed warrant. The shirt was ruffled at both wrist and throat and his *ensemble* was finished off with a *Cadogan* wig and a stylized mask that told everyone exactly who he was.

Drake.

I pushed into the crowd, threading my way through silk and satin. Each powdered face was a flicker of half-remembered familiarity, every hidden glance a whispered accusation. As the courtiers danced their choreographed reverie they made no attempt to avoid the woman in their way. Almost as if *I* was the ghost.Some laughed—a hollow sound completely devoid of mirth. Others whispered words I couldn't make out. Cold fingers brushed against my bare arms and the nape of my neck, but still I pushed on.

Because ahead and apart, standing like a lighthouse in the fog, was Rose. She stood still and poised, but something about her posture was a little too perfect, like a painted still life or a dressmaker's mannequin. Drake, damn him, hadn't moved either. Even his leering grin, like a knife at my ribs, was frozen.

And once again the music stopped.

The dancers froze around me and every mask turned my way. Knowing eyes burned holes in my self-control. They were many and I was one, but nothing could keep me from Rose and her tormentor. Nothing could stop me. Nothing.

I was...

14

I sat up, wide awake and terrified, my throat like sandpaper. My sleep-cast terrors had slithered into the shadowy corners of my bedroom, leaving behind them a collection of half-remembered fragments and the kind of aftertaste you don't shake. But there was still one fragment that refused to let go—the shrill chime that had sliced through the mournful flute like a poniard. Because somewhere, somehow, in those first numb moments of wakefulness, it was a bell that still rang.

The phone!

I threw off the bedclothes like they'd caught fire, hit the floor running, and ran to the bakelite telephone on the hallway table. My heart wasn't racing, but fear, tight and electric, still hit every nerve I owned as I snatched up the receiver and barked an impatient inquiry.

"It's me." Tamara's voice was shaky. "We've got a problem."

I pushed the remnants of my dream from my mind, slamming the door shut behind it. "What kind of problem?"

A click and then another voice. Male. Resonant, familiar, and dripping with smooth charm.

"The very worst kind," the voice said. "Your little game is over, Ms. Durant and you lose. Quit your investigation of me right now, or your friend here dies."

Another click and a flat, continual tone announced the call was done.

"Who was it?" Rose stood in the doorway to the second bedroom clutching the jamb, her wide eyes haunted.

"Tamara." I stared at the receiver like it might bite, and dropped it back into its cradle. "What time is it?"

Rose flicked her eyes down to the slim watch on her wrist. "Almost twenty-five to seven," she said. "Why? Is it important?"

"If I don't want to become a walking bonfire, it is." I stared down at the phone for a few moments longer before turning to face her. "Look," I tried to keep the urgency from my voice, "I know we said we'd talk. But something's come up and I need to go. Now."

"Without getting dressed?"

I followed her gaze down to my bare legs. At least I'd had the good sense to throw on a camisole and matching panties before retiring for the day. I threw a self-conscious arm across my chest. It didn't help all that much.

"Right. Clothes." I turned toward the bedroom. "Give me two minutes, but once I'm decent, I'm gone. I can't say how long for, but you'll be safe here. Lock the door behind me, and..."

"Don't let anyone in except you, Tamara, or Howard?"

"You got it. Keep an ear out for the phone too." I ducked into the bedroom and pulled on my street clothes. Then, a little more conservatively dressed, I made for the door.

But, before I could reach for the knob, a sharp, urgent, rat-a-tat-tat erupted from its other side.

"Charlie! It's Howard! Open up!" The big man's voice was breathless and panicked. I threw the lock, yanked the door open, and Howard Gold nearly toppled straight through me. The square-shouldered man was red-faced, his eyes wild, sweat ran down from his temples in tiny rivulets.

"It's Tamara," He gulped down air like a man saved from drowning. "Drake has her."

#

It all started, Howard explained, with a call to an old acting pal. A guy named Robbie Hurst. Robbie had an ex—one of the unlucky few who'd signed up for Drake's so-called *Treatment*. A dame who, supposedly, could dish all the dirt we needed. The trouble was, the ex got the wrong idea. She decided Howard must be a prospective customer, looking to wangle an appointment.

"For a consultation?" I asked, already dreading the answer.

Howard nodded, still wheezing like a broken radiator. "Yeah. Turns out Drake had a late-afternoon gap in his schedule."

I closed my eyes and let the weight of it settle in. "And I take it that was a gift horse Tamara couldn't resist."

"You got it. We figured you'd be... unavailable, given the, uh... circumstances." His eyes flicked toward Rose.

"Relax, Howard," I said. "Rose knows."

"She..? Really?" I let a single raised eyebrow answer the big man's question, and he exhaled like the secret had been holding all the breath in. Howard Gold might have had his talents, but secrecy wasn't among them.

"So?" I urged.

"Right... So she knew it might be a trap, and she wasn't exactly happy about it, but you know Tamara—show her any half-open door and she's already through it. She had that little gun she uses—the .22, but her going in solo still felt like too much—eventually, I talked her round enough for her to let me tag along. I mean, I'm no fighter—but a big, strong-looking man..." His words withered away as I treated him to one of my 'special' looks. "Anyway, we were directed to this place near Matson Park. Three stories of glass-and-concrete, with an underground garage, gardens big enough to get lost in, and more security than a bank vault. A guy wearing one of those 'Hand' rings answered the door."

If Howard didn't have my attention before he did now.

"We cooled our heels in the hallway for a while, then in walks this pretty little redhead—all pencil skirt and pen clicking efficiency served with a healthy side of condescension. She introduces herself as Ms. Pell, takes our coats, and glides us into Drake's office."

"The same place I told you Doc Rivers showed us?" I lit my smoke and waved the flame from the match. "All mahogany, marble, and menace?"

"I guess." Howard shrugged. "I know the good china was out alongside a plateful of cookies, as thin as lies… It was kinda like stepping into some Noel Coward matinee… anyway, Drake looks up from the report he's holding, flashes me a smile, and starts asking questions like where we'd heard about him, and what we were after. I played the washed-up actor looking to revisit the glory days, a part I know pretty well, and Tamara pretended to be my disaffected bride wanting the money success provides. Drake used the fake names we fed him like he'd known 'em for years."

I exhaled, slow and impatient. "Fascinating, but what say we skip high tea and get to the meat?"

"Well, after a few more rounds of soft-serve interrogation, Drake gets down to business. 'I believe I understand your needs,' he says. 'And yes, I can help you.' He hits a button on the desk to summon Ms. Pell who hands Drake a blue folder he flips through like an À La Carte menu. 'I see a Miss Nancy Keane referred you,' he says. 'Did she perhaps explain my process?' We told him she hadn't, figuring to get as much from him as he wanted to give. 'Well,' he purrs, 'Firstly, there's a fee that I ask for upfront, to cover certain costs, although the contract we will both sign guarantees a full refund if not one hundred percent satisfied. Until I have this… deposit, I'm afraid any magic stays in the hat.'"

"A contract," Rose's voice was sharp enough to shave with. "A Binding, then?"

I took a slow drag of tobacco. I'd figured about as much, but it was nice to hear the thought out loud. "And?" I urged.

Howard picked up a glass from the table and turned it in his hands a time or two. "Honestly? It was going great. We'd got the layout of Drake's place, saw firsthand how he lured people in, and even got the measure of the man himself. We told him we'd return the next day with a check and a pen and then it was all handshakes and smiles... we were almost through the door when the hammer fell."

He leaned forward, mimicking the smooth voice I'd heard over the phone."'Just one more thing, Mrs. Greene,' he says to Tamara. 'It's been a genuine pleasure meeting the both of you, but when do I get to make the acquaintance of your employer—the elusive Charlie Durant?'"

"Well, we pretty much sprinted out the door like all hell was chasing us. As we reached the outer door that led to the driveway, Tamara was only a half-pace behind me, hardly any distance at all, but I guess it was enough. I cleared the threshold. Tamara didn't." He paused, swallowing down the too raw emotions that accompanied the memory. "She fought Drake's men off, of course, but a meaty paw, as hairy as a gorilla's, clamped down on her arm and started to drag her back inside. Two more suited shadows peeled off the walls, and between them the goons pretty much swallowed her whole—it was like watching a pack of wolves hauling down a doe. The last thing I saw before the door slammed shut in my face were her stunned and pleading eyes."

Rose leaned in, her own eyes gleaming, her lips parted. "But you didn't leave her there, right?"

"No chance! I knew there was muscle gathered behind that door—three lunks at a minimum—probably more, but this is *Tamara* we're talking about." His jaw tightened, a flush climbing up his neck to bloom in his sculpted cheeks. "The door was shut and locked fast, but I threw my shoulder against the wood a time or two and on the third try something broke. I sprawled forward in a shower of splinters... only not *into* the house. I landed six yards further down the driveway, the shards of gravel biting into my hands and knees. It was like the house had swallowed me up and spit me out." He jerked a thumb toward the memory. "And behind me that damn door was still there, as whole and unharmed as if I'd never even touched it."

"But you tried again, right?" Rose's voice trembled. Hope

clinging to her like cheap perfume.

"You're damn right I did." Howard's eyes dropped to the glass in his hands as he gathered himself to continue. "I took a good, long runup, figuring momentum might break through whatever mojo Drake had cooking. It turns out it was a bad bet."

"Let me guess," I said, cutting off Rose's starry-eyed question before she could ask it. "Gravel again?"

Howard shook his head, a deflated, weary sadness slipping over him. "No. This time, the magic zapped me clean across the city—within the space of a second I go from barreling toward Drake's front door to near redecorating bare bricks in some Warren side street." He rose, staring at the floor like a six-foot-four schoolkid with a broken toy. "I could have headed back, of course, but you were closer, and I figured rounding up the cavalry was a better idea." His voice cracked. "You're the woman with the plans, Charlie, the woman who always knows what to do, so I figured it should be you calling the shots."

I let the silence breathe for a second. Outside, the city was tucking itself in for the night, the shadows getting longer, and Tamara was trapped in the lair of a beast who had to know I'd be coming to get her pretty soon. Guns drawn and fangs bared weren't about to cut it this time. I needed Plan B.

"Don't worry, Howard." I crushed my cigarette in the ashtray, gained my feet, and reached for my coat. "You made the right play, and you *know* we're going to get Tamara back. We need to be smart about it, though."

Howard flashed me the squint he reserved for ethics and arithmetic. "Smart being?"

"We follow your lead and get ourselves some help." I slipped on my trench and grabbed an old battered trilby.

Soft taps echoed against the window as if in agreement.

"We might be gone a while." I turned to Rose's wide-eyed stare. "So—"

"—Lock the door. Nobody in but you, Tamara, or Howard," she recited like homework.

I didn't smile. "That's right. And if we're not here by sunrise, head to Callaghan's and ask for Patrick. Tell him… tell him everything—and tell him I'll owe him a favor, too. He'll know what that means."

Rose only nodded but, as I pushed Howard toward the door, she added a few words that stopped me cold.

"Charlie," she called out. "Just… make sure you come back to me… okay?"

I couldn't think of a single goddamn thing I could say in reply.

15

"So, where are we headed?" Howard asked as the cab rattled into the rain-filled night. The rickety vehicle stank of stale smoke, tired leather, and the kind of soaked-in sweat that never quite fades. I cranked the window, more out of hope than expectation.

"Doc Rivers' place," I said. "Drake's got himself some kind of magic door, and the Doc represents our best shot at getting past it."

Howard's lips tightened. "Think he can whip me up a magic wand while he's at it? Something with a little heft?"

I tore my attention away from the ventilation. The big man was currently auditioning for stoic tough guy #1, but it didn't take much of a closer look to see the long shadows cast by the torch he carried for Tamara.

"No, that's not Rivers' style," I said. "The Doc deals in journeys. Point A to Point B, so, hopefully, he can put us on a road that avoids whatever voodoo Drake's got rigged up."

Howard grunted. "We could just blow that damn door off its hinges."

"Sure, if you like fireballs ricocheting toward your head." I winced at my own words. "No, this time we need subtle, and subtle's what Doc Rivers does best."

"Subtle like...?"

"I guess we'll find out. Just here please, driver."

#

The hour was getting close to unsociable, but I had an idea Kieren Rivers would still be up. An urgent tattoo on the door of the brownstone confirmed it. The door creaked open without a single sign of a human touch.

"Ah, Ms. Durant," the Doc's voice, butter-smooth and bodiless, came to my ear like a whisper. "I've been expecting you. Please, come through, my study is the second door on your right."

Howard shot me a glance, but we followed the directions of the disembodied voice all the same.

The room we found ourselves in was like something from an alchemist's dream.

"Given the urgency, we can dispense with the pleasantries." Rivers stepped out from behind a table on which a map, a compass, a candle, and a skull were arranged in some kind of pattern and lit a stick of incense. Scents of polished cedar and old temples filled the room. "I am, of course, already aware of the day's events."

Howard frowned. "How?"

"A wise man watches the wolves even when upwind of the pack," the doctor said, somewhat cryptically. "Unfortunately, I cannot accompany you on your mission to rescue Ms. Quinn, but it would be remiss of me not to aid you down a path I set your feet upon."

I bit down on my growing impatience before it could become an issue. "Then what can you give us?"

A flicker of a smile, thin and as dry as old paper, tugged the corners of the doctor's mouth. "Exactly what you came here for. A way past any wards or traps your adversary has deployed —a way to your friend. What you do once you reach her is, of course, your affair, although, personally, I'd advise stealth where possible, and your distinctive brand of violence where not."

"Always worked for me," I said. "So when do we make a start?"

The doctor raised a clenched fist and a sickly green light leaked from between his knuckles. "We already have," he whispered.

#

The ghost-light and the riverbed stink that accompanied it faded to dry air and the flat glare of a single bare bulb. I took a fast glance at the twelve by eight room Rivers' magic had transported us to. Whitewashed plaster walls dressed with dusty wine racks boxed us in. A fifth, free standing rack divided the cramped space, and behind us, a skinny, metal stair led up to a bolted steel door. It was the kind of place where vintage reds were left to collect dust, and they weren't alone.

Because in front of us, her back turned and her head lowered, knelt Tamara Quinn.

"Tamara," I whispered. "It's us. We're getting you out."

She turned her head and nailed me with a look that could have stripped paint. A fresh bruise decorated her right cheek like a bad watercolor. "Took you long enough," she snapped. She began to rise, but the chains cuffed around her wrists and ankles yanked her back to the concrete floor. "Drake has already asked me some pointed questions," she continued. "And, let me tell you, he doesn't enjoy getting 'no' as an answer. Tomorrow morning, I've got an appointment booked with a pair of pliers—Drake's scheduled to conduct that one personally—so, that gave me eight or so hours to get myself out of these chains." She held up a nail file. "And let me tell you, *that* was getting old."

#

Only an amateur leaves the keys to the cell on a nearby table and whatever else Drake and his boys were, they were no amateurs.

I crossed to Tamara to check her restraints. It was serious hardware. Thick cuffs secured both her ankles and her wrists, the shackles connected by a slim but solid chain that ran through an iron ring set in the concrete floor. The reasons a man like Drake might need a cellar rig like this were too ugly to consider, each scenario I imagined a hair worse than the last.

I shrugged the thought away and turned my attention to freeing my friend. No normal person could have possibly snapped the chains holding Tamara without the use of a pair of bolt cutters. It took abnormal me a touch over three minutes.

"Clear?" I asked Howard who crouched atop the metal stairs with an ear pressed against the steel door. He flicked me a curt nod, and waved us up.

Slow and stiff, Tamara limped toward Howard. I took one last look around the wine-soaked tomb and followed behind.

#

Beyond the steel door lay a kitchen straight out of a design spread. Big, polished, and smug about it, its light oak counters and sage-green cabinets were lit by the silver moonlight which shone through tall windows that graced the walls. The light and space they afforded were like a modern echo of Versailles' empty grandeur, only with cleaner lines and better plumbing.

Through the kitchen's outer door, star jasmine and night-dew-studded honeysuckle spilled across a narrow path. Howard brushed through this flora, launching a storm of droplets, and jabbed a thumb toward the corner. "Driveway's that way. A cluster of Drake's Hand boys guard the main gate, watching the road like something mean's due any second."

"And the other way?"

"Some tradesman's entrance, maybe?" Tamara shrugged. "Not that I'd count on it. The windows of Drake's office only showed us manicured gardens and thick, white walls."

"How tall?"

"The walls? Eight, maybe ten feet," Howard said. "But they were coated with this stuff slicker than a politician's promise and topped with enough razor-wire and broken glass to give a spider second thoughts."

I stared down the slice of garden Howard had jerked a thumb toward, weighing bad options against worse. The main gate meant speed, and, if we were lucky, surprise—a big 'if'. No, to have any hope, we'd need to...

"Wait!"

The voice was like brushed steel—clipped but kind of smooth. From the shadows of a nearby doorway its owner, a woman I'd seen once before, stepped out of the shadows. Gray hair. A trim suit. Cold eyes—it was the same dame who'd had a supporting role in the Doc's smoke-and-mirrors show—Ms. Barrett, Drake had called her.

"You won't make it," she said, her voice as calm as a ticking clock. "You can't. You've already tripped at least two silent alarms, so Mr. Drake knows you're here and so do his guards. If you head for the main gate, then it won't matter how quick or stealthy you think you are, this garden will be your grave."

As if on cue, the house lit up like Christmas. Barked orders erupted, followed by the click-clack of serious men prepping serious heat. Boots pounded floors. Flashlights carved the dark like prison yard searchlights.

The Barrett woman was right. There were too many men with too many guns. I might be an immortal creature of the night, but I'm not *that* immortal.

"Stick to the wall," Barrett said, talking fast. "Head to the rear of the house. On the way you'll pass two tall ferns by a stand of Japanese maples. Between the ferns, half-hidden in their shade, is the gardener's gate. It's kept locked, as a rule, but not tonight. From there, you'll hit road, and then you're on your own."

I squinted at her. "But why?"

"It doesn't matter. Just go. And make sure to stay safe... all of you."

I waved Tamara and Howard on, my eyes fixed on the gray-haired woman. "Thank you," I said. "Whatever your reasons, thank you."

She half-opened her mouth only to shut it again but, as I moved away, her hand found my arm. "Okay, but not here. Meet me at Callaghan's Champagne & Cocktail Lounge tomorrow night. Bring your friends. Do that and I'll explain everything—I swear."

Her eyes lifted from me, as if she sensed some presence, and I followed her gaze to the house's top floor where a suited man stood at a half-open window. In his left hand was a glass of something I hoped to hell was red wine.

I turned back to Barrett with a question on my lips.

But Barrett was gone.

#

I dropped Tamara and Howard at their respective doors and told the hack to take me home. What I wanted was the office and its familiar balms of alcohol, nicotine, and blood, but what I wanted didn't matter, not when there was a damsel I was trying my damnedest to keep out of distress waiting for me with a pocket full of questions I didn't know how to answer.

I paid the cabbie, cleared the stairs at a nervous trot, and patted my pockets for the keys I knew I'd given to Rose. Cursing my memory, I once again rapped on my own front door. "Rose, it's me," I said. A sentiment that's always true but never helpful.

A hollow silence was my only answer.

As the endless seconds ticked by tension spooled through me like film through a jammed reel. By the time I heard Rose's voice ring out from the stairwell behind me I was about ready to kick the damn door in.

"Charlie! You're back! I thought..."

"Never mind what you thought!" I spun toward the woman I'd sworn to protect. "I laid down the rules. Lock the door. Nobody in—"

"—Except Tamara, Howard, or you," she finished, cool as

the proverbial. “Yeah, I remember. But you didn’t say word one about going out.”

I opened my mouth to object, but she beat me to it. “Relax, Charlie. I only went to the store on the corner for some essentials—slim pickings at this hour, but it was the only place still open, so I picked us up a few sorely needed items." Rose clasped the bulky paper bag in her arms a little closer to her chest as she climbed the last of the steps from the street. "I was... careful.”

I shook my head—exasperation and relief doing the two-step in my skull. “Careful? No, Rose, you weren’t *careful.* You were reckless... thoughtless. I didn’t drag you all the way up here for kicks. I did it to keep you breathing. Nothing in any corner-store in the world is worth getting yourself hung upside down and gutted over.”

She didn’t flinch, not one iota.

“And what part of ‘keeping me breathing’ features me starving to death?”

“Huh?”

She brushed past me, unlocking the door with her free hand, and stepped inside. The paper bag hit the couch with a soft thud. “I'm guessing you don’t get too many guests, these days. Living ones, I mean. Your cupboards are practically bare, so if *someone* hadn’t bought some supplies, then the one of us who can’t survive on blood and is well and truly sick of breakfast sandwiches and cold burgers would’ve been chewing wallpaper by morning.” She glanced back, a blush rising in her cheeks. “Sorry. Poor taste.”

The small smile she tried for vanished, to be replaced by a keener, more curious expression. "*Do* vampires eat? I mean real food, not blood. Pastrami on rye, maybe? The odd slice of pizza?”

“Sure.” I shrugged. “I mean, give me a medium-rare steak with béarnaise sauce and a side of Pommes Anna over pizza any day, but yeah, we eat... if there’s something worth the eating.”

She nodded, slow and thoughtful. “Okay. And I guess I’ve seen you drink coffee, too... if I’m honest, it’s the smoking.” Her eyes narrowed. “If you’re dead, or... undead? Charlie, do you breathe?"

So we'd got to *The Talk*. It was a little ahead of schedule, but I'd known it was coming. I nudged the grocery bag out of the way and dropped onto the couch like a sack of bad decisions. Dawn was a whisper away, and that special ache that only the undead know was beginning to creak inside me.

"Okay, let's keep this straight and short. Yes, undead is the word, yes, I do smoke, no, I don't need to breathe." I cut off her interjection with a raised hand. "It's habit, that's all. Muscle memory inherited from when I was still a warm body. The lungs, the guts, the *machinery* is all still there, so eating, breathing, it's all still doable, it just doesn't *do* much, other than allow me to indulge my more mundane addictions—Nicotine, caffeine, and alcohol—the holy trinity of earthly cravings. I guess you could say breathing is the habit that feeds my habits."

"Right, but..."

I took an unneeded breath and cut to the chase.

"Daylight will kill me, fast and easy—if I step into direct sunlight I'm a pile of ash, and even the most overcast day would still see me get a slower but no less terminal case of sunstroke." I rolled my shoulder and reached across my chest, to knead the stiff muscles of my neck. "I don't have a reflection, a heartbeat, or a pulse." I continued, "and I can go unnoticed if I concentrate hard enough—not invisible, more difficult to see and hard to remember." I flashed her a dry grin. "It never works on cats for some reason—I'm also a lot stronger and quicker than I look—not comic-book levels, but more than enough to be handy in a fight. Oh, and I also heal pretty fast, especially after I've fed."

Rose's solemn gaze lingered on my face. "On blood?"

"Yeah. And it has to be human, too," I said as if I was ordering coffee. "Not that I have a choice in the matter. Either I feed or drink or whatever you want to call it, or I'm a bag of bones wrapped up in paper thin skin." I ran my tongue across my teeth. "It's more than survival, though. It's *desire*. A howling craving that scratches at the inside of my skull, just begging me to bite into vulnerable flesh—to drink and to keep on drinking until there's nothing left."

I finished with my teeth and licked the dryness from my lips. "Because that's the real thrill. The ecstasy of destruction. A high that never quits—that owns me, if I let it—that turns me into a monster who only exists to kill and kill again, ripping through flesh like paper and gorging on the warmest, freshest human blood way past the point of satiety—until the body it once fueled turns limp and lifeless in my hands." I let my eyes drop to the floor. "It's always there, Rose... prowling through my mind... whispering how good it would be to stop fighting and let myself feel that raw, animal high one more time."

I offered her the smallest of smiles. "But I can't... I won't."

Rose stared for a moment, her mouth open. "Wow," she said. "I never would have guessed."

"Good." I searched my pockets for a cigarette.

"How *strong* you are, I mean."

She stood and took a step toward the kitchen like the thought needed space. "How strong you *have* to be... I mean, I suppose, but... Wow!"

I looked up at her. I'd drawn back the curtain to reveal the monster inside me, and *this* was her takeaway? Even Tamara, the woman who'd gone from pointing a crossbow at my heart to being my closest confidante, had never reacted in *this* way.

Rose dropped onto the couch again, her legs folded under her like a school kid. "And the rest of it? Garlic? Holy water? Crosses?"

"Baloney." I grimaced, still raw from the wound I'd laid bare. "Stories made up to control the masses, and keep people scared and compliant. I used to wear a little silver crucifix myself, back in the day. It was an adorable little thing. I can't say it ever caused me much discomfort."

She chewed her lip. "Okay, but there's nothing controlling about garlic... is there?"

I snorted. "I don't know, maybe some enterprising merchant had himself a surplus to move. Not that it matters. It's all the same kind of nonsense. Hell, I grew up in the royal courts of

France and spent my first hundred or so years as a vampire drifting through most of the towns and cities of southern Europe. If garlic had been my Achilles heel, then I doubt I'd have made it past my first bistro!"

"I gue..." Her eyes narrowed. "Wait... You're *French!?*"

"Mais oui, Mademoiselle. Je suis Française," I executed a small, ironic bow. "Mademoiselle Charlotte Amálie Durant, third daughter of a no-name noble in the court of Louis XIV, the Sun King, at your service. A talentless woman born into meaningless, semi-luxurious obscurity, or so I used to think—a lifetime or two ago."

"Lifetime... Sun King." Rose's eyes sparked with realization. "Oh, that's right, you're old." She caught herself. "No! Wait! I didn't mean..."

"You meant old." I slumped against the arm of the couch and closed my eyes. "And you're right, I'm old—too old. I'm too rich in years and too soaked in loss. You see, age isn't just a number, Rose. It's a weight, an anchor that drags on you, getting heavier and heavier with every face, every name, and every scream. Age strips away any pretense of innocence, leaving only guilt and sorrow in its place. You think I'm strong, Rose—that I'm some hidden saint on the road to redemption, but there's no strength here, no goodness—all I am, all I ever *can* be, is a monster."

I opened my eyes to find hers waiting for me. She had drawn closer as I made my testimony of naked self-loathing.

"Nope, don't see it," she said, that soft, tobacco-brown stare burning into me.

"There's no monster hiding behind these eyes. No 'bad news'. All I see is a woman, playing the shitty hand fate dealt her and looking to beat the odds. A woman fighting to use the power of the demons inside her for something approaching good. You're no monster, Charlie Durant. You're the woman who beats back the monster." Her face lit up with something close to pride. "You're a goddamn *hero*."

Before I could protest she reached out, slow and deliberate, to brush a stray lock of hair from my face, her fingers lingering at my cheek like a pre-dawn breeze.

She was close now. Close enough that I could smell the perfume she hadn't worn that day—faint, dry, and floral. Her breath warmed my skin and, where our bodies met, I could feel the hummingbird flutter of her heart. A thousand incomplete thoughts raced through my mind—voices that were silenced by the rush of unbidden desire. I tried to pull away from her, but the couch had other plans.

Her lips found mine before I could untangle the words to stop her.

"Please. Don't." I whispered, my hand reaching up to cover hers.

But she did.

16

A firm, insistent knock at the apartment door yanked me from the arms of satisfied slumber. My robe was around my shoulders before my feet hit the floor.

Rose and I had fallen asleep in each other's arms at dawn, her heartbeat my lullaby, but Rose was gone.

The fading scent of skin-warmed perfume and the faint dip in the pillow beside my head the only remaining evidence she had ever lain, exhausted and satisfied, beside me.

I was alone.

A jolt of panic flared inside me as the last vestiges of sleep fled. I crept to the apartment door on silent feet. Dread twisted up my gut as flashes of a lifeless body—Rose's body—strung up like the Hanged Man of the Tarot and put on display. But there was no body anywhere in the apartment, and no sign of any kind of struggle, either. The penthouse was empty, but that wasn't nearly enough to ease the worst of my misgivings, because it still meant Rose wasn't there—and there was still someone knocking on my door who wasn't taking no for an answer.

I fumbled with the locks, my hands clumsy with unspent adrenaline and my mind racing with a parade of grim possibilities and as the final bolt slid back the door almost exploded inward and Tamara just about fell into the hallway.

"You're not dressed." Her words were a breathless, irritated blur. "Why the hell are you not dressed?"

"Just woke up," I muttered, raking a hand through my bed-tangled hair. "Last night was a pretty long day, if you remember."

"It sure was."

My gaze snapped toward the kitchen at the sound of Rose's voice in time to see the girl herself stroll into the sitting room carrying a thick sandwich and wearing what looked suspiciously like my shirt. She dropped herself onto the couch in a casual sprawl and a complicated surge of relief pulsed through me.

"You guys hungry?" Rose said with a needlessly knowing grin. "There's still a little pastrami and some cheese going spare."

Tamara gave her a long glance that walked the line between suspicion and curiosity. "No, thank you. Nice to see you've, uh, settled in though."

I don't blush—one of the factors of the whole undead thing—but my discomfort must have been about as plain as a neon sign on a desert highway. Tamara certainly caught it. Amusement glinted in the tall girl's eyes.

"Right… dressed." I brushed past her, ignoring her scrutiny as best I could. "What time is it, anyway?"

"About an half-hour since sundown." Tamara leaned into the doorway, flashing me a gleeful smirk. "A little early to head out, but we do have a rendezvous, if you recall."

I kicked the door shut and grabbed my clothes. "Don't worry, I remember." I shrugged on an unfussy white shirt and finished up with my pants. "Callaghan's. The Barrett woman. I don't remember her specifying a time."

"She didn't." Tamara's voice was raised enough to carry through to me. "But early will always beat sorry."

She had a point. Barrett had shown up just in time to steer us out of Drake's trap, and whatever her reasons, she'd taken a risk doing so. Maybe it was a setup—another misdirection, but maybe, just maybe, it was a crack in Drake's armor, and that made it a risk worth taking.

"If I *recall*," I said, fastening the last button and stepping into the sitting room, "she wanted to see all three of us, so, where's Howard?"

"I sent him ahead," Tamara replied, still entirely too pleased with herself. "If our new friend shows up early, I told him to keep her talking until we get there. Don't worry, though, I walked him through his lines and told him when to shut the hell up, too—made him repeat it back to me three times." Her smile curved into something wicked. "He's going to kill me when he finds out he missed this."

I shot her a glare sharp enough to cut glass and kept right on to the door.

"Rose," I called out.

"Stay put. Door locked. Nobody in. Mind the phone," she recited through a mouthful of sandwich. "Yes, ma'am."

#

Callaghan's was well within walking distance, although the city did its very best to make us second-guess our decision to do so. The remnants of a dirty rain still clung to the streets, and the sky was draped with low, sulking clouds that looked about ready to burst again. It lent the night a heavy, pregnant atmosphere. One underscored by a single unspoken question.

"Okay!" I stopped dead and turned to face Tamara, the weight of her silent interrogation too heavy to carry another step further. "All right, yes. I—"

"—Slept with her?" Tamara's grin, just as in my dream of Versailles, was all teeth and mischief.

"I… yes." I snapped off the word, tossing it over my shoulder as I marched on. Tamara hurried after me. "Okay, details, please, Ms. Durant. Who made the first move? Was it you? Was it her?"

"No!" I snapped. "No moves. Not from anyone. It just kind of… happened. You know?"

The vague nature of my confession stopped Tamara cold. She leaned against a lamppost with exaggerated patience and waited, forcing me to turn back. "Let's say I don't," she said.

"Why don't you walk me through it?"

"No!" I threw my hands skyward and let them rest behind my head as I paced out a tight circle. "For god's sake, Tamara, here I am, stuck figuring out whether last night was the best or worst of my entire cursed existence, and all you want to do is dig in the dirt for play-by-play details. Who kissed who? Who gasped first? Where did the hands land? I mean, come on, Tam, which of us is the vampire here, me or you?"

"Aww, Charlie."

"No, not 'aww, Charlie'. I'm struggling here, Tam. Really struggling. "Last night was..." I hesitated, searching for the right word. "...wonderful. But we both know it shouldn't have happened, and we both know why it can never happen again."

"But you want it to."

"More than anything." I sighed and met her unflinching gaze. "It's like you told me back at Callaghan's. You said she'd got to me... here." I tapped my chest, mimicking the same gesture she'd used. "Well, you were right. I've tried to fight it. God knows I've tried. But..." I searched the cloud-fractured sky for something like clarity. "And that's the problem, Tam. Because I could love Rose, and I mean, *really* love her. But I tend to break the things I love."

"The someone you killed?" Tamara said with unexpected softness.

"Yeah, the someone I killed." The image of Marie-Thérèse Bazinet, her skin fever-slick and her eyes filled with an unspoken plea, clawed its way to the surface of my mind. "No, I have to stop this, Tamara—before it's too late."

"And if it already is?"

"It can't be," I said, a little more forcefully than I meant to. "I can be what she needs while her life is at risk—protect her until this Drake mess plays out—but once it's done, I'll lay it out to her, clean and clear."

A heavy silence, filled with rain and restraint, fell over us. Tamara studied the crowded horizon, her expression unreadable, her schoolgirl enthusiasm gone.

"Sounds like you've got it all worked out, then," she said, pushing away from the lamppost like she'd finished a long shift. "But, for the record, I think you're wrong."

"Maybe," I muttered, falling into stride beside the dark-haired girl. "But right or wrong won't mean a damn thing if we don't see out our duty and put an end to this Drake character."

Tamara nodded. "Then what say we find out what this 'Ms. Barrett' has for us."

And, almost like we'd summoned them, the lights of Callaghan's Champagne & Cocktail Lounge loomed into view.

17

"My name is Dolores Evangeline Barrett. I believe you're aware of my association with Sebastian Drake."

She sat opposite us with her back to the door, a still life in grayscale. Her charcoal suit, twinset pearls, and square-toed shoes were all eminently practical. A cameo brooch perched at her throat like punctuation.

Her bearing was military-straight, her hands folded neatly before her like a schoolmarm. Everything about her told a story of stark, conservative precision. A story that clashed with the clientele of Callaghan's like the Spartans clashed with Persia.

"Perhaps," I said, tapping the last of my cigarette into the waiting ashtray and fishing for another. "But why not enlighten us anyway?"

Barrett's ice-blue eyes flicked to the door as it opened to admit two hard-looking men I recognized as *Domovoi* muscle loyal to Mother Yeager. "Very well," Barrett said, her attention returning to me. "I am Mr. Drake's personal assistant— his right-hand woman, you might say. A post I've held for some twelve years, although our relationship wasn't always so… defined."

"Romance?" Tamara's brow arched.

"Not quite." Barrett's lips twitched in cold amusement. "Although, I won't deny having once entertained the possibility. No, our arrangement has always remained purely transactional."

I let my eyes linger on her face. Her makeup was sparse, muted, and applied with the kind of restraint that favored discipline over vanity. Below it, her soft, pale skin bore only the lightest suggestion of time around the eyes and mouth. She wore her iron-gray hair in a severe bun that dared the world to call it old-fashioned. Taken together, the artfully artless effect spoke of both pride and control. It spoke of a calculated woman who knew the value of her looks and was determined to extract every last cent, and it made guessing the nature of her *transaction* with Drake pretty easy.

"You underwent 'The Treatment'," I said, giving the thought voice.

"I did." Her gaze darted to the door again. "I signed on the dotted line and paid in full. Of course, I was only a slip of a girl then. One more nobody in a chorus line of wannabes and never-weres—ripe fruit just waiting to be plucked."

"And?" I asked.

She sat back, the tension in her shoulders melting away. "And it was wonderful." An unexpected warmth bloomed in her cheeks. "Mr. Drake was so understanding. The way he smiled at me, the way he spoke... it was like he *saw* me." She caught herself, her cool poise snapping back like taut wire. "He gave me everything I'd ever wanted—sweeping golden hair, shapely legs that stretched forever, and full curves that would have made Titian blush." Her tone darkened. "But it was never enough."

"Enough for who?"

"Anyone." The snort of laughter that escaped her was bitter and breathy. "Don't misunderstand me, Ms. Durant, a pretty face, the right silhouette—it can take a girl a hell of a long way in a city like St. Germaine. A whole range of doors open with a flash of thigh and a lick of the lips. You can even pull the 'lost little lamb' card, if you're good enough. That one works like magic."

Barrett glanced down and adjusted the cuff of her blouse. "I played my own part to perfection," She said, her voice dulled by the memory. "The wide-eyed *ingénue,* all knowing smile and trusting eyes. It's what they wanted from me, and it's what I gave them—night after night and casting couch after casting couch—and, for a while, it worked, too." She paused, her jaw tightening. "But there were always other girls, each of them a dead-eyed sex-bomb waiting to explode. I'd say at least half had already taken 'The Treatment', so any edge I might have had was gone before I got it."

Howard stared at the older woman with something close to horror.

"But what about talent?"

"Ah, yes. Talent." She smirked. "The coin of the true artist. A rare commodity that remains unrealized until it's *seen.* I played the game, Mr. Gold. I flipped my hair, laughed just right, smiled sweetly, but not *too* sweetly, and hit every industry 'party' and two-bit audition for 'girl #2' I could stomach, going up against girls I *knew* I could out-act in my sleep—and all of it for just *a shot* at being seen."

I blew smoke at the ceiling and let her words settle over me like dust. "Then why fuel the same machine that chewed you up? You clearly hate the game, so why throw in with an enabler like Drake?"

Barrett inspected a fingernail with studied indifference. "Why?" Her voice was icepick sharp. "Because I wasn't getting any younger, Ms. Durant, that's why. Oh, sure, I could *look* twenty-five—I could even *act* it pretty well, but I never *felt* it—not in here." She tapped her chest. "I was getting tired. Thin. Used-up. You see, that's the real price of Drake's little miracles. A cost that's hidden deep within the fine print of his contracts, and never *ever* specified out loud."

She looked away again, her gaze fleeing from mine. "I went to him one last time, hoping for a patch job." Her lips curled into something that wasn't quite a smile. "What I got instead was a lesson on the cost of doing business."

"Meaning?"

"He laid it out pretty plain for me in that smooth, unshakable way of his." Barrett's jaw set like a lock. "Each Treatment requires a *Binding*, you see. A signed magical contract that can buy you anything you want—beauty, wealth, the whole nine yards. But the price of a Binding isn't measured in dollar bills. No, each signed contract steals a slice of the signer's essence—what some might call their eternal soul. *That's* what was wearing me thin. Not the pull of time... the gradual theft of my soul."

She met my scrutiny, her gaze unflinching. "I'd nothing left to offer and no way to beat him. So, instead, I threw myself at his mercy. I pretty much begged him for a taste of the power he had, and, to my surprise, he agreed."

"At first, I was given the administration work, the upkeep of the appointment book, ledgers, and client lists, the sourcing of rare *objets* for him to buy, but eventually, he started to let me observe him crafting his Bindings and taught me the intricate script. He even lent me just a taste of his power so I could, under his supervision, craft Bindings of my own. Eventually, I became his apprentice and the admin junk fell to a new girl—a vicious little social climber named Elizabeth Pell. You know the type. All shy smiles and ruthless ambition."

Barrett exhaled, flat and final. "And that's it. The whole damn story."

I traded a glance with Tamara and saw my own skepticism mirrored in her eyes.

"Not quite," the dark-haired girl said, sliding into the lead. "I mean, if it were, why would we be here?"

"Nothing slips past this one, huh?" Barrett's smirk was dry and derisive. "Fine, let's cut to it."

"You see, in my time working with Drake, I learned a few tricks. Not just which spells turned those brown eyes blue, or honeyed an ambitious man's words—no, I learned the true source of Sebastian Drake and all his power—and that's the reason I helped you free your friend from Drake's clutches, Ms. Durant, the reason I now need your help."

"Go on."

We were close to it now.

"I believe you have a client," Barrett said, her words slow

and careful. “A young woman named Rose Chamberlain. She’s probably told you of her encounters with Drake and every ordeal he's put her through—but I’m betting she never told you *why*.”

Barrett’s mask of cool control slipped a fraction, her gaze flicking to the door again like she expected trouble to burst through it. “Mr. Drake has a patron, you see,” she said, her voice barely a whisper. “Some nameless, formless entity that exists... elsewhere. It is this malevolent entity that grants him both his life and his power, and, in return, it demands a payment.”

“What kind of payment?”

I already knew where *this* was going.

“A blood sacrifice,” Barrett confirmed. “One made every six years, during the same lunar month Drake signed his own unholy pact.

"That’s the real depravity hiding behind his mask of urbane, sophisticated charm, Ms. Durant. He may feed off the insecurities of the desperate and the vain, victims who walk into his web of their own free will, but, in order for Drake to maintain his empire he must rip, with his own bloodied hands, the life, mind, and soul from a true and unsullied innocent.” She paused and took a sip of the water Howard had risked humiliation to fetch her. Cubed ice clinked softly against the side of the glass.“It’s always a young and beautiful girl he chooses—not necessarily a virgin, but a pure soul full of promise. Drake grooms this young woman. He instills fear, temptation, and despair within her and tortures her both physically and psychologically until she is finally ready to offer herself to him—the *pain* and the *surrender,* is the spice and the seasoning, his patron demands of him.”

Barrett took a deep breath and steadied herself against the table. “That’s the truth of Sebastian Drake, Ms. Durant. The monster that lurks within his tailored suit. A truth that, once I learned it, let me break free of his charms. A truth that led me to you.”

So Mackenzie Hoyte had been right. We were dealing with a raw power grab paid for in innocent blood.

Rose had been marked for death, a death soaked in pain

and perversion, simply because she matched the twisted appetites of whatever *entity,* as Barrett called it, Drake served.

I saw her as she had looked the previous night, curled up on my couch, with her legs tucked beneath her and her eyes dancing with mischief. I heard her laugh. I smelled the dry-spice of her perfume, and something twisted, sharp and needful, in my gut.

"*Life,*" I seized hold of the word like a lifesaver. "You said 'his *life* and his power', but what does that mean? Does Drake's unholy bargain include some kind of extended lifespan?"

Barrett almost looked impressed. "Immortality, Ms. Durant, or at least something close to it," she said. "Which brings me to the reason I need *you.*"

I watched a drop of water crawl down my glass. The bait had been cast. The hook was on its way.

"Magic has its limits," she continued. "It has to. In Drake's case, the invulnerability and immortality he sold his soul to obtain hinges on one condition hidden in the small-print of the Binding *he* himself signed. A provision so specific it reads like a joke."

I wasn't smiling.

"Understand, Ms. Durant," she continued. "Drake cannot be reasoned with. You cannot scare him off or blackmail him, and there's absolutely nothing he wants that he doesn't already have. You can try to hide your client away but he *will* find her, and if you think you can run, you'll find he can move faster. No, before the next full moon Sebastian Drake *will* kill Rose Chamberlain." She leaned forward her ice-chip stare flat and serious. "Unless *you* kill *him* first."

I stared at her. "But you said Drake *can't* be killed."

"He can't." Barrett met my eyes. "Not by any weapon or any person—not unless that person is already dead."

#

And there it was—the magician's silk lifted for the big reveal. I met Dolores Barrett's challenging gaze head on and held it.

"What do you mean *dead*?" Tamara's voice sliced the silence like a knife. "Dead is dead, and a corpse doesn't feature as much of a threat to anyone."

It was gallant of her, but pointless.

"Ms. Durant knows exactly what I mean and I suspect you do too." Barrett didn't even glance at Tamara. "But if you insist, Ms. Quinn, I'll spell it out. Your employer is a vampire—an undead predator with no heartbeat, no soul, and no place among the living. Qualities which make her uniquely qualified to end the reign of Sebastian Drake."

Howard looked ready to try some indignant bluster of his own, but I stopped him with a look and he settled back, frowning into his drink.

"Vampires aren't real," I said evenly. "They're just stories. Myths."

"And yet here you are," Barrett replied, as smooth as velvet. "Oh, I know all about you, Charlotte Amálie Durant. Even before your little invasion last night I knew who you were. You see, Mr. Drake tasked me to identify, evaluate, and catalog any and all possible threats that might impact his 'business'. Every danger I located got its own file, and every file was sent straight to his desk... all except yours."

She paused, her smile filled with cold triumph."No, you, I kept to myself. My ace in the hole. My 'just in case'."

"Why?"

Barrett's fingers tapped the table—slow and deliberate. "Why?" she echoed, the word clipped. "Why retain the details of the woman who, in a single night, slaughtered half the Royal Court of France? The woman who ripped through courtiers and servants alike in a massacre so horrific Versailles buried its memory deeper than the catacombs of Paris?" Her cold eyes flared. "Should I tally the bodies you left in your wake, Ms. Durant? Shall I detail your rampage across Rome, and Madrid?

Your sojourn into England? Your flight to The New World? Do I need to put a name to every man, woman and child you killed? I chose you, Ms. Durant, because of your unsurpassed talent for destruction, for your agency, for your appetite—you see, unlike the other creatures I cataloged, you don't sit on your power like some self-satisfied spider, letting others do your bidding for you. You *do*. You *act*."

I took a slow sip of my drink, the ice ticking gently against the glass. She'd done her homework alright. The Church called my undead debut—the rampage that followed Marie-Thérèse's death in an orgy of grief, rage, and hunger that only a newborn vampire could unleash—*The Masque of Blood*. Their cleanup was swift, clinical, and absolute. Every record was scrubbed and every witness silenced, leaving only one report—unread and unreachable, buried in the deepest vaults of the Vatican.

Or so I'd thought.

"Okay, so you looked me up." I ignored Howard's horrified expression. "But that was then and this is now. If you're hoping to recruit the monster who committed those crimes then I'm afraid you're a couple of centuries too late. I don't kill, Ms. Barrett. Not anymore."

"Oh, I know all about your *rehabilitation*," Barrett sneered, her voice dripping with disdain. "And there's no doubt you keep yourself on a leash, with the help of those 'friends' of yours, but, please, let's not pretend. You can't outrun what you are, *Charlotte. Amálie. Durant.* And what you are, were, and always will be, is a stone-cold killer. Nothing more. Nothing less." Her voice dropped, low and deadly. "But right now, you're a killer this world needs. The only creature with the ability, the opportunity, and the will to stop Sebastian Drake. The best, last, and only hope Ms. Chamberlain has. *You*, Ms. Durant. You, and *only* you."

Tears burned behind my eyes. It seemed, once again, fate had left me with no choice left to make.

"No," I said, my voice hoarse. "No, there's another way. There has to be."

"There is, Charlie." Tamara's hand slid into mine, firm and

sure. “And you know damn well we’re going to find it.”

Barrett rose from the table, gathering herself with practiced poise. “No, Ms. Quinn, you won’t. I wish another way existed. Truly, I do. But the only way to save your client is for your employer to become a killer again.” She pulled a business card from her purse and set it on the table with a precise flourish. “But, please, talk it over, think it through—turn over every rock and explore every option. When you finally accept the truth, you can call me on this number.”

She turned toward the door, her sensible heels tapping like a countdown. “But remember, Ms. Durant, Drake *is* on a schedule.”

#

As the door clicked shut behind Barrett, that final declaration hung in the smoke-filled air like the word of God.A hush settled over the three of us. Howard glanced at Tamara who stared at the door, willing it to swing open and give her something to punch. I emptied my glass and let the silence stretch on.

And the business card lay on the table like an unfulfilled promise.

“So what now?” Tamara asked. Her gaze didn’t waver from the door, but her words were meant for me.

I studied my empty tumbler. “Like you said, we find another way.”

“And if Barrett’s right?”

“She isn’t,” I said flatly. “She can’t be.”

Howard cleared his throat, his gaze not rising to meet mine. “Are you sure? I mean if she’s even half right, then killing Drake wouldn’t just save Rose. It’d be an ongoing public service.”

I set the glass down, a little harder than I meant to. “Maybe. But that’s the problem, Howard—because killing Drake isn’t where it ends—it’s where it starts.”

He blinked. “How do you figure?”

“I kill Drake, I save Rose, sure, but, where do I draw the

line? What happens when the next bastard comes along? And the next? And the one after that? How long until 'evil' becomes 'bad', or 'kinda bad', or 'wannabe bad'? How long until it stops mattering?"

"Sure, but he's only one..."

"No such animal." I tried my best to stay calm in the face of his nonplussed expression. "Your boss is an addict, Howard. I guess I should have made that clearer at orientation. I don't just need blood to survive— I *wan*t it. I crave blood, and I also crave the death and destruction that comes with taking it. It's something I'm on top of, right now, thanks to a little help." I shot Tamara a glance. "But one slip and we're back to Versailles and the Hell I unleashed there. One kill, for me, Howard, will always be one kill too many."

I wasn't sure if it was a remonstration or a confession, but whatever it was, it sank Howard back into his chair.

"I'm sorry." I offered him a weary smile. "It's been a long night and I guess I'm feeling the strain. What say we call it a night and head to the office? I think better when the walls know my name."

Tamara watched my face. "Yeah, and I'm thinking you could use a drink, too," she said.

My eyes flicked to the empty glass, and the parade of dusty bottles behind the bar, before I took her meaning.

"Yeah," I said. "I really could."

Tamara stood, brushed invisible lint from her coat and wandered toward the door. As she passed Howard, she gave his shoulder a light squeeze and a beat later, he followed behind, hesitating long enough to toss me one last sheepish glance.

I let the door swing shut before I dusted off my pants and did the same, but before I left, I tucked the card of Dolores Barrett into the inside pocket of my jacket.

A 'just in case' of my own.

18

Outside the single window of Charlie Durant Investigations, flickering neon bled across the broken city like old blood.

I turned away and slipped a hand into my pocket. The card was still there, a square of damnation sitting sharp-edged and smug against my ribs like an assassin's blade.

My mind rolled out a movie for me. A short loop of Drake slumped over his mahogany desk, his eyes wide, his throat torn open, blood leaking from him like an oil slick in shades of red. In my limbs and in my mind, weariness, bone-deep and existential, settled in and whispered its poison through every undead muscle, sinew, and synapse I own—an insidious, nagging urge to give in and be everything I was meant to be as I fixed my feet on the so-called easy path.

Except easy wasn't an option.

"So… options." It was Tamara's voice, about as casual as a loaded gun, that halted my downward spiral.

The tall girl held a chipped mug in her hand as she emerged from the back room. A mug that radiated a warm, metallic scent. I snatched it from her without a word, drank deep and the rush hit me, hot and electric.

"We could try another frontal assault." Howard did his best to pretend I hadn't just downed a half pint of some unknown donor's lifeblood. "Drake's magic door might be a no-go, but there's got to be another way in."

"You're focusing on the wrong part, Howard." Tamara perched on the edge of the desk, her arms crossed and her gaze cool. "It doesn't matter how, or even *if* we get in. Not if we can't..." Her gaze flicked toward me, dragging Howard's attention with it and a moment of perfect silence swelled, thick and pregnant, between the three of us.

I ran through my mantras until the spike of half-sated passions lent to me by the mug of blood dulled enough to let me speak.

"Okay, here's how I see it." I exhaled slowly. "We can't kill Drake." I met Howard's unspoken objection head-on. "We *can't*, Howard. Not without unleashing something a whole lot worse—but that doesn't mean we sit on our hands." I stood, rolling the creeping tension from my shoulders. "Rose was right. Moving her out of his way isn't enough. If Drake is even half as powerful as Barrett says he is, then there's not a bunker in the world deep enough, or any charm strong enough to hide her from him—no, we need to flip the board and make him play *our* game."

"And if that game ends with Drake's death?" Howard asked.

"It *can't*!" I set my empty cup on the desk, my hand trembling. "Barrett's selling us one solution, Howard—the *only* solution, but she's doing it too hard. No, that woman has skin in this game, an agenda— I can smell it."

Tamara's eyes narrowed. "You think she lied to us?"

I chewed it over for a second. "No... but I'm not convinced she told us the whole truth, either."

"Right, so our only source of solid information could well be tainted." Howard ticked off the points on his fingers like he was counting heads of cattle. "Drake already knows who, and most probably *what*, you are and is just about paranoid enough to see us coming a country mile away, and we haven't got much to throw at him as and when we do." Frustration crackled beneath his calm exterior. "All of which leaves us where, exactly?"

"About ten steps back from square one." I crossed my

arms, my thumb absently tracing the curve of one bicep. “And with the clock running down, too, because, if we take Barrett at her word, Drake’s got himself a deadline—the full moon. If we mean to strike first then we're going to need to move, and we’re going to need to get some ammunition.”

“Doc Rivers?” Tamara offered.

I shook my head. “No. He told us a while back there was only so far he could travel with us and I think helping us spring Tamara from Drake’s wine cellar was his last stop.” I glanced at the empty tumbler sitting beside the chipped, red-streaked cup Tamara had brought me. “There is someone else we might call on, though.”

“Oh?” Tamara’s eyebrows rose.

“Yeah. Two someones, actually.” Even as my body slowed under the dawn’s burgeoning weight my thoughts were starting to move. “What time is it?”

Tamara checked her watch. “A little under an hour ‘til sunrise.”

“Then I’m pretty much out of the game.” I exhaled and pushed myself upright. “Which means I’ll need the two of you to run some errands while I hit the coffin.” I fixed Tamara with a keen stare. “I’ll need *you* to check in on Rose. Give her the highlight reel from our meeting with Barrett, but don’t dig too far into the dirt. She doesn’t need any more nightmares."

"*You.*” I switched my attention to Howard. “I need to deliver two notes. Oh, and I want another copy of the apartment key made, too. I’m tired of knocking on my own damn door.” I crossed to my desk, hunting for a pen. “Once you’re both done, I want you to get some rest, but make sure to set your alarms." I found the pen and held it aloft like it was Excalibur. “Because, as soon as night falls, company will be coming.”

#

Vampires don’t tend to wear a lot of black, no matter what the movies might tell you. Browns, charcoals, a rifle green, or even a midnight blue are all far better for melting into the shadows of the night. Not that camouflage means much when, with a little supernatural effort, you can *be* the shadow.

Still, I guess dressing the part becomes something of a habit after a century or two, and habits that old die particularly hard. I pulled out a pair of charcoal slacks and a pistachio shirt that Tamara swore brought out my eyes from the small trunk we keep behind the sofa-bed in the back room. A broad black belt and some practical leather flats tied the look together. Tamara had left a note explaining she wouldn't be around to help with my makeup, but after two hundred years without the benefit of a mirror, I don't tend to wear all that much anyway.

Then, with a last useless sweep through my tousled hair, and a nod to no one in particular, I stepped into the office to greet the first of the night's guests.

#

"Well, I never... Charlie Durant! Don't you look the lady."

The words dragged up vague, uneasy memories of my dreams of Versailles and its whirling courtiers, memories I would've paid a fortune to leave undisturbed, but I put them to one side as I strode to the desk, took a seat, and met the cool, sardonic gaze of Patrick Callaghan.

"So *this* is the fabled office, is it? The nerve center of the whole operation?" He'd thrown himself into a chair and made himself at home as only he could, his familiar grin playing at the edges of his mouth. "Not bad. Could use a coat rack, or a rubber plant or something to fill the vacant corner behind the door, but it's got... atmosphere." The smile dropped from his face. "Want to tell me why I'm here, Charlie?"

"Not yet, Mr. Callaghan." I hunted for a cigarette. "I think I'd rather wait until everyone's here."

As if on cue, the office door burst open to admit Tamara and Howard, between them, his feet only just touching the floor, was a reluctant Mackenzie Hoyte.

"Patrick Callaghan," I said, raising my voice a little to drown out the academic's sputtering protests. "Meet Mackenzie Hoyte—former member of the Royal Historical Society, more recently head of the Archive Department at St. Germain's Mayoral office, and currently the city's foremost independent authority on the history and theory of magic including its associated grimoire, spellbooks, and codices." I switched my attention to the simmering, resentful academic. "Mackenzie Hoyte, allow me to introduce Patrick Seamus Callaghan, bar owner, businessman extraordinaire, and de facto head of St. Germain's premier criminal cartel."

Callaghan raised a bushy eyebrow, his habitual grin once again souring.

"What? I did say '*premier.*'"

Howard rescued a folding chair from the back room and set it next to Patrick Callaghan and Mackenzie, stiff-backed, still radiating waves of indignation, and eyeing the seat like it might just bite, sat down.

"Charmed, I'm sure," the wiry little man muttered in tones that said he wasn't.

"Now would someone please explain why I was abducted against my will at this ungodly hour and dragged here so unceremoniously?"

Tamara shook her head. "There wasn't any dragging. Mr. Hoyte made the trip on his own two feet and of his own free will—right up until I told him who else would be present. At that point he seemed to have some second thoughts." She offered Mackenzie a smile sweet enough to curdle cream. "I persuaded him he shouldn't."

"Yeah, your pet neat-freak was most *persuasive*," Mackenzie said, rubbing at his left wrist to make the point. "But, at the risk of repeating myself, why, exactly, *am* I here?"

"It's a fair question, Charlie." Patrick Callaghan said, his tone just this side of serious.

I sparked my cigarette into life, took a deep pull, and blew a cloud of smoke at the ceiling. “You’re here because I need help, and you two are my best shot at getting it.” I leveled my gaze at both men in turn to make sure I had their full attention and laid it all out—Rose, Drake, Dolores Barrett and her not-so-subtle ultimatum—everything.

When I finished, they exchanged a wary glance and sat back in their respective chairs, their movements almost synchronized.

“I said this business would get messy, Charlie,” Callaghan murmured.

“Yes, the affair does appear somewhat perilous,” Mackenzie agreed, his lips pursed. “Or ‘messy,’ if you prefer. I’m not sure what help you think I might provide, though.” He shot a thumb toward Callaghan. “Him maybe, but *me*?”

I met the academic's skepticism head-on.“That’s because you’re assuming I want firepower, which I don't—at least, not in the conventional sense.” I took a drag of my smoke before I continued. “Knowledge is power, or so those mysterious 'they' say, and right now Drake knows more about me than I know about him. It’s an imbalance I’d like to correct.”

“Weaponized information?” Mackenzie rubbed his stubbly chin. “Intriguing… I suppose I *could* be somewhat useful in that regard.” He threw a sidelong glance toward Patrick Callaghan. “Although now I’m not so sure about him.”

Callaghan rose, the slow burn of his temper flickering dangerously close to open flame. I stepped in before the spark could catch.

“Sit down, Mr. Callaghan, *please.* Mackenzie didn’t mean anything by it, did you, Mackenzie?” I didn’t wait for the answer. “Of course he didn't. He doesn’t know you like I do, that’s all. He doesn’t know about your contacts on this side of the veil *and* on the other. He doesn’t know that every secret this city holds, from guttersnipe gossip through to city hall plots, eventually passes through your hands.”

Callaghan sat, his anger guttering as quickly as it sparked. “All right,” he said. “Let’s say, for argument’s sake, I’m guilty of some or all of what you've levelled at me. What, exactly, is it you want from us, Charlie?"

"Like I said. Knowledge." I leaned forward, my jaw set and my gaze keen. "I want to know who Drake is, where he came from, what he's built, and exactly how he built it. I want to know about his power—both the magical *and* the mundane. I want to know its nature *and* its limits. I want to know every flaw and peccadillo the man has, and every fear that keeps him up at night. Hell, I'll take what he eats for his goddamn breakfast every other Tuesday if it helps."

Patrick Callaghan's eyes narrowed as if he was staring at something only he could see. "These are dangerous waters, Charlie—even for someone like me. If Drake has half the power you say he has and gets wind he's being looked into, there could be... repercussions. I've got my contacts when it comes to The Hand and I doubt this 'Drake' has any interest rummaging through my business interests personally, but the bar does look much better with all its windows intact, and I certainly don't need any extra heat from the local constabulary. No, I'm afraid if you want *my* help then you're going to have to make it worth my while."

"In what way?"

"Three things," Callaghan said, holding up his thumb, index and middle fingers. "First, when this is over, you tell me exactly what happened—and I mean all of it. No client privilege. No secrets."

I nodded. "Done."

"Second, you owe me a favor. A *real* one. And when I call it in, you don't ask questions, and you don't say no."

I hesitated. It meant a blank check presented to a dangerous mob boss, but what choice did I have? "Agreed."

"Third..." He leaned forward. "...when Drake's dealt with, you burn his whole operation to the ground, and I mean *everything*—but anything mundane left over, his hidden money, his client list and any dirt he's managed to dig up? Well, that becomes mine."

It was a heap of resources and a lot of potential for blackmail to present free of charge to a man like Patrick Callaghan, but at least I knew something of the man and his warped sense of honor. At least I knew where he lived.

"Done," I said. "And what about you, Mackenzie? What are your 'conditions'?"

"Only that you take this Drake down," Mackenzie said quietly. "The man is corrupting magic itself, Charlie. He's messing with ancient, possibly evil, powers to line his own pockets, and every contract he writes makes the next that much more acceptable. Every ounce of power he gets his hands on can only ever make a man like that hungry for more, if someone doesn't stop him..." He trailed off. "So, yes I'll help... If only for the integrity of the craft itself."

In the quiet that followed the two men exchanged another guarded look, but, this time, there was calculation and strategy hidden behind their silent glares. An understanding of a shared purpose undertaken for very different reasons.

"I guess we *could* come up with something," Callaghan mused. "If we pool our resources. I'd need a good twenty-four hours to shake my usual trees...you?"

Mackenzie nodded, his sullen defensiveness temporarily forgotten.

"Yes, I believe I can produce something of use by then. No promises on depth you understand, but... something."

Callaghan stood. "Then it looks like you have yourself a deal, Ms. Durant. We'll reconvene here tomorrow night... same time?" He glanced at Mackenzie, who nodded. "Good." Callaghan offered an open hand. "There will be a cost, though Charlie. If you manage to get yourself out of this mess you're in, you're gonna owe me that favor, and it won't be a small one."

Without any hesitation I took the proffered handshake.

"Yeah, I kinda figured."

With all the deliberate grace of a surgeon trying not to sneeze, Mackenzie copied this civilized little ritual and Howard showed the two men out, as they disappeared down the short corridor they were already deep in conversation.

"You think it'll work?" Tamara had settled by the window as quiet as a house cat, as the two men bickered.

"Has to." I watched my last, best hope cross the street below. "No information means no options."

"Well… one."

"Yeah." I stared up at the cloud-occluded moon. "Just the one."

"I'm not going to push you on this, Charlie. You know I never would." Tamara collected the abused saucer from the desk and started toward the back room. "But if you're forced to choose, and if, because of that choice, you lose yourself, then you ought to know *I'm* going to be the girl who comes looking." She paused, hovering in the doorway, her eyes hard. "You should also know that if there's nothing left for me to find, if there's no other choice but to put you down, then I'll be the woman holding the gun… just remember that."

I looked up at the woman I was so proud to call a friend, a cocktail of unnameable emotions churning in my breast. "Thank you." The two words weren't nearly enough, but right then they were all I had.

Tamara threw me a curt, wordless nod and disappeared through the door. I let my gaze dwell on the space she'd occupied for a moment and then a non-too-subtle need forced a question from my lips.

"What time is it?"

"Long past time you invested in a watch," she yelled back. "But if you're thinking of heading out you've got nothing to worry about, sunup isn't for hours yet."

I grabbed my coat. "Then I guess I'll see you tomorrow night."

"Do I need to ask where you're going?" I could almost hear the raise of her eyebrow.

"Not if you've got any kind of imagination."

19

A steady, rhythmic downpour of St. Germain's trademark rain left me more than a little damp as I reached the apartment, something Rose felt obliged to comment on.

"Charlie, you're soaked. Quick, get inside and out of those wet clothes." She caught my expression. "No, not like that!"

I crossed the threshold with a smirk and made to give her a soggy hug, but she danced away from it.

"Charlie, no! Come on, you need to shower and change. When you're warm and dry, maybe then we can, I don't know... snuggle?"

I watched her face, my clumsy attempts at playfulness arrested by the edge in her voice. "Something wrong?"

"No! Hell no." She sighed. "I'm tired, Charlie. That's all. Life's been pretty intense of late, and I guess it's catching up to me. I know I talk a good game, but there's still a lot I need to think about and a lot *more* that I can't *stop* thinking about."

A fresh pang of guilt flared inside me.

Here I was, so wrapped up in my own world of what-ifs and might-have-beens, that I'd almost forgotten who all this was for—had almost forgotten just how much Rose had been through.

"Well, the good news is we should have some solid, usable info on our Mr. Drake soon," I said as I hung my coat up behind the door and strode toward the bathroom to fetch a towel. "So, if the creep has any kind of exploitable weakness, we'll know all about it."

Rose tilted her head, her eyes narrowing. "I thought *you* were his weakness?"

Tamara.

I'd asked her to bring Rose up to speed regarding our meeting with Dolores Barrett while I retired for the day and apparently she'd done just that—and a little more besides. Again, I felt a flicker of unneeded jealousy ignite inside me.

"And I don't suppose Tamara mentioned why he might be mine?"

Rose nodded, a flush of color rising in her cheeks. "Yeah, she mentioned." She drew closer, taking the towel from my hands and reached up to rub my rain-damp hair. "The thing is, you're wrong... all of you." Her voice was soft but steady. "I know you've got your past, Charlie, but you've saved my life on at least two occasions now, and even if you hadn't, you're still the kindest, bravest person I've ever met. I think I'm beginning to know you, Charlie Durant, and I know you don't quit, not ever. That's why I know you'll beat Drake, save me and God knows how many other girls from an ugly, painful death, and then, as a finale, save yourself, too—I know you'll find a way back to the real you and all the people who care for you." She let the towel fall and met my flustered gaze "Which, just in case you hadn't worked it out by now, most definitely includes me."

Tamara's voice echoed in my mind. Different words that expressed the exact same unshakable belief. It was... terrifying.

"I only wish it were that easy." I said, a careless hand drifting to the small of her back.

She lifted her face. "But..."

It was such a small word, but it was plenty big enough to stay my hand.

"No, Rose." I turned away, threw myself onto the couch, and dragged a hand through my hair to avoid her gaze. "You talk about my past like it's something you can rationalize, but you've no idea what the word means. You *can't*." I looked down at my hands which remained rock steady, in defiance of my shaking voice. "When I became what I am, the need for blood and death *owned* me. I was new then, a perfect predator—vital, wild and fueled by unholy lusts." I swallowed hard, and looked anywhere but at her face. "You don't know the crimes I committed. The depravity. The..." I trailed off, choking on the memory. "It still gives me nightmares, even now."

Rose's brow furrowed. "But you must have fed since then... a bunch of times."

"Yeah," I admitted, "but never with the deadly abandon of those first nights. Not even at my worst. Not even when I tried."

"Tried?"

"Sure. Why not?" I shrugged, a gesture far too casual for the confession it shadowed. "I could never be human again. I could never be *good*, so why not be the worst? I crossed every line I could, indulged in every excess—all to recapture that first high, because that was all I had left." I met her stunned expression head on. "You think you know me, Rose. You think I'm some undercover saint, clawing her way back to grace—but you never saw the *carnage* of Versailles. You never tasted the fear of the ones I let live a little longer just so I could hunt them down all over again, never heard the screams of the children presented to court in their Sunday silks, only to be butchered before they could learn to curtsy."

Rose's face drained. "Jesus," she breathed.

"Yeah... and that was just Versailles. For the next hundred or so I toured the most crowded cities I could find—Rome, Naples, Lisbon, Amsterdam—and left each one a wanted woman. A few close calls later, I started to learn a little discretion and restraint. By the time I left the port of London for the New World, I was already a different kind of monster... and then I found Tamara."

Rose sank into the seat beside me and, for a moment, neither of us spoke.

"And the Bazinet girl?" she asked softly. "The girl Tamara said I remind you of so much?"

My gaze drifted to her face. It was true. Everything from the tilt of her head to the fragile determination of her wonderfully set jaw brought Marie-Thérèse Bazinet crashing back to life, uncovering memories I'd spent so many decades trying to bury, and loosening the walls behind which they were kept. Dismantling them, brick by brick.

"Marie-Thérèse Bazinet, that was her full name." I paused, trying to find the words I needed. "She was someone I loved more than anything else in the world." The image of Théri, so frail and sickly, her eyes begging me for salvation, appeared in my mind's eye. "Killing her was the worst thing I've ever done."

"Worse than the children?" Rose whispered.

"Yes," I said. "Because that was born from pure, vampiric need, but Théri I killed with a choice—the last choice I ever made as a human."

Rose looked ready to ask me more, but I stood and scooped the towel off the floor, letting the sudden motion break the spell.

"It's complicated," I said, my voice quiet. "And I'm too tired to tell you everything right now."

Taking to her tiptoes, Rose stretched up and kissed me lightly on the cheek."Don't worry, Charlie, I understand." Her voice was surprisingly gentle. "You go rest, Charlie Durant. I can't pretend what you've told me isn't a little scary, but it doesn't change anything... not for me." She tapped my chest over my too still heart. "The monster of Versailles doesn't live here anymore. And that means that when dusk falls I'll still be here waiting for the woman who does."

Her words were everything I could have possibly wished to hear.

It was a shame they weren't true.

#

Le Bassin du Dragon was always my favorite spot in the manicured haven of Versailles' famous gardens, but I never figured I'd lay eyes on it again. Certainly not in sunlight. But I guess in dreams anything is possible.

Shimmers danced and skipped across the surface of the shallow pool in which the infant Apollo aimed his arrow at the dragon Python—the death cry of the mighty beast transformed by the artifice of architect André Le Nôtre into a glimmering spout of water that split the sun into a million shards. And the sun, the real midday sun, lost to me over two centuries ago, burned down on me from a sky too blue to be trusted. My arms and shoulders started to prickle and flush under the relentless assault of the fiery orb. On my brow beads of slick, unfamiliar sweat bloomed like the first blooms of spring.

"Well, this *is* new," Tamara's voice, as dry and sharp as ever, cut through the surreal scene. I turned to the sound, greedy for the familiar in a world so strange. "Charlotte Amálie Durant," she teased, "stepping into the light and dressed like a lady for once. I… Wait… are you crying?"

I threw a hand up to my cheek and felt fat, trembling tears—tears borne not from grief, or rage, or even happiness, but from pure, broken frustration. Because, the sun, the heat, even the burgundy gown I was wearing, were a lie. A fantasy. A memory dragged from a past that died far too many lifetimes ago.

So why did it *feel* real?

"You're dreaming, remember." The lilting tones of Patrick Callaghan reminded me. "And *anything* is possible in dreams."

I turned to say something to him in reply, but he wasn't there—and neither were *Le Bassin du Dragon* or the cursed sun. Instead I once again faced the mirrors of *La Galerie des Glaces* where the graceful music played and, behind me, Rose Chamberlain danced with a bespectacled partner.

I spun and ran toward her, each step slower and heavier than the last, caught her by the shoulder and turned her toward me.

Except this was no dream-slick version of Rose Chamberlain. No, this was someone else entirely. A young woman whose face I could never, ever forget.

This was Marie-Thérèse Bazinet.

My Théri.

The woman I loved.

The woman I killed.

I saw her as I saw her back then, so beautiful, so delicate, and tore her away from the clutches of the man I could now name as Monsieur le Comte. The man who'd said he had a cure. The man who'd killed me and had forced me to kill Théri.

I grasped Théri's arm and spun her toward me, but she disappeared from my clutches like smoke, leaving me face to face with the strange scientist-nobleman who was root cause of every horror I'd ever endured.

Monsieur le Comte.

I tore at him, my fingers clawing at the black, domino mask he wore underneath his octagonal, smoked glass spectacles and found myself staring not at the trim, precise man I *knew* was beneath that mask, but at the smugly smiling visage of Sebastian Drake, the face of all my *current* woes. A cruel, barbed knife appeared in his left hand, even as his right rose to point toward the wall of mirrors behind me.

And, without moving a single step, I found myself standing not before the nearly immortal man who threatened all my hopes and all my dreams, but once more in front of my own, impossible reflection.

Only it wasn't *just* my reflection, because behind me, at my left shoulder, stood a masked young woman with honey-blond hair and tobacco-brown eyes. Rose Chamberlain or my Théri?

No, it had to be my Théri.

Or did it?

"And what of the mask you wear, my love?" The strange, double voice came not from the masked face in the mirror but somewhere else—perhaps everywhere else—and, as those orphaned words fell, the mirror rippled.

My reflection shifted and once again I was Charlotte Amálie Durant, lady of court, lips rouged, chestnut hair coiffed. And then the image twisted again. A creature with hollow cheeks, red eyes with slitted pupils, and a snarling, wolverine maw stared back at me. A thing of hunger. A creature of death.

Lady and monster. Both undoubtedly true. Both undoubtedly me.

Behind this dreadful, dual image two dancers, both female, both petite, both blonde, pirouetted in each other's arms. I turned and fled from the mirror and all the horrors it contained but within the space of five steps found myself running not *from* it but *toward* it—*through* it—running toward a lone woman in a burgundy dress who stood with her back to me.

I reached out to her, and the woman turned. Her mask dropped.

A horror of paper-thin skin, bruised and torn, was pulled tight across raw cheekbones. Bruises bloomed in shades of purple and gray on the cheeks and forehead of what could only be the living corpse of Marie-Thérèse Bazinet. Her hair, which had always been made of soft honey and warm sunshine, was dulled into dry straw. Weeping sores erupted among these cuts and abrasions that marked her skin like a dark constellation.

But far, far worse, were her eyes.

In the gossamer constructs of my memory those eyes existed as bottomless, tobacco-brown pools, filled with an amber-kissed warmth, that danced with unspoken mischief and glinted bright enough for me to fall in love again and again and again. But now those same eyes held all the tenderness of ice-cold steel. Gone was the gleam of shared secrets and the promises of more. In their place sat bitter cruelty surrounded by the thin lines of an enduring and undeserved pain.

#

I came to with the slow, heavy certainty that something was very, very wrong.

The dream still clung to me like cobwebs. Drake's face behind Monsieur le Comte's mask. A combination of the two very different men who played such similar games. My past and my present bled together in my mind's eye, but a dream is just a dream, and the agitation crawling beneath my skin was different.

It was real.

For a moment I didn't move, didn't breathe—I simply listened. Because there's a texture to silence, a weight—if you know how to feel it.

A master assassin in an empty house might be as quiet as the graves he fills, but there'll always be footprints in that silence — a subtle shift in the air, a too-careful breath, the unconscious shifting of weight from one foot to another— but as sleep and the remnants of my dream left me there was nothing. Not a sound, not a scent. Not even where there should have been.

I slipped out of bed, dressed without turning on a light and moved through the shadows like they were a second skin, ghosting through the bathroom, the hallway, the living room, and the guest room. Every corner was empty. There was no creeping assassin, no unexpected guest, only four walls, stale air, and a pit of dread burning like acid in my gut.

Because Rose was gone.

There was no sign of a struggle and not even a single hint of bloodshed, but the girl who'd come to mean so much to me was gone leaving behind the silent shape of her absence, the faint traces of her sweat and her perfume on my sheets, and her clutch, abandoned like a memory on the hallway table.

I flipped on the kitchen light, and immediately spotted a scrap of paper, propped against the toaster like an echo of the Binding that had been left for Rose.

My name was printed upon it in a careful, no-nonsense hand. I snatched it up and read:

> *Charlie—*
>
> *St. Jude's called. Grace is awake. She's screaming. Thrashing. Calling out my name, and coughing up blood like ink. They say it's killing her. They say they can't stop it. So although I know you told me to stay put, I can't.*
>
> *As I write it's still hours until sundown, and no one's*

picking up at the number you left me, so I'm leaving you to your sleep and taking a cab.

There'll be no stops and no detours, I promise. And I'll stay put at the hospital until nightfall—until you can come get me.

I'm sorry to leave like this, but I knew you'd only try to stop me. I hope you understand and can forgive me.

Oh, and just in case you missed it—I think I might be in love with you.

—Rose.

I crumpled the note in my hand, but the words still echoed, sharp and smooth, in my mind.

Rose had gone to St. Jude's.

Alone.

I understood the impulse, and, in her shoes, I might well have done the same—but understanding didn't equal acceptance. Because Rose was out there, alone and unprotected, and the phone call? That was a detail that stuck in my teeth like a splinter. Dolores Barrett had told us Drake's clock was ticking and that, if he was going to meet his deadline, he needed a *willing* sacrifice. It made the summons a coincidence I didn't like one little bit.

Some people wake up to coffee and sunlight. I wake to blood and broken promises.

I turned toward the window. There was no need to pull on the blackout drape. The burning ache in my shoulders was enough to tell me the accursed sun still reigned the skies, leaving the city and the hospital out of my reach. I tallied up all of the options I didn't have, crossed to the hallway, and picked up the receiver of the Bakelite phone.

"Charlie Durant Investigations," Howard announced in his best world-weary drawl. "No job too big. No fee too small."

"Howard, it's me."

"Oh... hey, boss!" I could hear the edges of his hesitation—like he wasn't sure which me was calling. "All okay?"

“Nope.” I pinched the bridge of my nose and puffed out a frustrated snort of worthless air. “Is Tamara there?”

“Yeah, she’s here. I’ll have to wake her, though.”

“She’s sleeping?"

“Yeah.” A flicker of pride crept into Howard’s voice. “She looked a little wiped, so I convinced her to lie down for a while.”

It seemed whisking Tamara from under Drake’s thumb had coaxed the smoldering torch he carried for her into full flame. And maybe, *maybe*, Tamara was finally letting someone look after her. In other circumstances, I might’ve risked a smile.

“Then I'm afraid you’re going to have to wake her,” I said. “Rose got a call from the hospital. Her sister, Grace is in bad shape, so Rose went running to her side—It could be a real emergency, but I can’t shake the feeling it might also be...”

“A trap,” Howard finished for me. “Got it. Don’t worry, boss, we’ll head over to St. Jude’s as soon as Tamara’s dressed.”

“Thanks, Howard. I’ll be with you as soon as the sun goes down.” Even *I* could hear the frustration dragging in my voice. “Until then, just... find her for me, okay?”

20

The main entrance to St. Jude's bore the same stripped-back utilitarianism of the back door we'd gathered around to meet Doc Rivers, but touched here and there with accents that conjured imagined memories of ancient Rome. It was an effect someone had tried to soften with shrubs flanking the stairs leading up to the front entrance, and hanging baskets of petunias and verbena suspended between its tall windows. Under a moonless sky and with the weight of my forced inaction still bearing heavy on me, those colorful flowers looked faded—a fitting metaphor for my mood.

I took the stairs two at a time and pushed through the heavy doors into a wide, high-ceilinged vestibule. White plaster walls and collared columns lent the place an air of dignity, and decorative friezes added a touch of artifice borrowed from some ancient forum, but the air still stung sharp with bleach and ammonia—an olfactory reminder of the place's real purpose.

Opposite me, beneath a wall-mounted clock, sat a reception desk. Two vases of the same petunias and verbena on display outside flanked the sole occupant of this front-facing counter—a nurse who gave me a look that burned with unfriendly suspicion. To my left, two long wooden benches, designed to give expectant fathers and worried wives somewhere to sit lined the wall. From one of them Tamara and Howard were already rising to their feet.

"Charlie!" Tamara's voice echoed gently in the cavernous space. "Thank God you're here!"

My unbeating heart lurched. "Trouble?"

She gave a slow nod, took my arm, and guided me to the bench. "Trouble," she said. "Or, at the very least, a mystery."

#

After my phone call, Tamara explained, she and Howard had moved fast. A generous, pre-arranged tip meant their cab driver pretty much ignored every speed limit and stop sign between the office and St. Jude's, but finding Grace Chamberlain had been a different story.

"We didn't know which ward, which wing, or anything." Howard's eyes still didn't quite meet mine. "All we had was a name, and the receptionist—" he nodded toward the woman behind the desk, earning himself a scathing glare. "—wasn't exactly helpful. It took more than a little relentless badgering to coax her into action. Eventually, she found some doctor, all white coat and stethoscope. We told him our tale, and he started to dig."

Tamara picked up the thread. "He called every ward, department, and treatment room he could and came up with exactly nothing." She shook her head, the gesture teeming with reluctant sympathy. "I'm sorry, Charlie... there's not a single trace of your girl or her sister anywhere in this hospital and there never has been."

#

I stared up at the plaster ceiling, letting the wall bear my weight, and tried to fathom the meaning of Tamara's revelation. Grace Chamberlain. The sister in the coma, the pawn Drake had used to force Rose's hand, wasn't here—had never *been* here. What did it mean? A hundred scenarios jostled for space in my mind, each a little more unwelcome than the last.

"It's Drake, right?" Howard said, tracking my thoughts like a bloodhound. "Some kind of illusion. Bait to draw Rose out, or a scam to put the screws on her. We know he's got the juice, not just face-lift hoodoo and glamours, real power, the kind that can fix the door thing and make him invulnerable." He threw me a quick glance that slid away before it could stick. "Well… almost invulnerable."

Tamara pulled an uncertain face. "It's possible," she said. "I guess, with magic, almost anything is, but why bother with illusion when reality works so much better? I mean, Drake doesn't shy away from inflicting the kind of pain Grace Chamberlain was in—so why not just *do* that?" Howard's brow creased, mirroring the confusion buzzing through my brain. "He'd have to spirit Grace away, of course," Tamara continued. "Erase the records and the memories of the nurses and the doctors, but Rose *knows* her sister… not her face—she knows *her*. So, presenting her with any kind of illusion would be a gamble, and I'm not sure Drake's the gambling type."

She licked her lips and looked at the floor. "Of course, there is *another* possibility."

"Go on," I said.

"You won't like it."

I sighed, venting both my pent-up frustration and growing fatigue. "Then let me guess. Your 'possibility' is that Rose, for reason or reasons unknown, has been lying to us from the start and t*hat's* why the records are empty, and why the staff are so ignorant of Grace Chamberlain and the sister who begged to stay with her—Grace Chamberlain isn't here because she was *never* here. That about cover it?"

"Yeah," Tamara said. "Pretty much."

"Then forget it, Tam, it doesn't hold. Sure, we've only ever had Rose's word for what happened to Grace, something we never even thought to verify, but why would she lie? It wouldn't buy her anything she wasn't already getting, and, as a story, it would be far too easy for us to unravel. She even left me a note this very night which pointed us straight to the one place she'd have to know we'd discover the truth! No, it doesn't track, Tam. Not one damn bit."

"But..."

"No, Tamara." I shook my head. "You know I've been crazy about Rose since the night we met. Hell, two nights ago, we lay in each other's arms—naked, exposed, and honest. I know that's the kind of intimacy that blurs the line between facts and feelings and makes everything I think tilted and biased—but this? This I *know*."

"How?" Howard asked. His voice was quiet, but the single word carried undeniable weight.

"Because this is what I *do*, Howard, that's how." I rubbed my neck and looked him in the eye. "It's not just the detective thing. It's what I've *had* to become. A woman who's careful. A woman who's learned to weigh her options, find patterns in the chaos, and assess the motives and character of those around her. To get by—to survive—I've had to learn to trust both my brain *and* my gut. And those are two things that tell me this is still Drake's game we're playing, and he's still the man holding all the aces."

Tamara's voice came soft. "Meaning?"

"Illusions, a mystical kidnapping, or a lying client, none of it matters because any way you cut it Rose is still missing. In my book, that leaves two possibilities. Either Drake has her, or, whatever the reason, she's on the lam and hiding out somewhere. If it's the latter, then we need to find her. If it's the former..." I let the sentence trail off. "Either way, us sitting here arguing plays into exactly what Drake wants from us... Delays. Distractions."

I paced away a step or two and turned back, sharply. "We can spend all night guessing what's real and what's not, or we can at least *try* to find Rose before it stops mattering. I know which option I'm taking. The rest is up to you."

Tamara and Howard glanced at each other, their thoughts following the same path.

Hesitation. Concession. Agreement.

"So, what do we do?" Tamara looked up at me, her expression a shade sheepish.

"If you're with me, we split the city up. We cover every bolthole and safe house we know Rose knows, and we do it now. We rule out the obvious and then, and only then, do we start testing Drake's magical defenses."

Tamara nodded but her eyes never left mine. "And what about your meeting with Mackenzie and Patrick Callaghan?"

I glanced down at the floor and swallowed a silent expletive. The intel the two men were gathering could be the secret to our success. It was a chance too valuable to skip.

"Alright. Then this is how we play it. Tamara and I will head north. You— " I flicked a sideways glance Tamara's way. "—to check my apartment, and me to hit the office and see what Mackenzie and Callaghan have for us." I turned toward Howard, catching the faint flinch that passed across his face as I did. "*You*, I want to go south and rattle Doc Rivers' doorknob a little. He might say he's out of the game, but there's a decent chance he's still watching over us. On your way, swing past Rose's apartment. It's a long shot, but if we skip it and that's where she is, we'll never forgive ourselves. There's a telephone at mine, one at Doc Rivers', and at least one of Rose's neighbors *have* to have one you can borrow for an emergency. If you find her—if you find any *trace* of her—call."

"Got it," Howard said, already shifting gears.

Tamara glanced away, her eyes narrow. It took another slow moment before she offered me her assent. "Yeah," she said. "Okay. Sounds like a plan."

"Then let's move." I stood and strode toward the glass doors, not needing to look back to know I'd be followed. "We'll reconvene at the office as soon as you're done.—be quick, but be thorough."

We crossed the threshold, swapping the clinical atmosphere for cool night air, and, for a few strides, we walked in silence, each absorbed in our own thoughts.

In the end it was Howard's inevitable curiosity that

bridged the awkward lull.
"You *slept* with her?"

21

I wasn't too surprised to find Messrs Hoyte and Callaghan holding up the walls outside the office door upon my return. Without saying a word, I unlocked the door and waved them in.

"Sit down," I said, grabbing a bottle and three glasses. "Drink?"Without waiting for an answer, I poured two fingers in each glass and handed them out like medicine. Both men took their brandy with a grace usually reserved for final requests.

I dropped into the chair behind the desk, knocked mine back, and looked them over.

"All business tonight, Charlie?" Callaghan's voice brimmed with lazy charm, but his eyes were sharp enough to bleed a person dry.

"All business, Mr. Callaghan and I've already had a long night, so you'll pardon me if I cut right to the chase. What have you got for me?"

Mackenzie Hoyte glanced once at his partner and cleared his throat. "I dug through everything I have—grimoires, codices, even the secret histories. Drake's name keeps showing up—never center stage, but always there, if you know where to look. In fact, the name features in the records of St. Germain spanning multiple decades—long before he made a single red cent from the silver screen crowd." He paused to let the weight of his words settle. "In fact, if we eliminate two or more individuals operating under the same name, in the same city, with the same modus operandi, Drake has been leeching off the folk of St. Germain for well over a century, perhaps even longer."

"So he's old," I said.

Hoyte nodded. "And in Caster society, old means *good*. Their little club's a vicious circle of friends at the best of times, and longevity is a rare and valuable coin. If Drake's been swimming beside those sharks for this long, then he's not treading water—he's circling up near the top of the food chain."

"Which is where I come in," Callaghan said, setting his glass down and leaning forward. "I had to ask some difficult customers some uncomfortable questions, but the story I got was always the same. Drake's the genuine article. He's got muscle on tap, and friends in high places. Real high, maybe City Hall, maybe The Three Families, it depends who's talking. He's a man who holds power in both hands—magic in the one, money and influence in the other." He jabbed his index finger into his palm. "But all of that power is either bought or borrowed like your source claimed—and *that's* the crack in his armor."

"Meaning?" I asked, trying not to let hope seep into me like warm whiskey liqueur.

"Meaning, we could, in theory, cut him off at the tap." Callaghan sat back, his gaze never leaving mine. "And underneath all the goons and the glamours you'll find a man just like any other. A man as vulnerable as our Mr. Hoyte here."

I leaned in, a flame catching in my mind. "And how, exactly, do we do that?"

Callaghan executed an ironic little bow and waved a magnanimous hand the way of Mackenzie Hoyte, causing the shabby little man to clear his throat again.

"Drake's magic comes through Bindings," Hoyte said. "Not all of them as strong as the example you brought me, but all branches from the same crooked tree—and it's not out of choice. It's a *requirement*. You see, as you were told, Drake must've signed a Binding himself to get his hands on that power. The fine print of *that* contract would stipulate what he owes, when it's due, and what happens if he comes up short—at a guess I'd say we're talking eternal damnation, or at least something close to it—which leaves us with two rather interesting options."

"Either you stop Drake from making Rose Chamberlain his appointed sacrifice before his clock runs down—" Callaghan cut in—"or you find and destroy that original Binding. Accomplish either of those ends, and the whole deal goes up in smoke, taking Drake's soul with it."

I leaned back, steepling my fingers under my chin.It was a lead, alright. One that dovetailed neatly with the intel obtained from the duplicitous Dolores Barrett, but the next answer would tell me just how big that lead was. "And how, exactly, do I *do* either of those things?"

Hoyte shrugged. "Well, on paper, option A is easy. You simply keep your girl out of Drake's reach until his contract expires."

The flame inside me faltered. "And option B?"

"A somewhat trickier proposition—first, you would need to find where Drake stashed his original Binding—and if he's smart, it'll be somewhere hazardous to the health of any undead intruders—and then you'd need to completely destroy it, and I don't mean with matches—Bindings are serious magic, Charlie, and if magic made it, you'll need magic to kill it. No, if it were me, I'd forget about option B, keep your client hidden away, and let Drake's daemon do the rest."

I gnawed the skin of my index knuckle, the hope I'd been nursing turning to ash inside me. "And what if he already has her?"

Callaghan studied me like a crime scene. "Then I'm sorry, Charlie. I really am. But if Drake's made a direct play for your girl, after weeks of feints and flimflam, it kinda smells like desperation, and in my experience desperation nearly always results in action."

I kept my eyes on the wall behind him, not trusting myself to reply.

"There isn't anything else, Charlie," Mackenzie's tone held

the soft fall of dirt hitting a casket. "I wish there were, but that's it."

Both men stood, adjusting their jackets and collecting their hats like mourners leaving the chapel.

Callaghan was at the door when he paused, his fingers resting on the knob.

"One last thought," he said, not turning around. "A whisper I've brushed up against once or twice. A whisper that says Drake's tied to something else—not his patron, or whatever, and not The Families either. No, we're talking something bigger. Something quieter. The kind of something that people don't like talking about."

I watched the back of his head like it might spill the rest, if I stared hard enough.

"Like I said, a thought."

#

When the door swung open again, it was to admit Tamara—rain soaked, windblown, and twice as moody as the night she'd emerged from. She peeled off her coat, slung it onto Callaghan's still-warm chair, and fell into the same seat, the rain practically steaming off her.

"Nothing," she snapped in answer to the question I hadn't asked. "Not one Goddamn thing was outta place. Rose's spare set of clothes were still folded neatly on the chair by the bed. Her perfume, her toothbrush, and some weird antiseptic soap I know isn't yours were all lined up in the bathroom as if they were waiting for an inspection, but of the girl herself? Not one Goddamn sign. Nothing."

I studied her face. There was something, alright.

"What?"

"I was thorough, Charlie. Every corner, every drawer, even under the bed. I don't know why I even thought to check there, but I'm glad I did. I found these." She reached into the damp folds of her coat and pulled out two pieces of familiar-looking paper.

"They kinda look like Bindings."

I took the proffered paper and unfolded it. The document did look very similar to the unholy contract which had hounded Rose like a curse for so long, but this wasn't hers. The layout was different. The symbols, dark, tight, and purposeful, were shorter and sharper and there was no dotted line lurking at the bottom to sign anything away on—just a subtle air of quiet menace dressed up in clean ink.

"And you found this under Rose's bed?"

"No... yours."

The revelation hit me like a slap.

"My... What?"

"You heard me. It was under *your* bed. In *your* locked penthouse. Behind all that Dvargn glass and enough enchanted steel plate to stop a whole battalion of Casters—a place only you, me, and maybe three others know exists."

I ran a hand through my hair and looked at the paper again, the saliva fleeing from my mouth. This was my own personal Binding. A Binding planted under my mattress like a bad dream with teeth. But to what ends? To leech my strength? To tire me out? To get into my head and cloud my thoughts?

"So Drake ghosts past every ward I've got. Through glass etched with the enchantments of the most cunning dwarven craftsmen and steel thick enough to shrug off artillery just to leave me a bedtime present?"

Tamara shrugged like the expression cost her something. "Drake got a Binding, a Binding that had been ripped up and binned on multiple occasions no less, into Rose's locked kitchen, and that's on the fourth floor. If he can pull *that* trick off, sliding these under your bed would be a stroll in the park."

Again, I got the distinct impression Tamara was leaving something firmly unsaid.

"And your *other* explanation?"

"You won't like it," she said, echoing the line she'd fed me in the foyer of St. Jude's.

"Rose, again? Really? Come *on*, Tam." I let my frustrated

sarcasm bite deep. "I know what happened at the hospital rattled you. Hell, it rattled *me*. But you've got to let this go. We're talking about the girl who almost fell apart telling us her story. The girl who was hunted, hurt, and very nearly worse by The Weasel. The girl *you* coached through her first taste of real magic, and who clung to you like a child after the Machine lit up her nightmares—and now you want me to believe she crept into my room in the middle of the day to lay *this* beneath my sleeping head?"

Tamara worried at her left thumbnail, her eyes scouring her hand like it held a map to somewhere better.

"It wouldn't have to be during the day," she said. "Rose has had unfettered access to your room for a while now."

"Okay, so she had *opportunity*." I leaned forward, my elbows on the desk. "But that still leaves *motive* and *means*. And there, Tam, you've got *nothing*."

Tamara's mouth opened again, but I cut her off before any more excuses could find their legs. "No. Look, I get it. I do. You want to keep me safe—keep me standing. But this *isn't* Rose. It *can't* be. Even if she had the knowledge and the power to craft something like this, it still wouldn't track. Why would she curse the person busting a gut to save her skin? Why would she vanish? Why would she lead us to St. Jude's and all the questions it opened up? No, it doesn't track... not one damn bit."

"But... "

"No, Tam!" I cut her off a little sharper than I intended. "Drake's still the play, here—all of this smoke and mirrors is some trick to keep us dizzy—to keep us chasing our tails. We know Rose isn't at the apartment, that's the headline here—she isn't there, she isn't here, and if Howard and Doc Rivers' radio-silence means anything, she's not at her place or the Doc's either —and that leaves only one other option."

I let my gaze bore into her, my voice a lit match."We need to stop stalling and pay Mr. Sebastian Drake a house call because I've got a few questions for that man, and I won't be asking nicely."

Tamara's lips pressed into a tight line. I could see the fight already forming behind her eyes. She wasn't sold by my logic, not fully, but when push came to shove and the fists started to fly, there was only one place she'd ever want to be.

"Alright," she said, moving to her feet with smooth grace. "Let's go get your answers. Not tonight, though. We're a man short until Howard makes the trudge downtown, and even if he came back with some of Doc Rivers' magic, we'd struggle to beat dawn's early light." She checked her watch to make the point. "No, we go, but we go at first dark. You, me, and Howard. All for one and all that jazz. But it's a rescue mission, and that's it. We get in, grab Rose, and get out just like you did with me. Agreed?"

"And if 'out' involves a fight this time?"

She flashed me a lopsided grin. "Then two guns and one bite-shy vampire will have to be enough, only this time it's more about getting *in* than getting out, because Drake's got himself a magic door, and he's got to be expecting us. That means every lock is going to be turned, and every hex humming."

She had a point. Drake's place was about as secure as Fort Knox, and without Doc Rivers' help there was no earthly way we could just walk in.

Or was there?

I grabbed my coat, fished in its pockets and, with a quiet surge of jubilation, found what I was looking for. "Well, Drake's magic door may be locked—" I brandished aloft the card of Dolores Barrett, a grim smile on my lips. "—but locked doesn't mean squat if you've found the spare key."

22

There wasn't a damn thing I wanted more than to storm Drake's lair with guns blazing and fangs bared. But the accursed sun still ruled the sky, and like almost everything else in this town, it didn't care what I wanted.

Tamara, on my suggestion, had gone home to catch a few hours of shuteye in a familiar bed, passing on the same advice to Howard. That left me alone with Barrett's card, the silence, and a world of helpless pessimism rattling around in my skull like dice in a rigged game.

It was down to me to make the call to Barrett, but not now. Not while my body ached and my brain buzzed with fatigue and frustration. Not while there was so much that could change. No, once Tamara and Howard got back, then I'd dial the number on the card.

I eased myself onto the office's fold-out, my bones grinding like worn gears. Too many trouble-filled nights and too many sleepless days sharpened the edges of my frayed nerves as I waited for the sky to give me the permission to go to war. Eventually, the kind of half-welcome sleep that drags you down by the ankles and doesn't let go took me, and I let it.

I slept—right up until the moment The Machine screamed.

The mahogany box, with its brass fittings and occult menace, hadn't made a single sound since the night Rose woke it but now, it howled for my attention. I shot away from the bed, my cold skin prickling like the air before a storm. I didn't want to touch The Machine—hell, I didn't even want to look at it, but I'd been in the business too long to ignore a scream in the night, even if that scream came from a glowing wooden box.

I reached out, slow and steady, and laid a single finger on the lid.

And my whole world collapsed.

#

It was late, long past sundown if my joints were anything to go by, but there was something different about the dark. Because I know darkness. I've walked arm-in-arm with mother night more times than I can count, and I know its palette. Midnight blue, candle-smoke gray, the sickly green artificial shimmer of sodium, the faint, fiery smudges of red and gold that clings to the horizon in the moments before dawn.

This wasn't anything like that. No, this wasn't a natural, normal *absence* of light. This was its *exclusion*. There wasn't a single glowing streetlamp, nor the soft trace of distant headlights—no moon, no stars. This was a pure and very deliberate darkness.

Almost as if summoned by my thoughts, a screech of fluorescence carved through the purposeful gloom on my left like a switchblade. A glare that was soon filled by the silhouette of a woman, her narrow shoulders stiff with tension. The coat she wore draped over those shoulders half-protected a white cotton dress patterned with red flowers from what looked like a run through a heavy storm. The hem of the dress still dripped with rainwater and a thicker, more viscous fluid that hit the threadbare carpet with wet, meaty smacks, releasing a vibrant coppery scent into the air.

The woman half-turned to check the hall behind her, and

I caught the footprint of her fear—the tremor in her too shallow breath, her stance, the clutch of her fingers around the doorframe.

Help me, it screamed.

Colors and feelings rushed through me in a broad, brushstroke jumble of sensations that were too vivid to ignore and too fast to hold.

But, as in my vision of the girl in the alleyway, I was just a frozen, helpless bystander, chained to the floor by The Machine's magic. I could *feel* the fear of the young woman. I could *taste* the tang of blood in her mouth and the sour bile riding the back of her throat as she stumbled into the dark room. I *knew* with absolute certainty that whatever was behind her was a thousand times worse than anything that could possibly be waiting inside.

Before she could shut the door on whatever nightmare was at her heels, a gloved hand imploded into the jamb like a crowbar, forcing it open and sending the woman flying in a sprawl of flailing limbs and screaming agony. I winced as something in her ankle gave way with a sound that danced down my nerves like a buzzsaw and tried in vain to call out to her, but, just as before, I had no voice.

That might have been the end of it, but the all too human instinct to survive at all costs doesn't care if your leg's busted and your odds non-existent. The woman scrambled back from the figure who followed her with surprising speed, wincing with every push of her injured leg. But her pursuer didn't make any kind of effort to rush toward her, and, somehow, that was worse. Because there was a patience in the blurred figure's movements. A cold certainty that knew it had all the time in the world.

I recognized the creeping nightmare in charcoal and static blur. It was the same flickering outline that carved up the girl in the alley. The monster whose murders The Machine kept throwing at my psyche. There was no face, of course, only leather gloves and the high collar of a trench coat turned up against some unseen storm beneath the shadow of a fedora, but the unhurried gait and the weight of presence stirred bitter memories within me—memories that didn't belong to the too-real vision.

Memories of Versailles.

Memories of Monsieur le Comte.

The terrified woman backed up until her spine pressed into the wallpaper, her breath exploding in tiny, ragged gasps. She threw up her arms in useless defense as the obscured phantom closed in. A wickedly barbed blade flashed in the cold light, slashing across the proffered palm. She screamed once, not in pain, but in shock and violation. Blood hit the carpet in fat, wet drops and jagged lines. She twisted to the side, trying to crawl away like a wounded animal dragging itself across the slaughterhouse floor, dark red streaks marking her slow, ungainly progress, and still, I could only watch on while this specter of painful death advanced on something so fragile and so scared.

Her attacker watched the sobbing, gasping woman too—a grim spark of satisfaction flaring inside the dead-eyed detachment.

I felt the perverse enjoyment, the dark thrill, the shadow of murderous intent.

I *echoed* it.

But watching can only satisfy for so long. Once again the assassin's arm straightened and the knife lashed out, slicing deep into the meat of the woman's thigh. She howled at the tearing, piercing impact, her voice breaking into jagged whimpers of pain and fear and curled to protect what was left of her vulnerable flesh, but it was too late. The blade flashed again and again, striking her in a frenzy of bloodlust. Her buttocks. Her arm. Her belly. All were slashed and pierced in a quick, steady rhythm that felt like more than needful fury.

That felt like *method*.

Like *ritual*.

The vision broke apart in front of me, fracturing like a broken mirror. White cotton and red blooms. Honey-blonde hair. The iron-rich scent of spilled blood. The smell of dry flowers on sunbaked linen. Sharp and sudden pain. A raw terror that was so very familiar. All this and more flooded my senses, but felt from the other side.

I was a helpless bystander no more.

I was *her*. A victim. Broken, bleeding, and dying.

Above me, stood the slender form of my killer, an insatiable need emanating in waves from the occluded, expressionist form. Not a need for sex, or death, or violence but a need for *control*. A need for *domination*—a need to own every single ounce of a person's terror, pain and misery.

As the understanding hit me, the scene lurched again. This time I looked *down*—down into dark eyes blown wide by fear and agony. Eyes that reached back to the day, the *moment*, I'd sworn I'd never let happen again. Eyes that told me I would. Eyes that told me I *was*.

The young woman reached out to me then, her fingers, slick with her life's blood, pleading for a mercy I knew I would never be able to give her. My gloved hand rose and, for one last time, the knife fell.

#

"Draw!" Tamara pretty much dragged my slack frame to the nearest chair and shoved the pad and pencil into my unresisting hands. "Do it now! While the images are fresh!"

I stared down at the blank page, my eyes swimming. Wherever she'd come from, Tamara was right. If the Machine had coughed up anything useful, we needed it, and fast—exorcising the memory would only be a welcome bonus.

"We..." she jerked a thumb toward Howard, looming at her shoulder like an expectant father. "... got to the door in time to hear the screaming, but too late to stop you." She leaned over to peer at the sketch as it took shape. "Another girl?"

"Yeah." The word tasted like ash in my mouth. "Except this time I think Drake might have found his mark."

" Rose?"

"I... think so. I didn't get a face, nothing clear, anyway. But the body, the hair, those eyes…" I trailed off.

"Yeah, but…"

"Another lookalike?" I finished the thought for her, pressing pencil to paper. "Another girl bleeding out in an alley like The Machine already showed us?" I angled the pad toward her. "No, because this isn't any alleyway. T*his*…" I tapped the image. "…is a place we both know far too well."

Tamara froze, her eyes wide. "Okay," she said, her tone fitted with a fine edge. "Then I guess we know where we're headed. Sundown's maybe twenty minutes away at the most, so finish up here and we'll make ready and meet you in the outer office." She nodded to Howard, and they left me alone, with only the sketchbook and the acid boiling in my gut for company.

#

Once more, a dead woman lay in the foreground of the finished sketch.

Her limbs were flung in cruel directions, her body, almost childlike in its size and vulnerability, ripped apart by scores of lacerations crowned by the final killing blow that had been delivered by a gloved hand.

By *my* hand.

The image, the *sensations,* still seared my memory like a brand. Blood, made dark in the muted light and already congealing, soaked the torn remnants of her white cotton dress, drowning its pattern of roses. Her face was turned away from me and half-concealed by a curtain of honey-blonde hair, but that ruined, unmistakable dress was identical to the one Rose had worn on the day she'd stormed out of Callaghan's and changed my non-living life forever.

"It's her, isn't it?" Howard's hesitant voice rescued me from the mire of my thoughts.

I couldn't answer him. I just stared down into the sketch. The numb, helpless dread I'd first felt in the foyer of St. Jude's crystallizing into something solid and real. The frame, the shoes, the dress, the place, it was all laid out in front of me. An unerring depiction of Rose's promised death.

"Yeah," I whispered as the silence held. "I guess so."

"Then may I suggest we make a move?" Tamara marched up to me like a storm, her hand dropping to my shoulder. "Like you said, The Machine only shows one possibility and we *might* still be in time to change that possibility... to stop it. Nothing's ever written in stone, you know that Charlie—and even if it were, you know we have the tools and the will to rewrite it."

Her words, meant to inspire some kind of hope, held one 'if' too many.

"I guess." I tried on a smile, but it came out crooked and weak enough for her to give my shoulder another squeeze.

"Well, I'm set." Howard closed the chamber of the revolver Tamara had dug up for him. "Locked and loaded."

"Me too." Tamara's hand left my shoulder as she stepped with purpose toward the door. "Charlie?"

I looked down at the sketch. "Yeah," I said, a tangled ball of helplessness threatening to explode within me. "Let's do this."

#

It was a ten-minute walk to Lawrence Street, and the building that housed my penthouse apartment—ten minutes that felt like a century on stilts. "And you're sure it was here?" Howard squinted up at the blacked-out window.

"I've lived, or, at the very least, slept, here for a couple of years, off and on." My voice held a brittle edge I didn't like. "The shape of the windows, the blackout drapes, the carpet that's worn a little thin by the door... yeah, it was here."

"But why?" The big man asked. "Why here, I mean?"

I shrugged, my tired mind too busy to care. "To make a point, maybe. I'm not sure it really matters."

"Then let's get to it." Tamara pushed past me, threw open the building's front door, and stalked inside. "You two take the elevator. I'll meet you there." She jabbed the call button, drew her weapon, and, without another word, headed to the stairwell.

"It's going to be okay," Howard said as we boarded the elevator car. "You'll see. We'll get there in the nick of time, like William Powell or Coop, snatch Rose from Drake's claws and ride off into the sunset...or, I dunno... the sunrise?"

I nodded in wordless, faithless reply. Howard had made enough peace with the monster I was to offer me a slice of his own backlot brand of false hope, but I wasn't buying it. Not tonight. The movies with their dirty glamor—their cowboys, gumshoes, and half-reformed gangsters with their last-minute rescues and sudden heel-turns—were reserved for mocked-up streets made of plywood and paint. In the real world there was no studio rewrite, or director to call 'cut' before the knife fell, and neither of us featured as much of a Gary Cooper. Hell, in a city run by powerful men with powerful friends, a reluctant vampire and an out-of-work actor barely rated a Jane Darwell between them.

"I know what you're thinking," Howard's best gravel-laden baritone cut in. "You think we're outclassed, outgunned, but you're wrong. Drake might be a spell-slinging demigod with a patent on soul-stealing, but the way I see it a slug to the leg still puts him on the ground."

"Leaving me to do the rest?"

"I guess." His eyes were softer than I expected and loaded with something close to guilt.

"Then remember to aim low," I said as the elevator rattled to a stop and we stepped into the hallway. "And for God's sake, shoot straight."

A sharp inhalation and a hail of muttered curses erupting from behind me announced Tamara had cleared the stairs in time to join the party.

#

The three of us took the slim, private staircase to my

apartment in lockstep. I wanted to kick the door in, hell, I *needed* to, but I held back and instead let my gaze crawl across the surface of the thing like a spider on the hunt. There were no scuffs around the lock, no scratches by the jamb, and all four deadbolts were sunk deep into the concrete wall. Everything looked exactly as it should be.

But it wasn't.

"Charlie..." Tamara's voice was a heavy breath behind me, the climb up the stairs putting a tremble in the hands that held her snub-nosed .22 and the spare key. "You're sniffing. Why the hell are you sniffing?"

My eyes never left the door.

"Because I can smell blood."

23

There were two dead bodies in the room and only one of them was mine.

The other, the naked corpse of what had once been a woman, swung gently from a thick coil of coarse rope tied around her ankles and looped through the central light fixture. Her skin, as pale and veined as cheap marble, was covered in a patchwork of slashes and ragged punctures as if some mad sculptor had tried carving her anew. But none of that, not the mutilation, nor the pallid, bloodless tone of death, was the worst of it—not even close.

Because, between her dangling arms, in the space her head should have been, a grisly inverted pillar of gore and vertebrae jutted like a skeletal hand clawing its way out from the pits of hell. Thick drops of blood dripped in a slow and steady rhythm from these torn remains, each landing in a clay bowl set at the very center of a chalk circle drawn beneath her with a wet and meaty *thock.* Outside the circle, at the cardinal points, arcane glyphs, like those of Rose's accursed Binding sat glowering with malevolent intent, and, resting on a velvet cushion to the side of the whole set-up was the Binding itself. Signed, sealed, and, with devastating finality, delivered.

The rest of the room was nothing short of apocalyptic.

By the wall between the door to my bedroom and the room Rose had taken for her own, a thick puddle of blood slowly congealed. It was a physical memory of the vicious attack that I witnessed—that I suffered—that I *perpetrated,* in my vision.

I could still feel the knife cut into my thigh, belly, and back.

I could still taste the terror of my helpless victim.

I could still *remember* her pain.

On the walls the arc of that cruel knife had left its signature in thin trails of gory calligraphy. A single handprint trailed from the midst of these lines into a smear that tapered and faded as it descended toward the floor. Underneath this gory trail, the baseboard bore scratches, so deep that one of them contained a broken shard of painted fingernail.

On the floor, a carmine sweep led to a dark, slowly congealing pool of blood near the overturned couch. A pool that was almost black at the edges. From there, the trail of destruction led directly to the suspended corpse, but, over every inch of the apartment, there were explosions of gore and blood that simply screamed their existence.

It was a Rorschach test I didn't need a shrink to decipher, and it was way, way too much.

I staggered back to the door. My eyes narrowed to hate-filled slits and my brow sinking as the sight and the *scent* hit me like a kiss from some long-abandoned grave. The undead thing that lived inside me stirred. My throat ached. An acidic saliva bloomed in my mouth as my head snapped up and the monster I truly am howled its unholy desires. The Thirst was a wildfire inside me—The Hunger a violent accompaniment singing out for destruction. For *release.*

And I *wanted* to set them free. I *wanted* to let them take me. I *needed* to...

Tamara caught hold of my hand and spun me around, pulling my head into the crook of her shoulder. Her hold was gentle, but more than firm enough to anchor me securely to her.

"Howard!" Her voice was muffled and distant, like she was speaking from an underwater grotto a million miles away. "Howard, it's too much! We need to get her out of here!"

I twisted, my muscles tensing, and hissed my frustrated rage and naked grief into the face of my closest living friend, but a second pair of arms closed around mine before I could claw my way out of her grasp. I grabbed blindly for a wrist, knowing I could snap it like a twig, but a heel struck my calf and my knees gave way. I crumpled to the floor, an unthinking thing of feral fury and needful rage and, before I could react, found myself half-dragged, half-carried away from the room which held such a visceral, corporeal nightmare for me.

Howard—it had to be Howard—hauled me through the door, and dumped me into the hallway like he was the hero in a war film, tossing a grenade away from his platoon.

"Come on, Charlie," Tamara's voice broke through the white noise screaming in my ears. The smell, the sight, the *pull* of the blood. It still called to me through the door Howard had closed behind us, blurring her words.

"Think," she continued. "Remember. You *are* Charlotte Amálie Durant. You *are* a good person."

I lay there, twitching; almost vibrating with need. The beast inside me shrieked with loss and rage, but, from somewhere deep within this maelstrom, I struck out and groped for the small, safe place where the woman I like to think of as *me* still waited.

It was faint, tiny at first, nothing but a single kernel of humanity tossed into the storm, but it persisted.

I persisted.

I was still there.

Charlotte. Amálie. Durant.

A good person.

I repeated the mantra over and over in my mind.

A plea. A shield. A whispered invocation of the me I wanted to be. And slowly, so slowly it hurt, the spark caught in the raging abyss. A dying ember of humanity. Faint but real.

Charlotte.

Amálie.

Durant.

With glacial reluctance, The Hunger and The Thirst receded. Not gone—no, never gone—but slowly coming to heel until I was so very nearly *me* again. A woman named Charlie Durant.

"Charlie? You with us?"

I realized Tamara's hand was squeezing mine tightly, a fearless, physical anchor weighted by friendship and trust, and let my head fall in a shallow nod, words still too much for me.

"Good." Her eyes scanned me. "The, uh, face thing's fading a little, too, but still, let's give it a minute, yeah?"

I flicked my gaze over to Howard. His face was as pale as moonlight.

"Thank you, Howard." I rasped, hating the growl that lurked beneath the sentiment.

Tamara rose and kissed the big man on the cheek. It was a quick peck, but heavy enough to put a little color in his cheeks. When she turned back to me, her eyes were solemn.

"You know we have to go back in there, right, Charlie?"

I raised an eyebrow.

"Clues. Evidence. Something that gives us Drake's next move. I mean, is this it? Is he done?"

"It doesn't matter, because I'm not done. I'm nowhere near done." My voice felt like broken gravel in my mouth. "Clues and evidence be damned. Drake dies... tonight!"

Tamara searched my eyes for a moment and then nodded, more to herself than in recognition of anything I'd said and half-turned away.

"Yeah, I figured you might say something like that," she said.

The kick she unleashed as she turned back toward me caught me behind the temple in a concussive explosion of pain. Electric flashes detonated behind my eyes, shattering my vision into swimming shadows. A harsh, metallic buzz filled my ears.

And the last thing I saw before the dark took me was the face of my oldest living friend, her expression unreadable.

24

Coming-to from being knocked out is like being dragged from the gutter by the roots of your hair. There's no soft-focus drift away from the sandman's clutches, only a fuzzy wrench back to cold, hard reality. My skull buzzed like a thousand bees had taken up residence. A throbbing hammer blow pulsed in my jaw, sending bright aftershocks racing toward my temple at irregular intervals. A gift delivered to me by a woman who knew how to make it count.

And then I remembered why.

"I need you to stay calm, Charlie." Tamara's voice came from somewhere behind me. "I understand if you're feeling none too friendly toward me right now, but there was no other way. I didn't want to, you understand, but every now and then we all have to do things we don't want to do."

I tried to raise my head, a few choice words of dispute on the tip of my tongue, but cool metal and thick leather bit into the skin around my skull, wrists, ankles, and chest, with no give and no mercy.

"No, don't try to fight it. You'll only hurt yourself." There was, perhaps, the ghost of an apology behind Tamara's words. "I had this set-up custom-made from Dvargn-forged steel and rune-bound, herb soaked leather. A precaution I hoped I'd never have to use."

I verified her words, testing each of the straps in turn before indulging in a little mindless thrashing. She wasn't bluffing. With no way to gain traction or leverage even my supernatural strength wasn't going to be enough to break me free.

"So what's the plan, Tam?" I inspected what little I could of my surroundings. From the dull glint of stainless steel beneath me, and the couchful of neatly folded bedding lurking in my periphery, I was strapped to some kind of gurney in the office's back room. "Are you going to leave me tied up here forever?"

"No, not forever." Tamara's voice said from the blind spot behind me. "Just until you calm down and start to think."

"I *am* calm." The lie tasted like smoke and bile in my mouth. In my mind's eye, a headless corpse turned like some grotesque wind chime in a room covered in blood and gore. "I'm about as calm as collected gets. But the time for calm is over. Sebastian Drake has to die."

The silence that followed was heavy enough to crush bones. I heard the slow scrape of wood on linoleum as Tamara pulled her chair closer and, a breath later, her face, framed by a cascade of dark curls, hit my field of view. Her stern expression was upside-down, like everything else in my world.

"But *you* can't kill him, Charlie," she uttered like she'd rehearsed the line a dozen times and hated every syllable. "And you *know* why you can't. Hell, *you* told us why you can't."

"This is different."

"Yeah, and that's what scares me." Her expression softened. "Rose is gone, Charlie. She's *gone*—and killing Drake won't ever bring her back or get her justice, and it can never mend the hole left in your life. You can tear out Drake's throat, but all it'll buy you is blood on your lips and a raging fire burning away what's left of your humanity—and that's when *everything* gets worse."

"Worse? For God's sake, Tam, how can anything ever be worse than this?"

"Have you forgotten the blood-thirsty *thing* we so nearly had front-row seats to back at your apartment? The out-of-control monster that you've been so scared of turning into for so long?"

I looked up at my closest living friend, tears boiling behind my eyes. "You mean the *thing* that could've stopped all this? The *thing* that could've saved Rose?" Inside me The Hunger twisted and snarled. "Is that the *thing* you mean, Tamara?"

She disappeared from my view again, her voice trailing behind. "Okay, then let's say you let the vampire take the wheel and kill Drake—when does the killing stop? And who does the stopping?"

"So, you think I should just leave it be? Just drop the whole thing?"

"No!" Tamara didn't raise her voice, not one decibel, but the single word dropped like a hammer. She stepped into view again, her face drawn with the kind of tired that digs deep into a person's soul—the same kind that was eating away at *me*. "No," she said. "You do what you do best, Charlotte Durant. You light a cigarette, pour yourself a drink, and start turning the wheels of that smart brain of yours—you work the angles until you find one that doesn't cost us *you*." She leaned down, the sheen of tears on her cheek. "We will put an end to Drake, Charlie, but we'll do it *together*. Just give us the time to figure out how... please."

I closed my eyes, letting my head sink onto the cold metal. Tamara was right, and I knew it. Heading straight for Drake, blood-mad and feral, would open a door I'd spent a lifetime nailing shut. A door I might never be able to close again.

"Okay." The word emerged cold and reluctant. "I won't pretend it'll be easy, or I like it, but I understand. So, as long as that evil bastard's still in our sights, I guess I'll play it your way. Now, how about untying me?"

A beat of thick and complicated silence followed.

Then, with slow reluctance, the strap across my chest tightened as the prong was eased from its punch hole. I waited for it to loosen again, but I waited in vain.

"Do you think I'm stupid?"

I risked a smile. "No, Tam. Not stupid. What you are, is *right*. Rose *believed* in me. She believed in the woman who holds the monster back, and if I'm going to justify that belief, I have to start now. There's nothing in the world I want more than to sink my fangs into the throat of the man who made such a masterpiece out of her murder..." I yanked on the chain of the visceral needs flaring inside me, swallowing back spit that tasted of iron. "... but you want stupid? Well, there it is. Rose would've wanted me to do better—to *be* better."

The air between us hummed with a heavy, crowded quiet that made words redundant.

"Wait here," Tamara said like I had a choice.

She disappeared from view again, and I heard a frantic, whispered conversation. Then Howard's rugged face filled the square of ceiling above me.

"I'm gonna untie you." The big man's glance flicked to the side. "Tamara's got her gun, and she says she won't hesitate to use it. I kinda believe her. I think you should too."

I remembered an unflinching stare aimed at me from behind a loaded crossbow. Yeah, Tamara wasn't a woman who bluffed.

"Fine," I said. "A little insulting, but I understand."

Howard bent to the task, his rough hands working each buckle from top to bottom. When all but my ankles were free I sat up, my spine crackling like a freshly lit cigarette. Tamara was straddling a chair cowboy-style, her eyes hard and her revolver trained on my chest—center mass, the training of the policeman's daughter—it seemed fair. After all, I was still the most dangerous thing in the room.

I rubbed my wrists. Not from concern for my non-existent circulation, but because the straps had been tight enough to cut into my flesh. "Nice setup," I said. "Had it long?"

"A while." Tamara's reply was as cool as winter. "It pays to be careful."

Howard undid the last buckle, and moved behind her, allowing me the space to swing my legs off the edge of the gurney. The muzzle of Tamara's .22 tracked me every inch of the way.

"Well, you're calling the shots." I glanced at the gun's barrel to stress the point. "Do I take it you have a plan?"

She shrugged. "Like I said, we work the case. With Doc Rivers absent, I figure Barrett is our best shot at getting to Drake, whatever her motivations might be. So, we follow Mackenzie and Mr. Callaghan's leads, track down Drake's Binding, use her to slip past his defenses, and hope the bastard bleeds like anyone else."

"Okay, that sounds workable." I grabbed a blood-bag from the fridge and pursed my lips, letting my thoughts click into place. "We'll need to find Drake's Binding first though, and we'll have to dodge a dozen snares and failsafes to get there—something we could really use Doc Rivers' help with."

"But like Tamara said, the doc's unreachable," Howard cut in. "There's no answer at the hospital *or* his brownstone. I guess the guy doesn't want to be found."

I paused, the blood-bag halfway to my lips. Inside, the gnawing need pulsed with dark impatience. "There is one other place he might be. Somewhere even his secretary doesn't know about. I found it once, thanks to a carelessly misplaced word and I know I can find it again."

I ripped the bag open and drank deep, the coppery warmth flooding my mouth like an electric memory.

"Where?" Tamara asked.

"The place the Doc goes when he needs to get away from the world. His haven if you like. It's a place you won't find on any map, or even any star chart, but I know where the back door is, and I know how to open it, too."

"And I suppose you want us to let you go all alone?" Tamara's voice was flat, her eyes sharp.

"It's a one-person job, Tam. Go in mob-handed and you don't *get* in. You remember Drake's magic door? How it punted Howard into The Warren? Well, that was a party gag compared to Rivers' setup. Trip his defenses, and you wake up in a Prague monastery or some Cologne brewery trying to remember what your name used to be."

Tamara and I locked eyes in a silent duel made of old trust

and fresh wounds. Neither one of us blinked.

"I'll go." Howard's soft, certain voice broke the uneasy standoff. "If you tell me the where and the how, I mean. After all, fetching the Doc was my job."

I nodded reluctant agreement. "Okay by me. I'll write down the location and some instructions—follow them close, though, because one mistake, and you'll be booking a flight home."

Tamara's jaw tightened. "And there's no other 'surprises you've forgotten to mention'?"

"No!" I flung a hand to the heavens. "You said it, Tam. Rose is dead. so, why would I blow my only shot at Drake? Why would I throw Howard, *Howard*, to the wolves?"

That landed. Tamara glanced at Howard, her mouth twisted into a pained line.

"I... I don't know, Charlie." She raked her fingers through her hair. "But after..."

I nodded, slow and solemn. "Don't worry, I get it. You can't trust me right now. Hell, I'm not sure I trust myself." I met the steady gaze of the woman who'd yanked me back from the edge of the abyss on so many occasions. A woman I trusted more than anyone else in my life, my death, and everything that existed in between.

"But think it through, Tam," I continued. "The blood-stained road I trod to St. Germain—the beast I caged—the leash I tightened... so much of that is because of you. So, no, I'm not okay—you know I'm not—but I know from bitter experience that pain lessens, and rage dims, and until they do I still have the controls you gave me. Drake *will* die for what he did, but he won't turn me into something worse along the way—he won't win." My throat caught as the raw emotion of my words caught up with me. "I'm Charlotte Amálie Durant." A single tear skated down my cheek. "And I *am* a good person. Sebastian Drake can't take that from me."

I moved a step closer to the woman I was so proud to call a friend, and she wrapped her arms around me. As her face pressed against my shoulder, I felt a sob rattle free from her.

"It's alright." My left hand slid the gun from hers with a gentleness neither of us questioned. "If the tables were turned I'd have done the same, maybe more. Now, what say we stop pointing guns and fingers and get back to what we do. It's way past time we took this murdering bastard down."

#

"These directions will take you to a disused warehouse you've walked past a hundred times before." I pressed the folded paper into Howard's calloused palm. "The incantations I've included will show you what's *really* there."

Howard blanched slightly. "And when I reach the Doc?"

I pulled another slip of paper from the desk drawer, licked the tip of my pencil and wrote a couple of lines. "Give him this."

"And you really think he can get us to Drake's Binding?" Tamara's voice was still a little raw from our reconciliation. Her mascara had not fared well.

I shrugged in answer. "We can hope." I glanced at the fading crack of light surrounding the blinds. "What time do you have?"

Tamara set the .22 on the desk like it was a sacred object and dropped into the chair behind it. "Approaching dusk."

"I was out that long?"

"I might've slipped you something." She had the grace to blush. "Just to help you sleep."

"...Long enough to strap me to a gurney." I allowed myself a brittle smile. "Don't worry. I understand."

I tapped the paper in Howard's hand to reclaim his attention. "If it's that late, you're going to need to move. The magic shielding Rivers' retreat is only crossable this side of midnight."

"Right," he spluttered with all the enthusiasm of a condemned man. "And you're sure you two will be alright?"

I flashed him a smile about a million watts brighter than I felt. "Sure, we'll be fine."

Howard glanced at Tamara who gave him a smile of synthetic reassurance. Then, nodding to nobody in particular, he tucked away the paper and headed out.

And then there were two.

#

"So what now?" Tamara asked with her trademark lack of preamble.

I folded my arms and leaned against the desk. "We wait until Howard returns, and then, depending on his success, we work the case, just like you said."

Tamara's hand drifted to the blotting pad, straightening it by a hair's breadth. A tell I'd seen a hundred times before.

"We went back," she said, eventually. "To the apartment, I mean."

"Oh?"

"Yeah." A flicker of amusement ghosted over her face. "I'm not sure Mackenzie will be talking to me for a while."

"You took Mackenzie?"

"Yeah, I thought he might see something I missed—magical stuff."

"And?"

She shook her head, "Nothing. Oh, there were hints... pieces that fit around the edges, but it wasn't any rite he knew of."

I let my tongue probe the inside of my cheek. Mackenzie Hoyte, a man who knew esoterica like a jazzman knew his horn, was puzzled. What could that mean?

"What did he say?" I asked. "Be exact."

"You're sure you're okay to hear this?" Tamara's eyes met mine for the first time since our awkward conversation began

"Have to be."

She stared at the manufactured chaos of the desk for a moment, and then, in hushed, hesitant tones, began. "The ropes, the bowl, and the chalk circle are all pretty much standard fare," she said. "As is the need to spill blood. But Mackenzie said too much of it was wasted—that, and there was too much violence."

I swallowed down the lump that caught in my throat.

"The blood wasn't simply offered up, you see—it was splattered across that room like a child's painting. Mackenzie couldn't understand why that should be… or why… Charlie, this is too much."

"No." I straightened in my chair. "Go on. Please. I need you to."

Tamara wiped her dry lips with the back of her hand. "The head," she said at last. "Mackenzie couldn't understand why Drake would take the head."

And there it was. A vivid, vicious memory, summoned by that single word and painted in shades of gore. Rose's body, hanging as pale as winter moonlight, the last drops of her blood…

Charlotte Amálie Durant. A good person.

"He'd seen ritual decapitations before." Tamara continued. "Apparently, it's a rare and powerful type of magic, and all sorts of dangerous… but this?" Her fingers clenched on the arms of the chair. "And the head should've been *used*!"

"Who's to say it wasn't?"

"It would still have been there. Removing it, even as a trophy, would unravel the whole deal. Mackenzie said it didn't make sense. Not magically and not logically."

I forced myself to think, tasting each half-formed idea. "Then there has to be another reason," I said. "Drake's old, remember. He's too good, and too experienced to slip up like this. Could it be something he *had* to do—something his daemon requires of him? Or could it be a way to mask Rose's identity for some reason? A way to throw us off."

Tamara shook her head. "No," she said. "Drake's way past keeping secrets. He left Rose's body where he knew you'd find it and didn't even bother destroying her clothes or that little half-moon scar on her shoulder. It's almost like he was sending a message to…"

"To me," I finished. "A message to *me*."

The silence hung for a beat.

"Maybe that's the bit we should be looking at. Maybe it's part of some dark pathology Drake buried so deep, even he's forgotten where it began." I felt the idea through. "Maybe our guy's a trophy taker like H.H. Holmes, or Jack the Ripper."

"Or maybe someone else intervened," Tamara countered. "Barrett, or that eager new recruit—Pell, I think her name was—or some competitor or disgruntled client looking to spoil his party. Any or all of the above could've had a motive."

I hit the desk with the flat of my hand, stopping Tamara dead. "No!" I tried to temper the wild edge in my voice. "However many maybes and could've-beens you dress it up in, this was Drake's doing—back-to-front and start-to-finish... It. Was. Him."

I drifted over to the window. Outside the night had begun to creep across the city, making it mine once more.

Across the road, a black sedan pulled up to the curb, and two men in equally black suits got out and crossed the road toward the office.

"...we'll get there," Tamara was saying, her voice a thread of hope woven from thin air. I peeled my eyes away from the suits and focused on her words. "I can't pretend to know what's going on in that head of yours, Charlie," she said. "But I know sitting still until Howard returns is eating you alive because I feel that too. Right now, though..."

I held up a hand, stopped her cold, and pointed to the frosted glass window of the office door.

"Something wrong?" she whispered.

"Maybe," I said, my voice low. "Hand me your gun, will you?"

Without hesitation, Tamara slid the .22 off the desk and into my hand. I crept toward the door, the weapon raised in one hand and the other hovering over the door handle. Tamara slid to my side.

"Hang on." She frowned. "Why does a vampire need a

gun?"

With a step back and a clean swipe I brought the barrel down against her temple. Hard.

"Because it's heavy."

25

"You don't like me much, do you?" Dolores Barrett asked me. It was forty minutes after I'd cold-cocked Tamara and I was sitting in the passenger seat of Barrett's Ford cabriolet, the canvas top unfolded to protect us from the elements as we sped toward the offices of Sebastian Drake. One call to the number on the card she'd slipped me at Callaghan's was all it had taken to arrange the ride, but I hadn't asked for the conversation.

"I don't know what you mean." I hunched lower, and watched the road slide by.

"Sure you do. You think I'm a cold fish only out for myself, and you're not entirely wrong—but everything Drake did to Rose? Leaving her decapitated corpse strung up where he knew you'd find it? That's not just unfeeling or selfish. That's evil. That's sick!"

A mess of Images swam before me, melding and weaving together. The blood-soaked room in my apartment.

Rose's body hanging like a marionette from the ceiling. The still, pale form of Marie-Thérèse Bazinet and the white sheet covering her. The single, crimson stain which marked the wound from which I'd drunk the last drop of her blood. Théri's death-scream, an agonized cry that was joined in terrible harmony by the voices of Rose Chamberlain and one Charlotte Amálie Durant, ripped through these uninvited memories—

screams on screams on screams, echoing with fear and rage and pain and grief.

And beneath it all—providing a grim accompanying rhythm—was the slow, steady drip of blood falling into a clay bowl—the smell all-consuming.

I clenched my jaw, forcing the visions away from me, and tried to replace them with the sunlight of Versailles, honey-blonde hair, and musical laughter.

"I always knew you'd come around," Barrett continued, my absence from the conversation unnoticed. "But I never realized what it would take." She smiled a rough approximation of warmth. "Sorry. For a cold fish, I talk too much."

I answered her smile with a miniscule twitch of my lips. It was too late for told-you-sos—too late for most things.

A taut hush held right until the moment Drake's oh-so modern headquarters loomed into view.

"You'll need to lie low from here on in," Barrett whispered. "At least until we're past the guardhouse. There's a blanket behind your seat. Do you want me to pull over?"

"I don't need a blanket," I replied. "But pulling over is an idea."

"Right. The invisibility trick… don't worry, I'm ready."

She wasn't, but, to give her credit, we only swerved slightly as I faded into the car's shadows. Her eyes flicked to my seat now and then, but as we rolled up to the gatehouse, the smile she flashed the guards who failed to see me was polished.

We coasted into Drake's underground garage like ghosts in a two-seater coffin.

#

I'm too much of an old-fashioned girl for cars to be my thing. They're just hunks of metal, their thrumming hearts and oil-slick veins a poor, mechanical imitation of life. There's no softness to them, no warmth—I guess that's a tad hypocritical.

But it didn't take any kind of aficionado to see the garage

brimmed with motorized money, each car as sleek as a predator. Almost like a bird, Barrett's head twitched from side to side, surveying for potential hazards. A guard. A mechanic. Anything. Satisfied, she nodded to herself and strode toward an elevator tucked like a guilty secret between a low-slung cabriolet and something slick and Italian. I trailed behind, wrinkling my nose at the layered stink of oil and wax.

Inside me, The Hunger roared, wild and clawing, drowning out *another*, fainter voice.

"All okay?" Barrett said, her brow creased.

"Sure," I stepped into the elevator beside her. "Just thinking is all."

"Oh?" The doors slid shut, muffling the garage's fumes and allowing different scents to bloom in the cloistered air—the smell of polished chrome and dark wood. The gray wool of Barrett's suit, the chemical bite of disinfectant. And all of it underpinned by something faint and floral.

I turned to meet Barrett's watchful gaze. "You don't think Drake could be wise to us, do you?"

She reached past me to press the button for the third floor. "No chance. He still thinks of me as his loyal, unquestioning servant, and you're supposed to be in your office, drowning in grief and liquor. Why? Cold feet?"

I shook my head, unsure what temperature my feet were.

"Good. Your retribution isn't much farther now." She erected her cold defenses again and strode from the elevator car. "From here on in, keep your pace brisk and your head down."

At the end of a slim corridor, a plain black door waited like the final note of a symphony. A door guarded by a suit wearing a familiar ring. I trudged behind Barrett, keeping my head down and my jaw set, an unwelcome tension tethering every step as I gathered myself for action, but as she had at the gatehouse Barrett intervened first.

I stepped through the door and onto a mezzanine above a broad foyer decorated in shades of streamlined elegance, the two levels connected by a wide, curved staircase equipped with a sinuous banister that caressed its climb like a lover's hand. It was all extremely tasteful, reassuringly expensive, and agonizingly minimal. If Versailles announced its grandeur in booming tones, here the conceit was whispered.

Moving with clipped stealth, Barrett led me to a smaller door near the top of the staircase, and then another, each door closely guarded and each guard overcome with a smile. Every part of me screamed the need to charge ahead of Barrett—to rip through the building in a wild and joyous bloodbath—but I didn't.

Because beneath those screams, the same small voice I'd almost heard in the elevator still nagged away, fraying the edge of my tired mind.

Eventually, we reached a room I'd seen a glimpse of in that other space Kieren Rivers had dragged the spectral forms of Rose, Tamara, and me to.

The office of Dolores Barrett.

The antechamber of the beast.

Barrett crossed to her desk, dropped her clutch onto it, and turned, her finger pressed to her lips.

"I know you want to charge in there and rip out Drake's throat," she pretty much whispered. "But, for now, I need you to wait here."

I raised an eyebrow, every fiber of my being vibrating with unsatisfied need. "Drake has a whole array of fail-safes designed to keep out unwelcome visitors, some of them magical, some of them not—but if you step through that door with bad intentions, you will die... and I mean permanently."

I nodded my reluctant acceptance, gritting my teeth against the baying cries screaming inside me. Barrett disappeared through the door, and I started to count the seconds,every tick of the clock an eternity, each passing moment an agony.

My gaze drifted around the cramped workspace, looking for something, anything to ground me.

The desk, buried in half-finished bindings I was going to

ensure would never be signed. The jacket and bag hung casually from the back of a slim chair. Female. Not Barrett's style. Possibly the belongings of the other woman. The woman called...

"All clear." Barrett's face appeared in a narrow gap between door and jamb. "You can come through now."

I reached for a cigarette I didn't have, and pushed myself from the desk, wishing to all hell I'd thought to stash a pack of smokes in my coat pocket and take on some blood. My tired mind was fighting hard against my unholy instincts even as my aching body was starting to fray at the seams. Never a good mix.

The seed of doubt planted in the parking garage elevator still gnawed at me, so close I could almost touch it. But it was a little too late for almost, a little too late for most things.

I gathered myself, swallowed an unneeded gulp of air, pushed through the door that would lead me to my prey and, for the second time in as many days, walked straight into hell.

26

A man with a gun closed the door behind me. Two more guards stood as still as statues beside the French doors, their black suits and signet rings all too familiar. A final pair of Hand goons flanked the ornate pedestal desk on the green rug I'd last seen during Doc Rivers' magic picture show and behind that desk sat Drake.

One hand of the well-dressed man rested lightly on Dolores Barrett's arm, the other clutched that of a redhead I assumed was the owner of the coat I'd seen in the outer office.

Elizabeth Pell.

"Ah, Ms. Durant," Drake purred, aiming for urbane charm and only missing by a hair. "Please... sit." He gestured magnanimously to the chair across from him. "I'd ask you to make yourself at home, but, well... context."

I glanced at the loose circle of armed mooks around me, measuring distances in my mind. "And will these gentlemen also be taking a seat?"

Drake flashed a full parade of perfect white teeth. "No. I think those 'gentlemen' should remain standing for now." He let go of the two women, slid a porcelain cup aside, and folded his hands in the space it left behind. "You've no doubt noticed my men are armed. I should probably advise you their ammunition has been specially modified with your visit in mind—silver nitrate, extract of *Allium sativum*, and just a pinch of rock salt—

not quite fatal to your kind, perhaps, but from the research presented to me, more than enough to incapacitate you." He smiled a plastic smile. "It should certainly afford my employees the chance to escort you out to the garden in time to greet the sunrise. Now, please… sit."

Without breaking his gaze I took the seat he indicated.

The Hunger stirred restlessly in my hollow chest.

“There, much more civilized. Tea? Wine? I have a very nice red laid down." He leaned back. "Although it may lack the, uh, *body* you’re used to.”

I kept my thoughts to myself, but my eyes must have flicked, for a second, to the face of Dolores Barrett.

“Ah yes, the incomparable Ms. Barrett." Drake said. "I imagine her inevitable betrayal must sting. All that talk of shared burdens and common purpose, only for her to lead you into my clutches like a Judas goat. But Ms. Barrett simply played the role I planned for her. The Mondego to your Dantès… Ephialtes at Thermopylae.” He smirked, pleased with this imperfect display of erudition. “And, while the notion of giving you two ladies a moment alone to discuss the matter may amuse me, I think I’ll handle her insubordination personally—assuming you don’t mind?”

He was baiting me—showing me how much he was in control, and it almost worked. Versailles and everything it held for me flashed before my eyes. The intrigues, the scandal, the man in the smoked glass spectacles, the poison, …

Théri

I pulled myself away from those dark memories to answer Drake’s question. “Oh, by all means.” I dressed my words in the same over-polite urbanity Drake was affecting. “Although I’m afraid Ms. Barrett may have to wait her turn, because tonight you and I have some business of our own.”

Drake’s smug, shit-eating grin calcified into something brittle and uncertain. “Oh? And what, ‘business’, exactly, is it you believe ‘you’ and ‘I’ have, Ms. Durant?”

“Oh, that’s simple.” I let my words fall with a contrived

polish, each syllable cool, deliberate, and precise, but inside me The Hunger grumbled and snarled like a half-starved dog. "My business is to kill you and yours is to die."

He flinched at that—only a flicker, but I caught it.

His cool, self-possessed mask cracked and allowed something real to peek through—fear and surprise—the specter of an unraveling composure.

"Of course." He tried his best to summon the assured smoothness again, but his *cordialité* was quickly losing its sheen. "And I'm sure you can appreciate why I might find such a transaction to be… inconvenient."

Inconvenient. The word, the very notion, coming from the man who'd stalked Rose Chamberlain through her nightmares. The man who broke her mind, butchered her body, and staged her remains so theatrically for me was like a slap. He had to know who he was talking to, he had to. He knew exactly who and *what* I was, and the best word he could conjure for the vengeance due to him was *inconvenient*?

The Thirst and The Hunger howled like wolves on the hunt. I tasted their insatiable fury at the back of my throat and crushed it with long-practiced restraint.

My eyes drifted over to the *objets* on the bookcase behind him—the box inlaid with ivory, the rod of jet—the mace-shaped artifact fashioned from wood and bronze, the pearl handled dagger resting on a red velvet cushion—and in the silence of my mind I repeated my mantra, again and again, letting the weight of the words ground me like anchors in a rising, inevitable, storm.

And then I realized Drake was waiting for a response.

"Yeah, having one's throat ripped out by a ravening vampire would put a crimp in most people's day," I said, my tone light even as my too willing mind supplied the vivid detail. "But let's talk about the 'inconveniences' that *you've* caused." I leaned in, tightening the space between us. "You, Sebastian Drake, twist dreams into nightmares. You grant wishes with poison. You feed the emptiest of desires. Inflate the most insatiable ambitions—

and in return you steal souls. Each Binding you write leeches away more and more of your victims' humanity until the young and vital become old and listless—become walking shadows that can only pray for death." I watched his face as each of my words hit home. It seemed like the air between us shifted and thickened. "You're a parasite, Drake. That's what you are. A contagion. A plague. You contaminate weak wills with illusions of power and beauty, and you send them out to infect others. Your 'customers' come to you to buy a dream, but in return you take everything that makes them *real*—You, Sebastian Drake, are a *disease!*"

He didn't even blink.

"And you fancy yourself the cure, I take it?" All traces of that broad, shit-eating grin were gone now, but his plummy voice remained clipped, and surgically cold. "Well. Let me tell you what *I* see, Ms. Durant. I see a hypocrite. I see a creature whose shadow falls far too long across this world's history, leaving carnage and death in its wake. So, no Ms. Durant you're not a cure, you're destruction. You're death dressed up in a pretty face."

His fingers tapped the edge of the document before him —an affectation that reminded me of Tamara's constant refinements, but perhaps, something more. "Charlotte Amálie Durant, private investigator and underworld dogsbody—*Mademoiselle* Durant. Third daughter of a minor noble in the court of King Louis the Fourteenth and author of *The Masque of Blood*. A vampiric killer with a body count that rivals pandemics. Europe, North America—a two century-long tour of blood-stained depravity. Oh yes, I've done my research, *Mademoiselle*." He looked up, and the broad smile returned, colder now and stripped of its pretension. "So, if I'm a sickness, Ms. Durant, then tell me, what does that make *you*?"

"That's not who I am," I growled. "Not anymore."

"Ah, yes. Of course." Drake's tone oozed with mock understanding. "You've changed, haven't you. You're a sinner turned penitent treading the slow road to redemption." He tilted his head slightly. "Tell me... has it ever occurred to you we might not be so different?"

Drake pushed back his chair and strode to the French doors, his silhouette carved into stark relief by the moonlight. He stared out into the night like he was searching for something that wasn't there.

"Unlike you I wasn't born into gilded luxury," he said at last. "No, I've earned every inch of what you see. Every dime. Every scrap of power. I rose through the ranks of Caster society not because of some accident of birth but because I *wanted* it. The hard knocks, the ridicule, the kicks and the punches, I let them shape me. I learned how to fight back, but with brains and will rather than muscles and sweat. I forged alliances. I betrayed trusts. I sold secrets and bought power. I felled mighty oaks and planted a million acorns." He barked a short, mirthless laugh "A harvest that took time."

He paused for a moment, dabbing absently at the corner of his mouth with his thumb. "Your years number, what? Two hundred and sixty, give or take a decade or two? Well, mine total one hundred and forty-three." He crossed to the desk, his index finger trailing along the letter rack's polished edge. "It's an impressive span by most people's count, but a span that has stretched, perhaps, a little too far."

Blindsided a little by this unexpected detour, I kept my mouth shut.

"*And this too shall pass.*" Drake exhaled slowly. The quote aimed seemingly at the still air of the room. "Second Corinthians, if memory serves. It's a sentiment I should, perhaps, have heeded a little closer, because more and more I find myself asking *why*? I mean was all the subterfuge and sacrifice really worth it?" He stared at the finger that still rested on the wooden letter rack like it was the only thing left in the room. "This sparkling world used to be something I dreamed of owning, Ms. Durant, and I came about as close as any man ever could. But now..." He tore his gaze away from the desk to meet mine, his eyes shining dimly with something that wasn't quite fatigue. "... now I find it bores me."

The conversation wasn't going the way I'd expected. Not by a long shot. And, from the looks on the faces of Dolores Barrett and Elizabeth Pell, I wasn't alone.

Once again, I cursed myself for not bringing my smokes with me.

"So what are you telling me?"

"That I'm done, Ms. Durant." Drake's voice was a shade too even. "I'm telling you I've had enough of the intrigues and the paranoia—that I've had enough of the Bindings, and more than enough of the empty vanity they enable."

I studied his face for anything that might betray a lie. A twitch. A blink. "And you think that buys you what?" I asked. "Leniency? Forgiveness? Do you really think that I'll walk away from this convinced that you're a changed man?"

"Yes." His voice carried the merest ghost of a sigh. "Oh, you have no reason to. I know that. But think about it. We have so much in common, you and I—the burden of too many years and too many lives left shattered in our wake. Haven't you ever wanted, just once, to set that burden down?" He exhaled softly. "You came here tonight to stop me, Ms. Durant, well consider me stopped. I beg you, don't add any more weight to your load on my account."

I rose slowly, keeping my open hands in view as I reached for the chair to steady me.

"You're right, of course," I said, my voice quiet. "You know you are. The crush of the years. The endless turn of the wheel. The loneliness. The longing for it to end. I know it far too well... but in my long and bloody life I've learned the best lies often come wrapped in truth, so it doesn't matter if what you say is ninety-nine percent God's honest. If the last drop is poison, the whole glass kills."

I met his eyes, my grip on the chair tightening until my knuckles turned white. "Not that it matters, because stopped or not, you're still the man who murdered Rose Chamberlain, and for that you have to die."

#

Before the last syllable landed, I was already moving. A right hook dropped the guard nearest the door, the force of the blow hard enough to pivot me in the direction of the wide-eyed goon stationed the left of Drake's desk. His head struck the polished wood with a hollow *thonk* as I tackled him, and he went down like a de-stringed marionette. Neither man had been given the chance to even raise their weapons.

Drake screamed, a shrill punctuation mark that broke the spell of stunned inaction and from the corner of my eye I saw Elizabeth Pell make a mad dash for the door. But I didn't have time for her.

One of the two guards stood by the French doors opened fire in my direction. The first bullet missed me by inches, but the second tore through my left shoulder, and pain flared like a lightning strike. It didn't take long before his colleagues followed suit.

Gritting my teeth, I vaulted onto the desk, dragging the unconscious body of the suit whose head I'd bounced off it's surface behind me, using his unconscious form as a shield.

He was only out for the count when I grabbed him but a hail of bullets meant it was a corpse I slammed into the goon stationed on the desk's far side in a collision that sent us both, the dead *and* the undead, sprawling to the floor.

And that left me with two.

Both men moved—not toward me, but *away*—falling back to buy space for a clean shot before I could get close and physical.

But it didn't matter.

I launched myself from the desk and landed in a tight roll. Three more shots cracked through the air, each bullet missing by a breath as I turned my roll into a lunge, driving my shoulder into the lead man's gut. We went down hard, me on top and him beneath me. Taking full advantage of our relative positions I drove my forehead into the bridge of his nose, and heard, or maybe felt, something crunch with an impact strong enough to make the guy fold like a bad simile.

His partner, a smarter man than any of his confederates, turned and ran, but I grabbed the gun the broken-nosed goon beneath me had dropped, and hurled it at his head like a fastball. The machined steel hit the running man's retreating skull with a sound like meat hitting marble.

And that took care of the guards.

I turned to the desk, fixing my baleful eyes on Drake, who was crouched behind his leather chair like a child hiding from thunder. The throbbing in my shoulder and the blood loss I could ill afford made my movements a chore. Each step I took fired a spark of fresh agony, but still I pushed forward, letting the pain keep me just sharp enough to hold back the growing tide of vital, deadly desire. The hunger for carnage flared within my breast. The Thirst for fresh, warm, human blood surged.

And buried deep beneath the twin needs that defined me, something else stirred, too.

"Do it!" The words belonged to the clipped tones of Dolores Barrett. Her urgent cry cut through the war raging inside me, stealing away my attention. Elizabeth Pell might have vanished, but Barrett, it seemed, had remained. She sat hunched in the corner of the room, her arms wrapped around her knees in an empty gesture of defense. Her eyes were wide and shining. Her right hand pointed at Drake. "You're the only one, remember," she continued. "The only creature on the face of this earth with the will and the ability to make this right—the only person in the world who can stop it from happening again. The only one!"

The words, jarring, brutal and too honest to ignore, crashed into me. In answer, the vampiric passions I'd held onto so tight for so long roared into full, undead life. The yearning, clawing needs to feast, destroy, and kill overtook me. My skin tightened and stretched, my fangs lengthened as the mask of humanity slipped away to reveal the nightmare I truly am.

Danger!

The silent voice, so long drowned by the unholy passions surging in my breast, sang out loud. I paused, frozen mid-step. In my too-still veins, adrenaline and blood-red need crackled with electric fire. It was a warning, of course, but not of any kind of threat from the man so obviously at my mercy. No, this was something else, something insidious. Something I couldn't name.

I shook my head in a vain attempt at clarity—a chance to give the more human side of me the opportunity to *really* listen —to listen and to think.

And that was when Drake made his move.

He scuttled backward, clawing at the bookcase behind him. Leather-bound tomes fell to the floor as his searching fingers closed around the mace-shaped *objet* I'd spotted earlier. As he climbed to his feet, he pointed the weapon—and I just knew it had to be a some kind of weapon, Caster-wrought and magical—at me, his hands trembling.

"Stay back!" he barked, his voice pitched high and raw. "I'll use it! I swear to God, I will!" The artifact bristled with sparks of arcane menace and, as if to underline his point. A crackle of blue energy danced across the brass studs at its head like a Tesla coil before fading away to nothing.

"He won't," Dolores Barrett said quietly from somewhere behind me. "He doesn't know how."

Drake's wild eyes snapped toward her. "*You!* You traitor!" he spat. "After everything I gave you, everything I taught you, *this* is how you repay me?"

"Why not?" Barrett straightened from her crouch and dusted herself off, her icy composure intact, her voice steady. "You sit there like a spider in your oh-so elegant web, spinning your lies, growing rich and fat while others bleed and suffer. I knew it had to end—that *you* had to end and tonight that becomes a reality. You say you want out of the Binding trade?" She nodded toward me. "Well, Charlie here is going to help you do that... permanently!"

Drake licked the corners of his mouth, his Adam's apple jumping as his gaze flitted between the two women he'd underestimated so badly. I took another step forward, preparing to loosen the final chains that held the beast. Inside me, The Thirst and The Hunger snarled and pulled, desperate for release.

In the last, desperate act of a condemned man, Drake threw the artifact at my face, but with not nearly enough force to stop me. His last, desperate gambit played out, he clattered to the ground. A broken, sobbing shadow of a man.

"Please," he whimpered. "Please, I'm begging you."

I didn't answer him. I didn't even blink. I simply let the red-eyed need for blood and vengeance roll through me in waves. My fingers curved into claws. My cheeks hollowed.

I could *hear* the hammering pulse of the prey at my mercy.

I could *smell* his fear.

"Do it, Charlie." Dolores Barrett's words arrived from a world away. "Do it! For her!"

For her.

The words echoed in the well of my cursed existence. The needful storm inside me howled, but at its center, another sliver of silent warning stirred. A warning that took me all the way back to Versailles and the man in the smoked-glass spectacles. The day I fell. The day I became a monster. The day I *chose.*

This time, I listened.

I took a half-step back as I fought for mental clarity.

Scattered pieces of information—things I'd heard in Tamara's broken admissions and Howard's quiet concerns, subtle clues buried in Patrick Callaghan's cryptic warnings and the urgings of Dolores Barrett, even the words of Sebastian Drake himself—all presented themselves for my inspection. These fragments spun... shifted... formed and reformed, and, at their center, like a still hub in a twirling cosmos, stood one forgotten phrase. A tiny piece of information, offered without thought, and never truly heard.

But now...

"No." I staggered back, reaching for the corner of the desk, my eyes wide. "No, but that would mean... wait... yes! The blood. Oh, my God. Can that be it? The blood? Is that what this whole thing is about? What it's *always* been about?"

"No," the voice of Tamara said from the doorway behind me. "No this isn't about blood. This time it's about stopping *you*!"

27

So, Tamara Quinn had come to put an end to me, exactly as she'd promised she would.

The Thirst and The Hunger clawed at the walls I'd hastily rebuilt inside me. My mind buzzed with a cocktail of dark passions and the single revelation that changed everything.

"You're armed, I take it?" I kept my voice as level as the prowling, salivating creature inside me would allow.

"Yup." Tamara's tone was tinder-dry. "With the very same gun you used to coldcock me."

I nodded. "And Howard?"

"Yeah, I'm armed too," the big man said, his voice heavy with reluctance.

"Alright, then." The mask of my humanity began to reassert itself, reshaping my features even as I spoke. "Then here's what I suggest. I'm going to turn around, real slow, and back up until I hit wall. I suggest Mr. Drake and Ms. Barrett take that opportunity to move over to you—everyone stays calm and everything stays coordinated. Agreed?"

The silence stretched to breaking point. I could almost *hear* the exchange of looks behind me.

"I guess," Tamara said. "But no tricks. I know *exactly* who and what you are, remember?"

I turned, my hands raised, my palms open, and there was Tamara. Her dark hair was pulled back in a loose cascade of gathered curls beneath a rain-damp fedora. A flash of bandage peeked from under the hat, but, thankfully, there wasn't a single trace of blood.

Small mercies, I guess.

"I'm sorry about the headache," I said, my words slow but my thoughts racing. "I didn't want to hurt you, but… "

Her eyes were steady, her gun aimed at my unbeating heart.

"… We all have to do things we don't want to?" she finished for me.

"I guess." My eyes dropped to the gun. "So what now?"

"Now? We go," Tamara replied. "And I mean all of us. Me, Howard *and* you. We leave Drake and his damn Bindings far, far behind us and never even *think* of looking back."

I nodded, more toward my own thoughts than her words. "And if I say no?"

"Then I shoot you, somewhere painful and inconvenient, and we go anyway." She held up a small case and I caught a glimpse of a silver coin identical to the ones Doc Rivers had used in his ritual. A coin that glowed with a soft, unnatural light. "This little doohickey doesn't care if the people it transports are injured," Tamara continued. "Or even dead, for that matter." Her eyes read the question that lurked in mine. "A gift. I guess Doc Rivers never did stop watching over us after all—for it to work, I'll need you to take a few steps toward me. Make them nice, slow steps."

I started to comply, my mind still smoothing the rough edges of my revelation, working the puzzle until every piece fit. Two paces in, I stopped.

"Five minutes."

"What?"

I met Tamara's gaze, trying to let my eyes convey everything I couldn't say. "Just give me five minutes to talk a few things through and hear myself think out loud. Give me that and I'll come quietly. No muss, no fuss. I promise."

Tamara's eyes narrowed, curiosity and suspicion battling

for the upper hand. "You got her covered?" she asked Howard, resisting the urge to glance his way.

"Yeah," the unease in the big man's voice was unmistakable.

Tamara's lips pursed even as the muzzle of her gun dipped. "Alright, Charlie. Five minutes. What you got?"

I tilted my head and stared at the ceiling, my tongue pressing against the inside of my cheek as I searched for a place to start. "Something's been off about this business almost from the start," I said eventually. "I think we both know that. Certain things didn't sit right... certain details. A word here, a choice there. Loose threads that didn't mean a whole lot on their own... but when woven together? I think I can finally see the shape of it."

"What are you talking about? What threads? What words?" Tamara's voice was sharp and impatient.

"Nothing really. Just passing remarks, strange omissions and odd coincidences—next to meaningless on their own, but put them together and they start to make a terrible kind of sense —and it all starts with one question. Who benefitted from the death of Rose Chamberlain?"

Tamara's brow furrowed. "Drake," she said. "Rose was his preordained key to power and immortality, remember? That's what this whole damn thing's about."

I opened my mouth to speak, but Drake got there first. "No!" the wild-eyed man shouted from behind Tamara. "No, she wasn't... I didn't... I swear it. I've never even heard of this 'Rose Chamberlain' before tonight!"

"Right." I stepped toward him, and he shrank back a little, his mask of urbane superiority long since shattered. "And I guess it wasn't you who haunted her dreams? That you weren't the shadow of impending doom that drove her right to the edge of sanity, so she'd be ready for the sacrificial knife? That it wasn't *your* laughter she heard echoing through her nightmares, wasn't your orange-scented cologne she smelled?"

Drake didn't speak. He couldn't. His trembling lips parted,

but no sound emerged.

"And the other girls?" I pressed on, my voice thick with the weight of memory. "The ones The Machine showed us being hunted down and torn apart like animals." The Hunger snarled in my gut as visions of blood on cobblestones and dead mouths frozen in silent screams danced before me. "I suppose *that* wasn't you, either?"

"No!" Drake, sweat-slick and panicked, shook his head vehemently. "I didn't… I couldn't. I won't pretend to be an innocent, Ms. Durant, but I was never the man who pulled the trigger. Never the one who held the knife. I have people for that."

"Of course you do." I let my words curl with bitter venom, "Getting those manicured hands dirty would never do, would it? It's not your *style*."

Tamara flicked a glance to the man cowering behind her, and I *saw* the gears of her mind start to turn.

"But that's the problem," I continued, my gaze returning to Drake. "Because I know of at least four young women killed in exactly that way. The last of them—a woman I actually cared for—was butchered and left strung up in my apartment for me to find like some sick joke."

"But not by me!" Drake yelled.

Inside me The Hunger surged again but I held its chains. I was Charlotte Amálie Durant, and for the moment at least, I *was* a good person.

"No?" I asked. "Then why was it your face Rose saw in her dreams? Why was it *you* The Machine showed Rose standing before her suspended body, holding a knife at her throat?" I stepped closer and Drake flinched away. "Rose Chamberlain is dead. Whatever excuse or justification you spin me, she's dead… and all because of *you*!" My chest tightened with a grief that could never, ever find peace and a rage that would never dim. I wiped my lips with the back of my hand, blinking through a flood of tears. "And for what, Drake? For greed? For ambition? For *power*?" I paused, letting that final word hang in the air. "Because that's what this whole thing is *really* about. Not blood, or death, or magic, or money. It was *always* about the power, and it still is."

I turned away from him, my voice a low growl. "Isn't it, Ms. Barrett?"

#

There was a moment of perfect silence. Dolores Barrett's mouth opened and closed with the rhythm of a fish dragged from deep water. Seven, maybe eight seconds later she found the composure to summon up some righteous bluster.

"Me?" She stuttered. "But what would I have to do with any of this? Drake's the man with the deadline and the power."

"Yeah," I said, The Hunger scuffling and whining beneath my ribs. "He is. All that power, so close I'm betting you could practically taste it. I imagine it just burned you up inside." I turned my gaze to Tamara. "I said Barrett had a dog in this fight, but the problem was we only ever saw half the picture. We were shown one crime, the imminent, prophesied murder of Rose Chamberlain, and we were never allowed to ask if there might be *another* crime... the planned and patient murder of Sebastian Drake!"

I stared at Dolores Barrett, a burning, ice-cold enmity in my eyes and every gaze in the room followed, each wearing an expression of confusion and shock.

"Drake had to die, didn't he?" I continued. "If you were ever going to get your hands on all that power and wealth, he *had* to be taken out of the picture. The only trouble was, to kill him you needed a weapon—the only creature in the world you could possibly manipulate into becoming his murderer. You needed me."

"Not the only creature," Drake murmured, his smug detachment a thing of the past. "But your name did appear on a *very* short list."

"List... right. Your list of potential threats. A list that became shorter and shorter as those threats were either paid off or put down." I turned to him. "Except, my name never got crossed off that list, did it, Mr. Drake? And why do you suppose that is? Whose job was it to maintain and manage it?"

"I told you," Barrett snapped, her ice-cold composure fraying at the edges. "You were my 'just-in-case'. My ace in the hole."

"Oh, I was an ace, all right. I was an undead killer with more blood on her hands than any arm. The perfect assassin. Except I was a monster in remission. A redemption you knew no amount of persuasion or pressure would ever make me put at risk. No, if you were going to get me ready for the kill, you were going to need to give me some serious motivation."

"Rose," Tamara whispered.

"Rose," I confirmed. "An innocent young woman dragged into a world she didn't understand and dropped at my feet.I turned back to Barrett. "She was bait you *knew* I could never resist."

Barrett's ice-chip eyes scanned the room, looking for a friend. Any friend.

"But how?" Tamara asked, stepping forward. "How could she know what Rose meant to you... what she *would come* to mean to you?"

"She couldn't have," I said. "Not with any certainty. But think about the way Rose looked, and the memories she stirred up for me. From the moment I saw her all I wanted to do was save her—to save the woman I'd failed so many years ago—the tragedy that defined my whole unholy existence, shaping every dream and haunting my every waking moment." I flashed a glance Tamara's way. "My guess is that was the point of the Bindings under the bed. To reignite those dreams and drag my past into the present."

Tamara frowned. "Alright... but the woman you told me about, the woman you..."

"...the woman I killed."

"Right, the woman you killed." Her eyes danced away before the glance could land. "That woman died centuries ago. How could Barrett even guess at what she looked like?"

"Um... I might be able to answer that," Drake's voice was

like a raised hand. "After your friend's, uh… visit," the expression he flashed Tamara was almost apologetic. "I had reason to access Ms. Barrett's files. There, in quite wonderful detail, were listed the history, known associates, and incorrectly rated threat level of one Charlotte Amálie Durant, and included in the biography was a drawing. A candid little sketch captured in pencil. Below it was a dedication. 'To C, with love eternal. T.'"

"Théri." The name fell from my lips like a eulogy. "Her name was Marie-Thérèse Bazinet, but to me she was always my Théri."

Tears slid down my cheek as I remembered her—laughing and gay, her hand moving deftly across the parchment to capture the image of her half-naked reflection. A private gift just for me, the woman who…

"She was the purest spirit I ever knew."

I forced my mind from the thought and returned my attention to Drake."But one summer, a disease came to court—a terrible wasting sickness. Those that it afflicted became walking, wasted shadows waiting to die. I remember lying beside Théri on the night she began to tremble and cough, and how quickly the sickness robbed her of her vitality, her light—her life." I paused, the memory falling across my thoughts like a pall. "Within a week, the woman whose passion and energy lifted my heart was barely there at all. She couldn't eat. She could hardly even lift her head. I brought every priest and every doctor to her bedside, but prayers and medicine did nothing, and that's when *he* appeared. Monsieur le Comte… the man with the cure."

I glanced over my shoulder, glaring at a past only I could see. "His cure was a serum that needed to be cultivated in living, healthy blood… my blood. He told me this patent miracle would lie dormant in my veins, growing in both strength and efficacy—borrowing from my vigor to evolve into the wonder that would end all of Théri's pain and suffering. He never once mentioned that the elixir was specifically engineered to react to a contagion he himself had designed—or exactly *how* it would end her pain."

The color drained from Tamara's face as realization

dawned.

"The 'cure' did save Théri's life, but the life it saved wasn't *her*. As her strength returned, she changed, devolving before my eyes into a ravening thing—an insatiable, insidious hunger wrapped in a woman's form... a monster that still bore my lover's eyes." I vented a long, slow, and entirely wasted breath. "I was her first victim that night. I was also her last. She clambered from her bed, her hair falling from her in clumps, her fingers cruel claws, her mouth split wide with rows of misshapen hooks and barbs, and flew at me. I raised my arms to protect myself, but her teeth pierced my flesh and her saliva mingled with my blood —and the serum that was still within it."

I looked up, met Tamara's eyes, and held them. "The combination made me into the monster I am today, but, as that initial surge of unholy strength and that first dire feeding-frenzy started to take hold of me, I seized hold of the poniard Monsieur le Comte carried in his belt and killed the only woman I'd ever loved. it was my final act as a human being, and the worst thing I've ever done."

"Touching, I'm sure." Dolores Barrett didn't even bother to veil the contempt in her voice. "But it proves what, exactly? That I know my history? That I've seen a sketch? Drake saw that drawing too, if you remember. If you're searching for a monster, Ms. Durant, then I say look again."

"No!" The word pretty much exploded from me. "No, It's *you*!"

Charlotte... Amálie... Durant.

"I think, somewhere deep down inside, I always knew it was you—right from the very start—but even if I hadn't, you told me as much yourself."

"I... *What*?!" Barrett's face twitched with the barest flicker of doubt.

"Tonight, in your car," I said. "As you drove me here to be your executioner. *'Stringing Rose Chamberlain's headless corpse in a place he knew you'd find her.'* Those were your words—but I only ever told you Rose was dead. I never told you *how* she was killed, and I never said *where* we found her... so, how did you know?"

I took a step toward her.

...A good person.

"After all, Drake hires others to do his killing for him and keep his manicured hands nice and clean.

He wouldn't... he couldn't... expose himself to that much mess, that much *blood.*"

As I voiced that final word, the final piece of the puzzle fell into place and a shockwave of clarity surged through me, rolling through the grief and loss filling up the hollow place where my soul should sit, and igniting the wild, unstoppable desires that dwelt in its place. The mask of humanity fled from me in a burst of vicious fury. Every suppressed desire, every ounce of the bloodthirst I kept so tightly caged, exploded in a wildfire of vengeful lust that could have torn everyone in the room apart.

If not for Tamara.

"Charlotte. Amálie. Durant."

Unflinching, she stepped forward, her hands gripping my shoulders, anchoring me to her calm resolve. "You are Charlotte Amálie Durant!" She repeated. Her voice, echoing from so very far away, rung with unshakable belief. "Remember, Charlie, remember! You are Charlotte Amálie Durant—and you are a good person."

I stared uncomprehendingly at her—through the storm, through the madness, but she didn't flinch.

"Charlotte Amálie Durant," she repeated. "A *good* person!"

Six words. Six simple words, spoken not as a plea, but as a *certainty.*

It shouldn't have worked. It nearly didn't, but that sentiment, those words, were enough to pierce the maelstrom of deadly desires and reach the last shred of humanity hiding inside.

I dropped to the floor, allowing grief to eclipse the rage and the need. Raw sobs wracked my body. Tears streamed down my hollow, bestial cheeks. Tears for the love I'd lost. Tears for the humanity ripped from me. Tears for all the unnameable women who died because of me.

"Please," Barrett had retreated to the room's sole door, her composure gone, her expression frantic as she faced the reality of the monster she'd provoked. "

Please. You don't understand," she stammered. "It wasn't me. It wasn't! I *swear* it wasn't! On The Bible or anything you like! *I did not kill Rose Chamberlain*!"

"No, I know you didn't." I lifted my face to meet her wild-eyed stare, letting the hatred that burned like white-hot ash in my gut fuel the controlled fury of my words. "You couldn't have killed Rose Chamberlain, because Rose Chamberlain never existed."

28

A moment of uncomprehending silence settled over the room as every eye turned to me, each individual waiting for an explanation. I stood as tall as I'm able, licked my lips in an attempt to find some kind of equilibrium, and began.

"The blood."

The single word, like hot, jagged burning gravel, stuck in my throat.

"The blood should have told me everything… but I guess that was the point."

"I'm sorry, you've lost me." It was Tamara who broke the uneasy hush. "What blood? And how can a woman we *spoke to*, have never existed?"

"Getting there." The glance I shot her pretty much begged for patience. "But blood is where it starts. Blood, and a body hanging in a place I was always going to find it. *Why?*"

Tamara opened her mouth, but I held up a finger to stop her.

"I happen to know the average human body holds between nine and twelve pints of blood, depending on the height, weight, and sex of the person and the blood that decorated my apartment so thoroughly had to add up to nearly every drop of it—*why?*"

Tamara's brow furrowed. "The fight the machine showed you…"

"Okay, there was a fight. A vicious, one-sided assault. But no fight on earth could account for the sheer *volume* of gore and gristle spread so far, so wide, so... *artfully*. No, the charnel house we walked into wasn't the aftermath of any kind of struggle. It was *staged*—meticulously, skillfully staged—and all to provoke one very specific reaction."

"You turned." Howard's voice was small and quiet. "Changed, I mean."

"Exactly... Barrett couldn't risk me recovering my senses enough to truly look, to truly *think*—and *that* was the point —a diversion—one designed to bypass my more human, more rational mind and speak directly to the bloodthirsty creature I keep locked up inside. A diversion that used the horror of my past, and the wreckage of my future, to fuel a creature of unstoppable vengeance. But, oh, if I'd only *seen*."

I swept my gaze around the collection of confused faces. Dolores Barrett's discomfited expression told me only she knew where this was going.

"The body matched Rose's height and build," I continued. "And without a head it *could* have been Rose, but there was one fatal flaw." I turned to Tamara. "It was you who pointed it out, although you didn't realize it at the time. At the office, after Howard left on his fool's errand, and we danced around the subject of the body and all it meant, you mentioned a scar."

Tamara's eyes narrowed

"Yeah... below the left shoulder. A faded half-moon. The bottom part was mostly slashed away, but it was there."

"But Rose didn't have any scars. Not on her shoulder. Not anywhere."

"You're sure?"

"We laid in each other's arms for one beautiful, impossible night," I said, swallowing down a spike of bitter pain. "I could trace you every contour of her body, every inch of her skin. *There was no scar!*"

Tamara's frown deepened, her mind working the implications. "Okay, so the body wasn't Rose's." She spoke cautiously, feeling her way through it. "Which would explain, I guess, why the head was taken... but then *who was it?*"

I let my attention linger on the increasingly troubled Dolores Barrett, fixing her with a venomous stare. "I don't think we'll ever truly know. Oh, we could trawl the missing persons lists, but I'd guess more than a few petite blondes get swallowed up by this city—way more than ever get reported let alone searched for—we witnessed three of those deaths ourselves."

"The Machine!"

"Yeah, those too-real, implanted sensations gifted to both of us by The Machine—all those girls, each murdered so brutally, each so very like Rose—we never understood what those deaths meant. We never realized. We never *saw!*"

Tamara's hand flew to her mouth. "Oh," she breathed.

"I'm sorry, but I still don't realize or see anything." Howard squinted at the wall behind me as if the answer might be scrawled there.

"Barrett needed a body," Tamara said, haltingly. "One that matched Rose, or, maybe... Marie-Thérèse?" I flashed her the briefest nod and she continued. "She'd have to be young, of course, and not too tall, with a lack of tattoos or piercings, and no obvious imperfections. A blonde would be ideal, I guess, just in case a stray hair was ever found—I guess it's a harder shopping list to fill than you might think."

Howard shook his head and blinked, confusion still clouding his handsome face. "Okay, so the body wasn't Rose. I get that," he said. "Sort of, anyway—but we still *met* her. We still *spoke* to her. We..." his eyes flashed my way."...we still *touched* her."

"A hired dupe?" Tamara offered, her brows drawn. "Some kind of actress, maybe?"

"No," I said. "Not exactly... but consider Dolores Barrett. What power, borrowed or not, do we know she possesses? What *skills* does she have?"

Tamara's lips parted in a soft, stunned 'Oh'. "But you don't mean... no. She *couldn't*... could she?"

"A washed-up actress, eaten up by jealousy and mediocrity. A woman Drake coached to change people's appearances—their faces, bodies, and hair color—if she learned to transform someone else's appearance so completely..."

"Then why couldn't she do the same to herself?" Tamara's almost shouted the conclusion. "It was *her*! Dolores Barrett was Rose Chamberlain!"

"I am right, aren't I?" I turned my gaze to Drake. "The skills you taught her, the power you lent her... she could conjure up the face and figure of a ghost captured in a pencil sketch."

"It would be tricky." Drake's voice was still strained. "But it would be possible." He was a shadow of the assured, dangerous man who faced me across his desk now, his cool sheen gone. "We are sometimes asked to work from photographs—this actor's chin, that model's hair, that kind of thing. A pencil drawing is less ideal, but still doable. The most difficult part would be the comprehensive nature of the transformation."

I turned to Dolores Barrett. A woman who, even in a room full of people, suddenly looked so achingly alone.

"*Comprehensive*." The word slipped across my tongue like poison. "Yes. Because the way you *inhabited* 'Rose'—the way she looked. the way she spoke, her every gesture and expression, the fear in her eyes—In other circumstances, I might be tempted to give you a standing ovation."

"Oh, come on!" Barrett's words were frantic and breathless. Her eyes flitted wildly, looking for any kind of escape. "Do you really believe what you're saying? Do you think I'd go to such unbelievable lengths to kill the man who gave me everything? That I'd spend who knows how long transforming myself into a reminder of some long-lost lover? Do you really think I'd scour the streets for lookalikes? That I could force myself to sleep with a creature like *you*?"

I turned the insult away. "Yes, I do. I think you'd do all that and a lot more besides," I said evenly.

"But you're missing the point. I don't *think* anything... I *know*!"

Barrett's mouth opened and then shut again without a word escaping.

"Little things." I held my thumb and forefinger a judicious inch apart. "Tiny, really. Like how, outside Drake's gatehouse, you knew all about my little vanishing trick. A trick only Tamara, Howard and one other person were aware of." Barrett's cool composure was starting to creak anew, so I pressed on. "Then there was the way 'Rose' blurted out Théri's name. *'The Bazinet girl I remind you of so much,'*. I assumed Tamara spilled that little detail when she visited the apartment, and, of course, you were more than happy to help keep me assuming." I paused for a second, letting the tension ramp up. "The trouble is, Tamara had never heard the name Marie-Thérèse Bazinet... not until tonight."

"Not once." The certainty in Tamara's voice rang out like a bell. "You told me about the girl you killed, but you never once mentioned her name, and even if you had, I wouldn't have shared it. Not with anyone."

"Then maybe you misheard her." Barrett's voice pitched high and brittle. "Maybe you only heard what you *wanted* to hear, or maybe... I don't know... maybe Rose heard it someplace else."

I took another slow, deliberate step forward, my eyes drilling into hers."No. You know exactly where 'Rose' got hold of that name. My dossier. The dossier *you* assembled. The file that gave you the key to break down my resolve and close the trap. The research that uncovered the name Marie-Thérèse Bazinet... and then there's the perfume."

"The perfume?" Again, her face twitched.

"Yeah, the scent she wore so liberally on that first night at Callaghan's. The fragrance which lingered more subtly on her skin every night that followed. It was a good choice. Elegant. Haunting. Like a desert wind through a Parisienne garden—but no amount of your carbolic soap could completely erase such a scent for an undead creature with heightened senses." I let a small, weary smile I didn't feel creep across my face "The ghost of it even followed you into Drake's garage elevator—I couldn't place it at first, but now, with everything else..."

I felt the room tighten, even as the facts stacked up.

Tamara subtly shifted to her right, and Howard to his left, cutting off access to the door. Only Drake stayed put.

"Sounds like you've got a case." Tamara's voice was achingly calm. "So, what do we do with her?"

"What you stopped me from doing to Drake," I growled. The restraints I'd held so long were starting to fail as The Hunger—The Thirst—T*he Vampire,* threatened to slip free. "Barrett played me... she played all of us. She made me think this cold, dead heart could learn to love and live again." I could practically *taste* the panic radiating from the frantic, silver-haired woman before me. "Rose might never have truly lived, but this is still the woman who killed her, and for that... she dies."

As the last word fell Dolores Barrett's composure shattered and instinct took over.

Fight or flight.

Choosing flight, she ran—not toward the door that Tamara and Howard guarded, but straight at me—straight p*ast* me.

I should've seen it coming. But blood loss and the dual burdens of naked emotion and raw revelation were enough to make me slow. Before I could react, Barrett dove to the floor behind me. When she scrambled to her feet again, the mace-like *objet* was clutched in her hands.

"Oh, no," she panted, her face flushed with manic heat. "Someone is going to die here tonight, but it won't be me. Drake might not know how this device works, but I do. I researched everything about it—just as I did for every relic, threat, and every sap who ever walked through that door." She cast a bitter glance toward Drake. "And all for a man I'm worth a thousand of."

I stepped between Barrett and Tamara, taking her out of the artifact's crosshairs but keeping Barrett in mine.

"It could've been yours," Drake said quietly, from somewhere behind me. "The money. The power. As much as you wanted."

"When you felt like it?" Barrett barked a raw, jagged laugh. "If I asked nicely? If Elizabeth Pell didn't get there first? No, I couldn't let that happen. So I summoned your Patron, performed the rites you kept so transparently secret, and signed my very own Binding—a Minor Binding, only a sliver of temporary power but more than enough to pull off my transformation into that vapid little whore. But when you die..." She glanced at Drake. "...When your Binding ends, I inherit the rest. The magic. The invulnerability... Everything. I was always your rightful successor, the woman who should have had it all." She hefted the weapon. "And now that's exactly what I'm going to get."

She turned her focus to me. "This can't kill Drake," she said, lifting the artifact to her shoulder. "But it's more than powerful enough to take care of you and your friends—unless you do what I want."

The air around us crackled.

"I won't kill him." The Hunger snuffled at its cage, but I kept my voice steady and defiant. "I won't. Do what you want, but I'm through being your assassin."

"No!" Barrett snapped. "No, you are *not!* I invested in you, *vampire*. I spent time, effort, magic, and so, so much care to prime you for the kill. You *will* make good on that expenditure."

The air around her shimmered and her features melted back into Rose's—that familiar, intoxicating smile on her lips.

"Do it, Charlie," she whispered in the voice of the girl who'd been created for me. "You couldn't be my savior, but you can still be this. My dark, avenging angel."

The illusion crumbled, and the eyes that glared at me once again held the cold fire of the woman who killed my hope of a future. "It took more than I ever dreamed to get you here," she said. "Becoming that vulnerable little tramp, so helpless and alone. Employing The Hand to terrorize 'Rose' into signing that useless piece of paper—The Bindings. The dreams. The disappearance—it was an intricate plan—an almost perfect plan—but it doesn't matter now. Because you're still here, and I'm still calling the shots. So *I* say when you're through." She took a slow step forward, sparks dancing across the artifact's head as it swayed between me, Tamara, and Howard. "Now make with the fangs, or Howard here dies first."

For a second nobody moved. An almost palpable tension rippled through the room, wire taut and diamond hard. Howard's jaw set in an expression borrowed from a hundred silver screen heroes.

"Do it!" Barrett screamed at me, her shrill voice shredding the air. "Do it or your friend is *dead!*"

To underscore the threat, she fired a burst of crackling energy at Howard's feet. The big man cried out once, sharp and pained; the near miss carrying enough force for him to crumple like a discarded sheet. Behind me, Tamara gasped and pressed something cold and metallic against the small of my back. A subtle, unmistakable message.

Once again I felt a storm of dark passions stir within.

"Then stop with the theatrics and do it," I said, capturing Barrett's full attention. "None of us get to walk out of here, anyway. So what's the difference?"

"The difference?" Barrett's frozen, arrogant smile returned. "Why, none at all, Ms. Durant." She stroked the weapon. "You trusted the wrong person, all those years ago—a mistake that cost you your lover—and now, for the same reason, you get to watch two more of the people you care for die."

"Wrong." I shook my head, a rueful smile tugging at the corners of my lips. "You almost did it, Dolores. You thought you'd managed to free the urges to kill and consume that I've kept caged for so very long, but you were wrong. Not that it matters."

I took a slow step forward and another to the right, the weapon in Dolores Barrett's hands tracking me all the way. "You wanted it all, Dolores... but you get nothing! Nothing except this!"

Tamara stepped smartly into the space I'd vacated, the little .22 revolver I'd left so carelessly on the office desk loaded and cocked. Barrett turned at the sudden movement, but with a sharp bark of finality, the gun still spat its deadly payload.

Dolores Barrett snapped backward as if yanked by invisible strings.

But she still managed to fire the Caster artifact one last time.

29

"No!" The word burst from me, primal and desperate. "Tamara! No! What have you done? What have you done?"

I raced to her side, moving with neither grace nor thought, reaching her a half-second before Howard, and stared into the unseeing eyes of the greatest friend I'd ever known, still so knowing, still so alive, still so Tamara. Where the energy of the mace had struck, a wide, irregular scorch mark penetrated through the three layers of clothing she'd worn over her torso. There wasn't a single mark on her exposed skin, and not a single drop of blood, but from the stink of cooked meat, from the way her head lolled to the side as I turned her over, and the sightless stare of her eyes, there could be no doubt.

Tamara was dead.

And that thought—those three words—were enough. As if a key had been turned, The Hunger, the vibrant, howling need for destruction escaped. I turned my head away from Howard Gold, and the eloquent, almost gentle emotion displayed on the big man's face. Grief and mourning would happen, but those slower emotions would have to wait, because lying on the green rug by the over-large desk was the woman who couldn't.

The woman whose machinations had brought us to this point. Dolores Evangeline Barrett, the woman who tried to make me a killer. The woman who killed Tamara Quinn.

She groaned softly as consciousness slowly crept back to her. A stain of the deepest, most vibrant red blossomed over her left shoulder where the bullet had struck—the shot had come from six feet or so, but even at that range and even with the training of the policeman's daughter it hadn't found its ultimate mark.

I strode toward her, the endless screaming desires for blood and violence rising within me even as my fangs and claws descended. But even with a bullet in her shoulder Barrett was fast. She scrambled away as I closed the short distance, trying desperately to put the oversized desk between us, but I didn't rush, despite the passions surging in my breast. The memory of all those girls hacked to death in dirty alleyways and the slow, methodical steps of their killer made each prolonged moment feel that much more fitting—and so, so much more delicious.

I could see the helpless dread in the eyes of the silver-haired woman. I could almost *taste* the fear emanating from her in waves. Two more steps and I would be beside her. Two more steps and I...

And for the second time that night, a gunshot rang out.

Dolores Barrett, the woman who had been the author of so much misery, the woman whose pride and ambition had so very nearly driven me to betray so much, lay still. Her arms had settled by her side like a cruel parody of a soldier on parade, but her face—what was left of it, stared straight up at the ceiling—staring forever into blind infinity.

I stood for one frozen, uncomprehending second, Dolores Barrett been shot, she'd been killed, but by whose hand?

Then I turned and saw Sebastian Drake. The spilled gun he'd rescued from the floor still extended before him like an accusation. In his eyes, the same dull confusion that was so slowly dissipating from me shone like an echo.

"I... I had to." The words, reluctant and uncertain, tumbled from him like they belonged to someone else.

"Oh?" I kept my voice carefully non-committal.

"Yes!" He glanced at me, and then back to the corpse. "She played us, Ms. Durant. She played us both—and she almost won, too." He wiped away a thin line of drool. "If you hadn't seen through her nested deceptions, I'd be en route to an eternity of torture about now, and you'd be a ravening, feral monster, hunted down by the only friends you have left." With every word, his certainty seemed to grow, the armor of his urbane sheen slipping imperfectly into place. "Yes, if you ask me, I've done us both a favor."

"I don't care."

Before he could take his eulogy of justification any further, I set those three simple words in his way like a roadblock. The storm of vampiric cravings breaking enough for the distraught and exhausted woman beneath to lay it out plain.

"I don't give a damn for your ifs, and your might-have-beens," I continued. "If it wasn't for you—your corruption, your Bindings, your greed and your ambition —then would Dolores Barrett have followed you so far? Would anyone have died here tonight or any of the nights that prepared it?" I didn't give him time to answer. "Consider this your notice to quit, Drake. Pack up, lock the doors, and walk away to that quiet little life you say you want. Because if I hear one whisper that you're still in business I'll be back, and, whatever the cost, I'll put an end to it all—I'll put an end to *you*!"

I made a point of turning my back on him, not giving him the satisfaction of any kind of reply, and took the few steps to Howard, who was still kneeling beside the fallen body of my best friend.

And that's when I heard the hum.

#

The Caster artifact Dolores Barrett had been holding was in Drake's hand, its crackling mace-like head leveled at me.

"No," Drake said. "I'm sorry to disappoint you, Ms. Durant. Truly, I am. But I can't allow that. My 'retirement plan'—a few idyllic years away from the tawdry, empty values of this world—was a wonderful idea to float in front of a vengeful vampire who had the power to kill me. But if the exploits of the late Ms. Barrett had anything to teach me, it's that my power isn't some burden to be set down. It's something to covet—something to *protect.*" He stroked the artifact like a pet. "Especially now that I know how this thing works."

As those final words landed it was as if something snapped deep inside me. Not the supernatural yearnings of the vampire. Not The Thirst or The Hunger, something that was far more intrinsic, something that was more... *human.*

I launched myself at him.

We hit the ground hard and my fists flew into him. I struck him. Once. Twice. A third time. A fourth. The Hunger howled its savage approval. Blood spilled down his chin, and the scent of life rose into the air, the smell rich enough for The Thirst—that unyielding desire to feed on living, human blood—to finally surge to the fore. I wanted to drink the blood of the man at my mercy—wanted to drain the very last drop and watch as the light faded from his eyes.

I raised my head and screamed a snarling, guttural roar no human throat should ever make and the vampire answered. My true face melted away my humanity, my fangs descending like drawn daggers. I stared down at my broken, bloodied prey and braced myself for the final strike.

A strike that never came.

Instead, firm, unyielding hands dragged me away from Drake. I struggled, flailing against the unwelcome intervention and saw the face of the man who had dared to stop me.

Howard.

"Don't." His eyes, made moist and sore by the fall of tears, locked on to mine. "I know, Charlie. Christ, I know. But stop for a second. *Think.* Why did Tamara come here tonight? Why did she try to kill Barrett?" He shook his head in weary frustration. "It was for you, Charlie. Because she believed in you. Because she knew you were more than the soulless killer Barrett tried to turn you into." His voice cracked under the weight of emotion. "But she saw past all of that. She saw the woman behind the monster—she saw *you*, and that's why she stepped so decisively between you and Barrett."

I shoved him back. "Move," I hissed. "Move or I move you."

He staggered away from me, but recovered quickly enough to force himself into my path again, staring into my eyes with misplaced courage and naked, unshakable faith.

Inside me, rage, grief, hunger, and vengeance screamed, but Howard's quiet belief spoke louder.

Charlotte Amálie Durant. A good person.

Tamara's mantra, *my* mantra, cycled in the hollow spaces of my heart—powered by the big man's steady gaze—stitching together everything fury and loss had torn apart.

A good person.

I took one step forward, and then another, but he didn't move an inch.

A good...

It was such a small, undemonstrative thing, but the unflappable, immovable display of faith from the man who'd once shown me such wariness was everything. My legs gave out as I reached for him, and I dropped to my knees.The Hunger and The Thirst dissolved inside me. Howard didn't hesitate. He knelt beside me and wrapped me in his arms. I tried my best to fight my way free, but my fight was done. He held me close, and I collapsed into him, clinging to his strength and warmth, sobbing like a child who'd lost the world.

"Touching," Drake's words echoed Dolores Barrett's, but, whereas her voice had been cold and haughty, his was thick and slurred. "Such a shame it's all for nothing."

As one, we turned.

Drake was standing again, but only just. His face was a patchwork of bruises, his nose a ruin. Blood dribbled from the corner of his mouth. His right arm hung limp and useless and, behind him, the Caster artefact lay abandoned on the floor. In its place, was Tamara's .22, its muzzle aimed squarely at Howard's head.

"Against the wall," Drake barked. "Both of you. Now."

#

Tamara was dead, Rose Chamberlain—the girl who never was—was gone. And now a gun was being aimed at the only friend I had left.

I retreated from the lure of unwise action and did as Drake said, backing up until I felt thick wallpaper against my back. In my mind's eye, the man in the smoked glass spectacles peered at me from the shadowed corners of *La Galerie des Glaces,* his head tilted in that same bloodlessly inquisitive way. '*What now*?' those eyes said. '*What will you do now?*'

"Good." Drake's voice had once again regained some of its poisonous poise. "Now, if either of you so much as twitches, Mr. Gold, here dies."

The threat rang true.

This close, the bullet didn't need to be well-aimed, and no matter how fast I was, I knew I could never reach Drake before he squeezed the trigger. Not with the blood, loss, and grief pressing down on me like wet stone.

"I never wanted any of this," he said. "But you have to understand, Dolores Barrett's treachery needed to be repaid." Drake's bruised eyes lingered on the pistol in his hand like he was seeing it for the first time. "But just imagine," he murmured.

"Imagine what?"

"The power." His voice held a soft reverence. "So explosive. So immediate. So… final." He licked another bead of saliva from his lips—mania burning red and sullen in his eyes. "Such a small thing," he said. "So dull—so ordinary.—but held within it, the power to end lives." He let out a slow trembling breath. "I've chased power all my life, Ms. Durant. Ever since I was a small and sickly boy. I was always hiding, always running away… but I was *clever*—I gathered secrets, made deals—but even as my power and my wealth grew, I stayed in the shadows and gave the orders, but tonight?" His fever-bright eyes rose to meet mine again. "To-night *I* pulled the trigger. *Me! I* took a life and *I* felt what real power truly is!" He grinned, his teeth pink with blood. "And now I get to feel it all over again."

I looked away, not wanting to bear witness to the madness twisting his features. "I'm sorry, Howard," I whispered. "If I'd been smarter, quicker..."

Howard stopped me with a shake of his head."There's nothing to be sorry for, Charlie," he said. "I wouldn't have missed these last few months for the world. I've seen the unreal, done the impossible. I found out where I belong and who I belong with—you might have hired me to be the face behind the desk, the Charlie Durant people expect to see, but for one brief and brilliant moment I actually made a difference... I mattered." He turned his eyes to Drake, a wistful smile playing at his lips. "So, I guess if this is where my story ends then at least I can say I lived a little before I died."

Drake wiped the blood and spit from his face with a shaking hand, the madness in his eyes glowing brighter and brighter.

His mouth stretched into a grin sharpened by delirium.

"A pretty speech, my friend." He thumbed the hammer, and the soft metallic click echoed like a death knell. "But it changes nothing. You see, *she's* the threat." The gun swung from Howard to me.

This close and this still there was no way he could miss. The round would tear through my skull, scattering memory and whatever soul I had left into the ether. No amount of vampiric resilience would be enough to repair that.

And a helpless realization, true and redundant hit me. Because it wasn't Barrett who was to blame and it wasn't Drake. It never had been. It wasn't even Monsieur le Comte, the man with the smoked glass spectacles.

It was *me.*

I'd called Drake a sickness, but I was the true Patient Zero —the carrier of an invisible affliction that leeched the life from everyone I'd ever loved. So, if there was any kind of judgement to face, it was only right I should be the one to greet it.

The barrel of the .22 with its single dark and endless eye stared me down and in silent peace I waited for the bullet.

But it was a bullet that never came.

#

I tore my gaze from the barrel of the gun and let it ride up to the face of my destruction. A look of frozen, uncomprehending terror stretched across the face of Drake. He quivered once, his eyes shining bright in fear and pain. Whatever was happening to him wasn't by his design, and he certainly wasn't enjoying it.

I put aside my self-recrimination and listened. A thin, keening whine cut through the silence. A shrill cry that came from the Caster artifact abandoned on the floor behind Drake. A fierce, pale-blue light emanated from the relic. A glow that pulsed as steady as any heartbeat.

I turned to share my discovery with Howard and perhaps offer him a warning—but my words were strangled before they were even halfway formed. Because, with a gossamer explosion, another glow burst into life. A softer, more subtle echo of the same light emanating from the relic in Drake's hand. This new illumination seeped around Tamara's lifeless body, encasing her in a soul-shaped shroud as ephemeral as starlight and then sank into the carpeted floor beneath her.

My eyes snapped to Drake.

The terrified man was still locked in that B-movie shooter's stance, but there were tears running freely down his cheeks now.

From the corner of his lips, a thin line of spittle began a slow, almost timid, descent.

But it was his feet that really caught my attention, because the same spectral light that enveloped the Caster relic and the body of Tamara shone around them like a spotlight—a spotlight that was *rising*.

The glow climbed Drake's legs, snaking around each limb like glowing smoke, and, as each ephemeral column rose, it multiplied, branching out like capillaries from a blood vessel. When this network of glowing miasma reached his gut, Drake's back arched and a shudder of pain flashed across his face. His screams were stolen from him, but his eyes locked onto mine, and there, in their frantic, agonized gaze, I saw a silent plea:

Help me!

But it was too late for help, and far too late for second chances. Maybe if I'd had the time to consider Drake's claims of kinship and shared burdens more fully, maybe then I might have tried to save him. But for Sebastian Drake, *maybe* could never happen.

Even as the consideration bloomed in my agitated mind, the strange mist-light spilled over Drake's shoulders and down his arms, up his neck, and across his cheeks, the tendrils splitting again and again like the heads of some ancient Hydra. One serpentine wisp vanished into his left nostril. Yet another slid into his mouth. Others slipped beneath his eyelids and into his ears—and still others burrowed into his flesh itself.

Sebastian Drake, his arm still raised and his pistol still aimed my way, began to glow from within. The serpentine light that had overtaken him spilled from his mouth, his ears, his eyes. Taut contractions of stone-like stiffness—the very enemy of vibrant life—rippled through him.

And there, right before me, Sebastian Drake—the man who was all but immortal—died.

#

I stood numb and unfeeling. The enormity of what I'd witnessed washed over me in waves of ice-cold fire. My mouth worked soundlessly. My hand reached blindly for Howard. Every nerve in my body screamed with static.

Sebastian Drake was dead.

It defied explanation.

"What the...?" The rest of Howard's sentence died in his throat, cut short by a sharp, electric crack which dragged our attention to the statue-like corpse still frozen in its deadly intent.

Because the statue-like corpse of Sebastian Drake was glowing again.

The brilliant aura intensified, gathering into a concentrated sphere that hovered above him. I raised an arm to shield my eyes from this midnight sun, but it was useless. The searing brilliance flared, stretching into a thin column of cold, flickering fire. A spire of pure, ethereal energy.

And then, as suddenly as it had burst into life, the flaming pillar dimmed and fell, becoming a soft, powder-blue mist that covered Drake from head to toe and shoulder to shoulder. A mist that held something else.

At first, it was only a suggestion—just a half-formed silhouette in the center of the haze, but, as if approaching us from across some fog-strewn battlefield, it solidified little-by-little into the too-heart-breaking form of Tamara Quinn.

She stood tall and proud. So very strange, and yet, at the same time, so hauntingly familiar. Her pupilless eyes—eyes that were filled with the softest, purest light, swept over Howard before drifting onto me.

And then she smiled.

30

Three weeks plodded by in the pedestrian way weeks often do. Night followed night and day followed day. Normality, or at least something like it, slowly enveloped the grief still burning like a silent scream beneath my skin, but somehow, I survived.

I owed a lot of that to Howard.

The big, square-shouldered man could've vanished, leaving the office and the broken woman haunting it far behind him. I wouldn't have blamed him. Not for one single second.

But he didn't.

"Hey," he said, his voice tight as he opened the door to the office that first time since the events of Drake's office. "I guessed I'd find you here."

It wasn't the wildest of deductions. My apartment had been given the full crime-scene scrub, thanks to the unexpected compassion of a certain Irish mob boss. Every wall, every floorboard, had been scoured until the place gleamed like a showroom, but there are some stains that never wash out. The walls, even the air itself, still held so many memories of everything I'd done and everything I *wished* I'd done. It was almost as if the suspended body of the girl who never was, the girl I hadn't saved, still hung there, casting a suffocating, indelible shadow.

"You okay?" I asked, partially to banish the unquiet thoughts.

"You know I'm not," he shot me an insincere grin and eased into the client's chair, setting the cane that supported his injured leg aside. "Same as I know you're not. I guess I just figured we could be not-okay together"

I flashed the big man the first smile I'd managed in weeks.

I hadn't gone to the funeral, of course, late afternoon being a touch too early for me, and I hadn't really said goodbye, either. The presence of Tamara still hung a little too substantially in the office of Charlie Durant Investigations for that. The files she'd organized, the last of the three blood bags in the fridge, all of it sat a half-inch this side of too much. I wasn't exactly a stranger to loss, but Tamara's death, well that was a fresh wound.

And it hurt Howard, too.

"We could've made it, you know," he said, almost as if he'd read my mind. "Tamara and me, I mean. At least... at least I think so." He took off his hat and ran the brim between his fingers. "I mean, there never was a 'her and me', but if I'd asked. If I'd said..." He looked up at me, blinking back the promise of tears. "You know?"

I opened the second drawer of the big desk, rescued the too-empty bottle, poured us both a drink, and slid a glass his way before he could object.

"I know," I said. "And maybe that was enough. Maybe that potential was part of what brought her back to save us both."

"Then it was her?"

"Had to be. We got so caught up in Drake's 'can only be killed by a dead man' clause that we never stopped to consider if that qualification fit anyone else, but I guess a royally pissed-off ghost ticks the box fine." I took a long sip from my glass, resisting the urge to drain it completely. "Mackenzie says the weapon Drake used was a Caster artifact called '*The Traitor's Mace.*' He's digging up more intel on it, but he thinks it could have the power to somehow resurrect its victims... the power to resurrect Tamara just long enough to save our sorry hides."

I swirled the liquor for a second, watching the way the

amber liquid reflected the muted light. "But if you ask me, it was something more."

A long silence followed. A silence broken by the *clink* of Howard's glass as he set it down.

"She was wrong, you know," he said, eventually.

"Tamara?"

"No." A tired smile touched his lips. "The Barrett woman. She had her opinions about you. What you are... *who* you are, but she was wrong, and I guess I was too Both of us saw a glimpse of your different sides—the living, feeling woman, and the snarling, ravening vampire—but neither of us saw the whole." He looked at me, his eyes all sad seriousness. "I underestimated the monster in you, but Barrett? Well, she underestimated the woman."

I set down my own glass and rubbed some of the aching guilt from my temples. "It's a nice thought, Howard, but the truth is, she played me like a fiddle," I said. "Barrett told us she was an actress, and it turns out she was a damn good one, too. The way she touched me, the way she held me, it all felt so... real." My thoughts drifted, unbidden, to that unforgettable night with Rose. "But I don't think she ever took her eyes off the prize. Not for a single second."

We fell into a bleak silence, each of us staring into the remnants of our drinks and the weight of all we'd lost.

As the seconds ticked by, Howard cleared his throat. "Anything interesting come across the desk?" he asked, trying his hardest for casual. "Anything you might need a little help with?"

I arched a brow. "Is a case really what you want to be thinking about right now?"

"Well, it beats thinking about anything else."

I nodded my understanding. "There's nothing," I said eventually. "Not interesting *or* otherwise. I haven't been what you might call 'open for business' these last few weeks, if you catch my drift."

"But..."

"No, Howard. Look, I get it. You want something in your

life that isn't about the sucking wound Tamara's death left in your heart, but is this really the time or the place? Here... where it all began?"

Howard lowered his eyes, studying the thin carpet.

"I don't know, Charlie. Maybe not. But it's either this or auditioning for more of those lousy commercials, and after Drake, I'm not sure I want anything to do with that world ever again." His eyes rose, his voice steadying. "Your world might be dirtier and scarier, Charlie, but at least it's real—at least it means something—Tamara would want us to make that count, would want us to make a difference. She'd want us to go on... together."

I turned toward the frosted door, watching the passing headlights catch the reversed words etched onto the glass:

CHARLIE DURANT INVESTIGATIONS

"The work will be hard," I said, remembering the very first conversation I'd had with Howard. "The hours are terrible, and I can't promise you anything close to a steady paycheck."

"I know, boss," Howard said through about half a smile.

I walked to the door and held it open with mock formality.

"Then welcome aboard, Mr. Gold. You start first thing tomorrow night."

Howard rose and, with a grin, tipped his hat. "I look forward to it, Ms. Durant."

I watched the big man limp down the shallow hallway, toward the stairs, poured myself another brandy, and drifted toward the window. Soon, he'd cross the street to hail a cab, leaving me alone again, with only my thoughts, and the distant, thrumming heartbeat of the big city night for my company.

"Well... not quite, Ms. Durant," said the ghost of Tamara Quinn. "In fact, I don't think you're ever going to be alone again."

www.ingramcontent.com/pod-product-compliance
Lightning Source LLC
LaVergne TN
LVHW091126080826
845145LV00008B/2061